MURDER
AND
LYRICS

LACYNDA MATHES

This is a work of fiction. Names, characters, places, and incidents are products of the author's imagination or are used fictitiously and are not to be construed as real. Any resemblance to actual events, locations, organizations, or persons, living or dead, is entirely coincidental.

World Castle Publishing, LLC
Pensacola, Florida
Copyright © 2024 Lacynda Mathes
Paperback ISBN: 9798891262461
eBook ISBN: 9798891262478
First Edition World Castle Publishing, LLC, August 5, 2024
http://www.worldcastlepublishing.com

Licensing Notes

Cover: Cover Designs by Karen
Cover-designs-by-karen.com
Editor: Karen Fuller

Dedicated to the love of my life, David Alan Mathes.
I'm so happy we chose each other.

PROLOGUE

Gabriella was sitting in the car waiting. She called for her son. He had little league practice in half an hour. She got no response. She honked the horn. He came out of the house, his cleats slung over his shoulder.

"I can't find my shoe, Mom," Gavin called.

"What do you mean? How do you lose a shoe?"

"I don't know. I took them off in the garage and left them in the basket by the door. Now there's only one shoe."

She huffed and turned off the ignition, "So help me, God, Gavin, if I come in there and find your shoe in that basket, I'll make you clean the garage."

But the shoe wasn't in the basket where they threw their shoes before walking into the house. Nor was it in Gavin's bedroom and not in his closet. They scoured the house. Gavin's right shoe of the pair they had just bought…$152 for Nikes, not that the money mattered that much…was just gone.

CHAPTER 1

Deb placed the window box full of mums on the rail of her tiny balcony and sighed. This wasn't the home she'd planned on. She'd thought she and Gavin would buy a house together when she'd placed her house on the market. She'd thought it would be in Batavia, where she'd lived her entire life. She hadn't anticipated a headhunter for the University of Mary Washington offering Gavin a position as a professor in the Criminal Justice Department. She'd known he held a doctorate in criminology, but it had never occurred to her that he'd ever do anything other than be a police officer. It didn't seem to have occurred to him, either. But the offer was genuine. She wasn't convinced he hadn't ultimately accepted the offer because of her, despite the hours of their discussing it. He'd been shot. And after what happened to Mark…she was afraid that he was letting her fears guide his decision.

Mark. She had loved him…or thought she had. Whether it was true love or just a connection that filled an emptiness in her, her feelings for Mark had been real. Real enough to sacrifice her marriage over. But were she to have met Mark today…she'd choose Gavin.

That was why she was here. She'd follow Gavin anywhere. Even to Virginia. Even if she believed he was making a mistake.

It hadn't been so bad in July and August. Dan and Miranda had spent the summer at the beach house in Colonial Beach. She'd had a support system. But Miranda had been accepted at Northwestern. She was starting law school in Chicago. They'd made arrangements for Jason to spend one weekend a month with Dan and Miranda. Dan would come to them. He was the one with all the cash. Gavin had protested that he could afford to take Jason home, but Dan insisted that it wasn't Gavin's responsibility. They'd adjust as needed. Now that the plan was in motion…she was feeling a little anxious, a little isolated.

She stood back, as far as she could anyway, on the small balcony and admired her handiwork.

"The flowas are pretty, Mommy," Jason proclaimed from the balcony door.

"Yeah, not bad, huh? Kinda homey," she agreed.

"Hello!" came the exuberant voice from the sidewalk below them. A woman was standing there waving up at Deb and Jason. She was dressed professionally and probably about Deb's age. Deb had turned 31 in July. "Hi! I'm Fiona Hendricks. I live under you."

"Hi. I'm Deb. This is my son, Jason. Nice to meet you, Ms. Hendricks," Deb called back. "We're still unpacking, but would you like to come up for a cup of coffee?"

She felt a little silly, inviting a complete stranger into her apartment, but she'd seen Fiona and her children going in and out of the apartment below them, and the woman seemed friendly. She was craving a little adult female conversation. The woman gave no indication that the invitation was in any way too forward or out of the ordinary. She smiled as if that was what she was hoping to happen and replied, "Love to. We'll be right up."

Deb pulled off her gardening gloves and smoothed her hair before walking inside her apartment and making her way into her kitchen. She washed her hands and then started a pot of coffee. Not a minute later, Fiona was knocking on her door. She had two children with her. Deb opened the door, welcoming them into her apartment.

"Hi! I'm so glad I saw you out there on your balcony. I've been looking for an opportunity to introduce myself!" Fiona announced, walking through the door. "Oh, this is Mavis. She's five. And this is Christian. He's three."

"I'm three," Jason said, jumping up and down.

"Wow! Three! Same as Christian! That's amazing!" Fiona crooned, putting her hands on her knees and leaning to look Jason in the face as she spoke to him.

Deb smiled. "Hello, Mavis. Hello, Christian. Would you like a snack and a juice box?"

The children looked to their mother for approval. Fiona nodded. And they clamored to the table. Deb pulled some string cheese, apple slices, and three juice boxes out of the refrigerator and three plastic plates out of her cabinet. She placed some cheese and apples on each plate and set a plate in front of each child. Then she returned to the kitchen, pulling two mugs from the cabinet. "How do you take it?" she asked her guest.

"Creamer, two sweet n' lows," Fiona answered. Deb handed her the coffee.

"I'm going to warn you. I am not the greatest in the kitchen. My friend, Miranda, has been teaching me over the summer, but my coffee is hit or miss," Deb laughed.

"I'm sure it's fine," Fiona said, taking a sip and coughing. "Just a little strong."

Deb grimaced. "Sorry."

"I needed a pick me up anyway," Fiona laughed. "I work 3 to 11 at GEICO. Maybe I can take a thermos to go."

"You're working on Labor Day?"

"Hmmm. Yeah. Customer Service. Double time and a half," Fiona winked. "How about you? What do you do for a living?"

"Oh, nothing. I mean, plenty, but not outside the home. I worked before I married my ex, but I was pregnant when we got married, and he was okay with my staying home with Jason, so...I probably won't until he goes to school."

"You said ex. So, I take it the dreamy guy living here with you isn't Jason's father," Fiona leaned in, hoping for something good.

Deb blushed and smiled. "No. Gavin isn't Jason's father. But he's great with him. So's Miranda, the friend I mentioned. She's Dan's, my ex's, new wife."

"Ah. That's nice that you all get along. I wish me and my ex and his paramour could do that. Too bad she's a raging bitch, and he's a giant ass." She burst out laughing.

Deb snickered.

"Mommy, we finished our snack. Can we go play in my room?" Jason asked from the table.

"Sure," Deb answered. "Put your plates in the sink and juice boxes in the trash."

Fiona smiled approvingly. "He's sure a well-behaved kid. Maybe he'll be a good influence on my monsters!"

The children did as they were told and ran off down the hall to Jason's bedroom.

"I'm single at the moment, myself. Christian's dad is in the Marines. I met him in Quantico. You'd think I'd have been old enough to know better by then, but...c'est la vie. He's an okay guy. Pays his child support on time. But, as they are apt to do, he moves around a lot. He's at Camp LeJeune now. He's a little younger than me, too, truth be told. Mavis's dad is the giant ass. He owns a body shop. He's always late on his child support, and he never shows up on time. I made the mistake of marrying him. He never took it seriously. He started dating the paramour, Trixie, before I moved out. She had moved in by that evening. And my oldest, Jeff…he's ten…his dad teaches at UMW. He was the best of the three. Unfortunately, he already had a wife. I found that out a little too late," Fiona explained. "Wow, I just unloaded my dumpster fire life on you. Sorry."

"Your kids are clean, well-fed, happy, and loved. You are the first friendly person I've met in the apartment complex. Besides, I have my own dumpster fires to tend to," Deb answered.

Keys rattled in the door. It swung open. "Hi, Honey. I'm home!" Gavin called playfully as he entered and closed the door behind him. He held up a bag of groceries. "Got the charcoal and steaks."

Gavin, at 36, 37 next month, was 5 years older than Deb. He was an incredibly handsome man, more Mexican in appearance than Irish, belying his name. His near-black hair was cut short but curly, with just a few hints of silver starting to appear around his ears. His complexion was tawny. His facial features were chiseled. His eyes were a cat-like golden brown. He ate right and exercised, so he was lean and muscular. At 5' 11", he wasn't as tall as Deb's ex, Dan, but he wasn't short. His smile took Deb's breath away. Actually, everything about him did.

They had only known each other for six months when they had decided to live together, and they were still getting to know each other. They hadn't thus far found any insurmountable issues. He was quiet and circumspective in nature. She was loud and brash. He was smart, well-educated, and ambitious. She wasn't stupid but less motivated. She hadn't gone to college. After graduating high school she'd worked at Macy's until she'd gotten married. Her ex-husband had been happy to have her stay home with their child. He was a traditional kind of guy. Even after they had divorced, after she cheated, he supported her. When he unexpectedly inherited a large fortune, he'd changed their settlement to reflect his wealth, and she was free to continue staying home with their son. Gavin supported her decision, any decision she made, actually. He respected her autonomy. It did leave her feeling a little inadequate, but that was her issue, not his and not theirs. They both felt some survivor's guilt over their relationship, given they met when Deb's boyfriend, a police lieutenant, was killed in a mass shooting. And she felt some jealousy over his last relationship with a woman, Shannon, with whom he had lived with for 4 years before they split rather "unamicably." The fact that he didn't talk about it was maddening.

"Hi, Sweetheart!" Deb replied. "Let me introduce our downstairs neighbor, Fiona Hendricks." A chorus of giggles and thumps came from Jason's room. "And those would be her kids, Mavis and Christian."

"Well, hello, Fiona. Gavin Mahoney. Nice to meet you." Gavin leaned across the counter and kissed Deb. He nodded to the cup of coffee Fiona was drinking. "Brave woman."

"Shut up. I'm getting better."

"Sure. If you say so," he teased.

"Ah, Geez. Look at the time," Fiona exclaimed. "I gotta get my kids to the sitter and get to work. Thanks for the jet fuel…I mean coffee." Fiona winked at Deb. "Kids! We gotta go to Miss Nancy's. Come on."

CHAPTER 2

Gavin rolled over and found Deb watching him.

"Hey. Everything okay, Babe?" he asked groggily.

"Everything's perfect," she whispered. She reached out and traced the scar on his shoulder, where a bullet had grazed him in May. He pulled her close, nuzzling her neck, making her giggle.

"I know, I've said this ad nauseum, but you didn't have to quit because of me. I was scared seeing you injured, but it's important that you're happy."

"I'm happy. I promise," he said, kissing her.

He thought she was about to say something else, but suddenly, there was a banging on the door to their apartment. "Deb! Gavin! Help me! Help! Please!"

"Fiona!" Deb exclaimed, sitting up and looking at the clock, which read 2:18 am.

"Stay here!" Gavin warned, grabbing his weapon from his gun safe. Deb followed him to the bedroom door. He made his way to the apartment door. He looked through the peep hole and then unlatched the chain, swinging the door open.

"Gavin! Help! Please! Jeff's missing!"

"Jeff?" he asked, as the frantic woman collapsed into his arms. He turned to look at Deb. Jason emerged from his room.

"What's happening?" the child asked, rubbing his eyes.

"Nothing, Honey. Mavis and Christian's mommy is upset. Go back to bed. I'll be right there," Deb replied. Then, turning to Gavin, "Jeff's her oldest child. He's ten." She ushered her own child back into his room.

"Come in, Fiona. First, where are the other kids?" Gavin asked.

"At the sitter's. I pick them up at 6 am," she wailed.

"Okay. Good. Now, sit down. Take a breath. Deb, get her some water." He led the distraught woman to the sofa and set his gun on the coffee table. Deb went to the kitchen and poured a glass of water from the Brita pitcher in her fridge. She rushed to the sofa and placed the glass in the woman's shaking hand. Fiona took a sip.

"When did you last see him?" Gavin asked.

"Friday. He was at his dad's. He says he dropped him off at my house at 7, but I was at work. He said that wasn't his problem. I didn't know he was going to do that. I'd have had him take him to Nancy's if I'd have known. He was supposed to be with him until Tuesday morning because of the holiday. And after work, I went out with some of the girls for a couple of drinks and karaoke. I got home at 2 and saw his backpack on the floor in the living room. So, I called his dad to yell at him for leaving him at my house when I was at work and not even telling me. He told me he was asleep and to call him in the morning. So, I went into his room to check on him, and he wasn't there!"

"Have you called 911?" Gavin asked.

"Oh my God! I'm so stupid!"

"No, you're scared and panicky. I'll call," he reassured her.

He grabbed his phone and made the call.

"Fiona, Gavin is an ex-police officer. He's a Criminology professor at Mary Washington. He'll help you. Okay? I need to go take care of Jason, but I'll be back as soon as I can," Deb explained. "Trust me. I know exactly how you feel. Jason was kidnapped in May. I promise I'll be right back."

Fiona looked at her new friend through her tears and nodded. Deb ran to Jason's room to comfort her own child.

The Fredericksburg Police responded quickly. They knocked at Deb and Gavin's door in less than five minutes. Gavin opened the door and let them in. The responding officer looked familiar to Gavin. He stared suspiciously at the weapon on the coffee table.

"It's mine, Officer…Vance, isn't it? I am an Illinois State Trooper, or I was. I'm currently teaching Criminology at UMW. You're in one of my classes. I took it out of the gun safe when she banged on my door at quarter after two in the morning."

A second officer approached and whispered something to the first. "When did you last fire that weapon, Sir?" the officer asked.

"Yesterday morning at the range. Why?" Gavin asked. He had a sinking feeling deep in his gut.

The second officer whispered again.

"Do you own a shotgun?"

"No. I own that weapon and two rifles. The rifles are locked in a gun rack in our closet. I keep the handgun in a gun safe by my bed. No shot guns."

"Are your weapons registered?"

"They are."

"What are they asking about your guns for? Why aren't they looking for my son?" Fiona screamed. Turning to the officer in charge, she cried, "Why aren't you looking for my son?"

Gavin read the answer in the officer's eyes.

"Damn!" he whispered. "Fiona, come sit down, Honey."

"No! Why aren't they looking?" she implored.

He frowned and took her by the elbows. "Please. Sit

down."

She allowed herself to be led to the sofa and sat, looking at him and the officers, scared and confused.

"We found a juvenile male body in the apartment complex dumpster," the second officer announced. "He's been shot with a shotgun in the chest."

"No!" Fiona screamed and collapsed, sliding off the sofa to the floor.

CHAPTER 3

Gavin watched them pull the boy out of the dumpster. He was wearing one tennis shoe. His other shoe and sock were missing. One little foot, five perfect toes. His heart broke looking at that foot. Other than the missing shoe and sock, he was fully dressed in a pair of jean shorts and a red tee shirt. His brown hair was cut neatly above his ears. He was a beautiful child with a cute splattering of freckles across his nose. But the foot. The foot would haunt him.

As he stood back, behind the police line, watching, he noticed the police officer who'd first announced the finding of Jeff's body in his living room half an hour before speaking with the Chief of Police, a rank he recognized from the insignia on his uniform. The officer pointed toward Gavin. They spoke for a second or two more, and the Chief marched over to Gavin.

"Professor?" he said, "I'm Chief Lindstrom."

"Hello, Chief. What can I do for you?"

"Funny you should ask."

"How funny?" asked Gavin, concerned.

"Well, our head investigator resigned nine hours ago without notice. And I actually had your credentials on my desk. I was going to wait until morning to contact you about the job. But then we went and pulled the body of a ten-year-old boy out of your building's dumpster," Chief Lindstrom iterated.

"I have a job, Chief," Gavin said.

"And you can keep it. We've already cleared our offer with the University. You were our choice before this happened."

"Gavin," came Deb's voice from above their heads. He turned and looked up at the love of his life. "Take it," she said, tears streaking her face. Then she looked back over her shoulder at the woman wailing on their sofa. "Please."

"I guess I'm accepting your offer, Chief."

"Great. Can you spare a few to come get sworn in and get your badge and service weapon?"

"Now?"

"No time like the present."

"Can I change out of my sweatpants first? Maybe put on some shoes and socks?" He looked down at his bare feet and wiggled his toes.

"Sure. But make it quick. We need you immediately."

Gavin nodded. "Be right back."

One little bare foot. Five perfect little toes, he mused as he turned and bounded up the stairs to his apartment to get dressed.

By 7 am, he was fully sworn in and had a shiny new shield, a new service weapon, and a uniform that mostly fit to wear as well as one ordered that would definitely fit. He was also handed the keys to a service vehicle, a shiny Charger emblazoned with Fredericksburg Police Department insignia. He walked out with Chief Lindstrom at 7:30 am for a press conference, introducing him as the new head detective. The Chief touted his resume and advised he'd be jumping in headfirst with the murder of the child found in the dumpster at 2:30 that morning. Gavin answered what questions he could and advised that the public would be kept informed, but at this time, he had not had time to review the case fully. Nothing quite like being thrown to the wolves in a uniform that didn't quite fit.

He was still teaching two classes every day at UMW. Instead of heading home, he went to the school. As he walked from his office to the classroom, he found the officer who had questioned him at 2:30 falling into stride beside him.

"Good morning, Detective Mahoney. Um, I mean, Professor," he said.

"Good morning again, Officer Vance."

"I wanted to apologize for this morning."

"What for? Doing your job? You asked valid questions based on the information you had."

"Thank you, Sir."

"Tell me what you found out about the boy in the dumpster, Vance."

"Yes Sir. His name was Jeff Webster. His mother is Fiona Hendricks, a customer service rep at GEICO. Works 3 to 11 shift. We verified she was at work. After she went to a local karaoke bar with three friends. Two half-siblings at his mother's. They were at the babysitter's. Father is Fillmore Webster, a History Professor here. Stepmother Claudia Webster, two older half-siblings, one younger at dad's. They were all home. Webster says he took Jeff to his mother's house yesterday evening at about 7 pm after the boy and his wife had an argument. He says he didn't want to go to the babysitter and claims he wanted to go to his mom's, promising he'd call to let her know he was there. He says he watched him unlock the door and go inside. No record of Jeff actually calling his mother. Did you or your wife see or hear anything, Sir?" Officer Vance extolled.

Gavin smiled. "You're going to do well in my class, Vance. No. We went out to dinner. Because my girlfriend is beautiful and amazing in every way, but she can't cook. She burned the steak I brought home earlier in the afternoon. We left at about 5:30 and didn't get home until after 8. We got her son bathed and in bed by 9. We watched television. I reviewed my notes for the class we're walking to. We went to bed around eleven. I never heard anything. You'd have to ask Deb, but she never said she heard anything out of the ordinary. Certainly not a shotgun firing. We had no idea Jeff was home alone. Do we have a time of death?"

"Not definitively, but based on body temp and lividity, the coroner estimates between 9 pm and midnight. His laptop is missing, along with that shoe and sock. They weren't in the dumpster or the apartment."

"Hmmm. Check on online activity. Based on his state of dress, I'm guessing he wasn't sexually assaulted, but verify that with the coroner."

"Plus, he wasn't shot close range…not a big enough mess. But whoever did it must have been a good shot. The distance would support your theory about him not being assaulted."

"Yeah. I think he was hunted, Vance. We have our work cut out for us."

"Are you assigning me to the case, Sir?"

"Sounded that way to me, Officer Vance," Gavin affirmed.

"Thank you!" Vance exclaimed a little too loudly, drawing eyes from the full classroom as they walked through the door.

"Officer Vance, stick around after class. We need to go see Professor Webster."

"Yes, Sir." Vance found a seat at the back of the classroom but was clearly the envy of the class.

CHAPTER 4

"Professor Webster wouldn't be here today, surely," Rudy Vance observed, trailing behind Gavin's long, quick pace.

"One wouldn't expect so, but that is his parking space, and that is his vehicle parked in it," Gavin said, pointing at the black Lexus parked in the indicated space.

They made their way to Dr. Webster's office. He was a tall, thin, bespeckled man, in his early 50s, balding but not bald. He looked like a man who had spent his life in academia. He was in the process of tearing his own office apart at the seams.

"Where is it? Where is it?" he cried over and over in between his open sobs.

"Dr. Webster," Gavin said calmly, in his soothing voice, his talking to the victim's family voice, the voice he used to question them without them realizing they had been questioned.

Dr. Webster looked up at the uniformed man and the student behind him. He sat down at his desk and buried his head in his hands, leaning his elbows on the desk. "He only had one shoe. They said the other was missing. Just one shoe," he said as his tears fell and his shoulders shook. "I was so stupid to leave him. I shouldn't have let him. I shouldn't have let him."

Gavin stepped forward and placed his hand on the professor's shoulder.

"What about the shoe, Dr. Webster? What are you looking for?" Gavin asked, quietly, compassionately.

Dr. Webster looked up and took a handkerchief out of his pocket, a habit Gavin shared, and wiped his eyes and then his nose. "A letter. I got a letter on Friday. Here at the office. I didn't understand it. It was just a piece of sheet music. Music and lyrics. No explanation. Nothing attached. I tossed it aside."

"I don't understand, Dr. Webster," Gavin said, moving a stack of mail around on the desk. Then he saw the envelope that had slipped under the desk. He picked it up and pulled the folded stack of sheets out. Sheet music. No note. No explanation. Just as the professor had indicated. He nearly dropped it when he saw the title of the song: "One Shoe Blues," by B. B. King. "Whoa!" he exclaimed.

"That's it! You found it! You found it!" Dr. Webster said, grabbing Gavin's hand.

"Yes. I found it. This is evidence, Dr. Webster. Can I have it? Or do I need to call for a warrant?"

"Take it. Please. You can get DNA off the envelope or stamp, right? It can help you find the monster who killed my baby boy, can't it?" he pleaded.

"Maybe. Maybe." Gavin replied, placing the letter in an evidence bag he pulled from his pocket, thankful he was in his dress uniform, complete with gloves. "We need to ask you some questions, Dr. Webster. I have to get this to the lab and review other evidence. But this young man is Officer Rudy Vance. He's working on your son's murder. Can he talk to you now, Sir? You never know what may help us in our investigation."

"Yes. Oh, of course. Thank you. Thank you so much, Detective. Dr. Mahoney, isn't it? I saw your name in our staff and faculty notes and on the news this morning."

"Yes, Sir," Gavin replied, flinching at the unfamiliarity of the "doctor" moniker. He'd quietly had his doctorate in

Criminology for the better part of four years now, having earned it from Northern Illinois University. He had never felt the need to flaunt it. In fact, he felt talking about it might even have been a detriment. And yet, here it was, out in the open, even garnering him a degree of respect. "You've got this interview, Rudy. I really have to get to my new office at headquarters. Holding down two full-time jobs isn't as easy as it looks. Especially on three hours of sleep and when I was only planning on one." He winked and slapped the young man on the back as he exited.

CHAPTER 5

Deb got all three children down for a nap. She was watching Fiona and Fiona's kids. Fiona was finally asleep, too, thank God. Deb sat on her sofa and took a minute to breathe. She felt completely helpless despite doing everything she possibly could to help.

Her phone rang, and she realized she had fallen asleep.

"Hello, Dave. He's not home. He has his phone with him, though," she answered, noting Gavin's father was calling.

"What the hell, Deb? He's the head detective at the Fredericksburg PD?" Dave bellowed into the phone.

Deb winced. "Yeeeeeaaaaaaaah," she replied, holding the phone away as he yelled.

After a few seconds, she held the phone back to her ear. "It just kind of happened, Dave. I'm sure he just hasn't had time to call. You see, I made a friend yesterday. Our downstairs neighbor. And then, last night, her son was found murdered in our dumpster. The Chief approached Gavin at the scene with the job offer. And I…I told him to take it," she explained.

"Is he still teaching?"

"Yes."

"Is he happy?"

"He says he is, but I'm willing to bet he's a lot happier today than he was yesterday."

There was a long silence. "Yeah, me too," he finally said. "Are you okay?"

She smiled. "If he's happy, I'm happy. I'm scared, but I can live with that. I always could. He just wouldn't listen."

"Well, he loves you. And you love him. So, when are you going to get married? Gabriella and I want grandkids."

Deb laughed. "Dave, Molly has three kids. You have grandkids." She put her hand to her stomach, covering her secret, the one she'd tried to tell Gavin last night before Fiona banged on their door. "Besides, you don't have to be married to have kids. I got married because I was pregnant before, and it didn't turn out well."

"Ah, Honey. That was because you got married because of the baby. It wouldn't be that way with Gavin. You'd be getting married because you love each other."

"Maybe," she smiled.

"Maybe nothing. He's not getting any younger!" Dave laughed. There was another moment of silence. "When are you due, Sweetheart?"

"I should know better than to talk to cops. Late April, I think. But keep it to yourself, Granddad. I haven't told him yet."

"I promise. I won't even tell Gabriella."

"Well, I should hope not. I wouldn't get the chance to tell him if you did."

"Tell me what?" Gavin asked. She hadn't heard him come in.

"Busted," Dave said. "I'll talk to you later. And him. Tell him to call me. But after you talk to him. Bye, Sweetheart."

"Who's Granddad?"

"Your Dad," she said, putting her phone down.

"Sure. Three times over, but why would you call hi…" His voice trailed off. "No? Really?"

She smiled wryly and bit her thumbnail. "Yes. Really.

That okay?"

He grabbed her hands and pulled her up, and kissed her on the mouth. "I do so love a man in a uniform," she said, smoothing his jacket shoulders. "This man, anyway." She smacked his shoulder. "Hey, what are you doing home in the middle of the day?"

"I'm beat, Babe. I've put in a full day. I'm old. I like being head detective. I can point my protégé in the right direction and take a nap."

"Oh, you have a protégé already?"

"Uh-huh. Good kid."

"You picked that suspicious fellow last night who questioned you about your weapons, didn't you?"

"Rudy Vance. Yep. How'd you know?" he asked, lying down on the sofa and closing his eyes.

"Because the day we met, the day my boyfriend had his brains blown out by a sniper, you questioned me about my ex-husband's possible motives."

He grinned and grabbed her hands, pulling her down on top of him. "Well, it worked out well for me. I got the girl and a best friend. And now I have my own family."

His phone rang. "Ah, my mother. Dad held out for all of five minutes! Hi, Mom."

Deb's phone beeped. She read the text, "Sorry, Sweetheart. I got busted, too." She burst out laughing.

CHAPTER 6

"You really love him?" Mark asked, stepping out of the darkest corner of the bedroom into the light.

Deb smiled. "I really do."

"Did you ever love me?" he asked, sitting beside her on her bed.

"Of course, I did. I still do. But it is different with Gavin."

"Why?" he asked.

"I wasn't myself. I needed help. I wanted so desperately to be happy."

"So you were with me because you had lost your mind? That's great, Babe. Thanks."

"I wouldn't go that far. You were fun and handsome, and you were there when I needed you. I'll always love you for that," she pleaded.

"But you wouldn't love me now?"

"That's not fair, Mark. You're not here. He is," she answered.

"He deserves to know that you would choose him. I deserve to know, too. All I ever wanted was for you to be happy!"

She bolted upright at the sound of Gavin's phone. She looked around the room. It was just a room. No dark corners. And no Mark. But of course, there was no Mark. How could there be?

There was Gavin. Strong, calm, steady, smart, handsome as hell. A tear ran down her cheek. She was caught between the dream and the reality. She was overwhelmed by her own emotions for the man who was really there. He loved her. But she couldn't let go of her survivor's guilt. Was Mark okay? Was it unfair for her to be happy? The phone rang again.

"Gavin, Honey. Your phone," she said, shaking him gently.

He stirred. "Hmmm? Oh. Okay. Mahoney," he said, answering the call. He sat up quickly, throwing off the covers and swinging his legs off the bed. "Yeah — I'll be right there. — Got it. — Yes, Sir, Chief. — On my way." He stood and went to the closet, opening it and pulling out his uniform that he'd pressed and hung in there just a few hours prior. "Go back to sleep, Honey. I gotta go to work," he said, dressing quickly.

"Break in the case?" she asked hopefully.

His silence was heartbreaking. "No," he said finally. "Another body. Professor Lourdes Marcon, Art History. Her teenage daughter's body was found at James Monroe High School."

"Any reason to think it's connected to Jeff's murder?"

"Other than she's the daughter of a UMW faculty member? Not at the moment."

"But it is. Isn't it?"

"I'm willing to bet it. I'm pretty sure we're dealing with an honest to God serial killer, Deb." He slipped on his shoes and sat on the end of the bed to tie them.

He stood and leaned down to kiss her.

"Don't you want me to put on the chain?" she asked, starting to rise.

"No, Honey. Go back to sleep. Bob can lock up behind me."

"Uncle Bob?" she asked, confused. Uncle Bob was in

Chicago.

Gavin nodded his head toward the bedroom door. Sure enough, Bob Zamphir stood in the door jam. He'd previously gone by Bob Walters, but recently, he'd made the oddly independent choice to change it back to Zamphir. It was odd because Bob usually followed Frank, but Frank was still using their mother's maiden name of Walters.

"Crap! Uncle Bob!" she jumped. "What on Earth are you doing here? And when will you ever knock?"

"Gavin doesn't mind," he said, stepping forward. "I'll be honest. I thought it would be less fun than it was scaring Dan, but watching you react to his not reacting is even more amusing."

"Happy to amuse you," she replied, rolling her eyes.

Her uncle chuckled.

He stepped back to allow Gavin past. Gavin clasped his shoulder. "Keep her safe, you creepy ole vampire," he teased.

"You know I will," Bob winked.

CHAPTER 7

Seventeen-year-old Yvette Marcon had been a bit of a tomboy. She was the starting forward on the James Monroe High School Girls Basketball team. She wasn't just athletic. She was a jock. She assured her mother that she was indeed a girl, but she wasn't girly. She never wore dresses or skirts. She wore her hair short, her nails trimmed, her shoes…well, she liked sneakers. She didn't mind pink, but she hated frills. She owned exactly two pieces of jewelry: an antique locket her grandmother had passed down to her and her medical alert bracelet advising of her allergies to peanuts and penicillin. She only ever wore the latter. The former she kept in a box in her sock drawer. She'd hit a growth spurt at age fourteen that increased her stature from a thin 5'4" to a very thin 5'11" at seventeen.

Her body was found in the dumpster at James Monroe High School by the janitor at 5:30 am. He'd come in early to clean up after a pep rally held at the school the night before. She had been shot by a shotgun, like Jeff Webster, not at close range, but by a very good shot. But, unlike Jeff, it was clear Yvette was not wearing her own clothes. She was dressed in a black Lurex sparkly mini dress. She had been dressed in this outfit postmortem, as the bodice covered the fatal wound to her chest, and while it was blood-soaked, there were no tears in the fabric where the buckshot would have blasted through to cause the corresponding wounds beneath the dress.

Knowing what to look for, Gavin had asked Lourdes Macron if she had received a letter containing sheet music in the days preceding the murder of her daughter. She confirmed she had received a letter with no return address, postmarked in Fredericksburg at her UMW office Saturday. It had contained only sheet music with the music and lyrics to "Beautiful" by Christina Aguilera.

Gavin sat at his desk, examining the envelopes to the two letters closely. The killer had used forever stamps. They could have been purchased anywhere. There was no saliva on the envelope seal. The killer had used the self-adhesive kind. But the handwriting could give him a clue. He couldn't analyze the handwriting for personality traits. He wasn't sure he even put much stock in that sort of thing, but he could determine some things. He was certain the same person had addressed both envelopes, and the writing was oddly familiar. The killer wrote left-handed. He wasn't eliminating right-handed people, but the killer was either a leftie or ambidextrous. The killer used a black gel pen that leaked a little. So, he or she wasn't fastidious.

Maybe the killer was a singer? As far as he could tell, the lyrics were more important than the composition in the staging of the bodies. A non-fastidious, left-handed, or ambidextrous singer with a connection to UMW. It was a start, at least.

He glanced at his watch. He had to get to campus. He had his other class in an hour. He dropped both letters back in the evidence room and was heading out to the Charger. A young desk duty officer raced after him. "Detective Mahoney! Sir!" she called.

He turned to her. "Yes?"

"I'm sorry, Sir. I wanted to catch you before you left the building. You've had your calls held all morning. Your mother has called…" She glanced down at her message pad. "Twelve times this morning. She says she needs to know if it's a boy or a girl." She looked up and blushed. "Congratulations, by the way. I have a toddler myself: a boy, Davison. He's a handful."

He laughed, relieving her anxiety a little. She giggled back. "Well, next time she calls, tell her it's the size of a black-eyed pea right now, but as soon as we know, she'll know," he answered. "I should apologize in advance for my mother."

"Oh. And your father called three times. He wanted me to remind you to apologize to me for your mother." She handed him the stack of messages. He shook his head and walked out the door.

He shoved the messages into his pocket as he opened the car door and climbed behind the wheel. The University was just a few miles away. It took him less than five minutes to get to his office.

He had just settled into his office and sat down to review his materials for his class when his office phone rang. He sighed and picked it up. "Mahoney.— Yes, President Marshall. — Sure. I'll be right there."

He reached into his pocket and felt the messages. "Ah, this is why professors' offices are always so messy," he grumbled. He tossed them into his "in" basket and headed out the door.

As he shut his door, he noticed Rudy Vance coming toward him.

Rudy smiled and waved. "Good morning…um. You know I don't know whether to call you Detective or Doctor Mahoney."

Gavin laughed. "Doctor in class, detective in public, and just Gavin in private."

His protégé beamed, "Thanks, Gavin."

"What can I do for you, Rudy?"

"Oh, I have notes from my interviews with the Webster girl's family for you."

"Great. Walk with me. I've been summoned to the University President's office," Gavin offered.

"Sure. The stepmother, Claudia Webster, says she did have an argument with Jeff that afternoon. She says it was Jeff's idea to be taken back to his mother's early. The argument was over…Jeff's shoes."

Gavin stopped walking and looked at Vance. "His shoes? Really?"

Rudy nodded. "She says Jeff wanted to wear those…and I quote… "garish canvas things" when she had bought him a much nicer, "expensive" pair. She thought the boy had given the new shoes to his friend, Harley Brown."

Gavin started walking again. "And who is Harley Brown?"

"Um, the little sister's, Mavis's, father's girlfriend's son."

"Well, that's not complicated at all," Gavin snickered. "Sounds like my life."

"How so, Gavin?" Rudy grinned.

Gavin burst out laughing. "My girlfriend's father was my Tia Tami's first husband. So, my cousin Brandon is my girlfriend's half-brother, for starters."

"Starters?"

"Yeah, we don't have time to unravel that string, Rudy. Bob, I hope you didn't drive that hearse on campus today. I'm on my way to meet with the President of the University about a serial killer. I don't need to explain a visitor driving an antique hearse to see me," Gavin said, looking straight ahead.

"I'm sorry, Gavin. Who's Bob?" Rudy asked.

"I am," said a voice from the other side of him. He turned to see the man walking silently beside them.

"Ahhh! Geez! Where'd you come from?" Rudy cried, jumping.

"Chicago," the man answered, matter-of-factly.

"Rudy, this is Uncle Bob. Bob, Rudy. Deb okay?"

"Oh, yes. I was creeping out her friend Fiona, and given the woman's current state, I thought I'd be of better service elsewhere. I drove that horrible minivan. Though, I do believe the hearse is part of Fiona's issue with me."

"Ya think?" Gavin said, winking.

"He drives a hearse?" Rudy asked, confused.

"A 1964 Cadillac Hearse. Yes. It is a beautiful vehicle," replied Bob.

"May I ask a question?" Rudy asked.

"What have you been doing up to this point?" countered Bob. Gavin choked on his laughter.

"Um. Yeah. Asking questions, I guess."

"Well, carry on, young man," Bob said with a flourish.

"Are you dressed up for a costume party? Halloween isn't for a couple of months yet."

"This is how I dress," replied Bob, sticking out his chin.

"In all black, with a waistcoat, a gold pocket watch, a black bowler hat, a curly mustache, and a black walking stick? Huh. I thought you were dressed as Dick Dastardly."

Gavin burst out in full laughter. "Dick Dastardly! That's a good one."

They reached the President's office, and Gavin left the two of them outside the building.

CHAPTER 8

Shortly after Bob left, Fiona's mother arrived, having driven all night from her home in Fort Meyers Beach, Florida. Deb was happy to be a support for her new friend in this trying time, but she could barely keep her eyes open. The pregnancy was kicking her butt. She honestly didn't remember being this tired with Jason. So, as her friend was being consoled by her mother, she sat down on the sofa with her son and put on a "Scooby Doo" movie for him.

Once again, she found that she fell asleep sitting there as the movie had progressed way further than she had expected, when there was a knock at her door. She heaved herself to her feet and went to the door, looking through the peephole. She didn't know the woman, but the man was the apartment manager. She unhooked the chain and opened the door. "Hello," she greeted the visitors.

"Ms. Bradley," Mr. Ford began. "Do you know anything about a hearse parked in the parking lot?"

Deb sighed. "Sure. It's my uncle's. He's visiting from Chicago. It's in a visitor's space, isn't it?"

"Oh, yes, it is. It's just inappropriate for that type of vehicle. We don't permit commercial vehicles to be parked for extended periods in the visitor spaces," Mr. Ford elucidated.

"Oh no, it's not a working hearse. It's a restored vehicle being used for transportation. Its plates are not commercial. It's actually quite nice," she explained.

"Really? Who drives a hearse? It needs to be moved off the premises!" scoffed the nasty woman.

There was something about the way the woman held her face, like she was smelling something foul, that pushed Deb's buttons. "I don't think so. The vehicle is properly registered, in working order, and parked in a visitor's spot. It doesn't even leak any fluids. We pay our rent on time. Our lease allows us to have guests. If you don't like the hearse, avert your eyes. He'll only be here for a few days. Now, unless you have a valid complaint, my son's movie is ending."

"Ms. Bradley, it's just with the unpleasant business the other night. The hearse is frightening other tenants."

"Mr. Ford, I daresay the murder of a child is very frightening. My uncle wasn't even here then. Neither he nor his vehicle have anything to do with that. So, I suggest they focus their fears elsewhere." Deb started to close her door. The woman stuck her foot in the way and shoved the door back open.

"Look here. I have lived in these apartments for fifteen years now. This is a quiet, respectful, professional community. I don't know what that husband of yours does, but I hear him leaving in the middle of the night ever since that poor child… and now that…horrible vehicle! I'm five minutes from calling the police!"

"Go ahead. Ask for Detective Gavin Mahoney," Deb said, crossing her arms.

"Right, the new head detective at the FPD? The man on the news? What do you think he'll do for you?" sniffed the woman.

Mr. Ford blushed. "Mrs. Thompson. Detective Mahoney lives here."

"Does he, now? Well, maybe I will call him then. He MAY

be interested in the activity in this apartment," she huffed.

"I'm sure he is since it's his apartment. Move your foot," Deb said.

Mrs. Thompson looked at Mr. Ford. He nodded. "Yes. Here. In this unit."

The woman slid her foot back. Deb closed the door with a firm push and reattached the chain.

Then the woman screamed.

"Oh, dear Lord!" exclaimed Mr. Ford.

Deb grinned, undoing the chain and swinging open the door. "Hey, Uncle Bob. Come on in." She glared at the woman, closing the door after her uncle glided in past the troublesome woman. She kissed him on the cheek. "I love you, Uncle Bob," she laughed.

Wordlessly, he smiled at her and winked.

CHAPTER 9

Having reassured the University President that he was indeed doing everything he could to catch the killer, and while Gavin preferred the exact contents of the two letters be kept confidential, he recommended a general warning should be issued to faculty and staff that any unsolicited correspondence containing sheet music should be reported to the police. Students unrelated to faculty or staff did not appear, at this time, to be a target. With the President, Gavin helped draft a letter and press release to that effect.

Gavin walked out of the President's office to find only Rudy waiting for him.

"Where'd Bob go?" he asked, walking up behind the younger officer, who was talking to two pretty girls. Rudy jumped for the second time that morning, this time spilling the Coke he'd purchased while waiting.

"Jesus!" he bellowed, wiping the spill from his shirt with his hand. "You and your uncle sure do sneak up on people, Gavin."

Gavin chuckled, "He's Deb's uncle, not mine, but you need to be more observant, Rudy. So, where's Bob?"

"Count Dracula stood there still as a statue for fifteen minutes, not sayin' a word. Suddenly, he announced that Deb needed him at home, and he left. He reminds me of somebody. I just can't put my finger on it. He's one creepy son of a…"

Gavin smiled. "Bob and his brother, Frank, take great pleasure in creeping people out. It's an act, Rudy. They were in the circus as kids."

"The Great Zamphirs!" Rudy blurted, snapping his fingers.

"You know about the Great Zamphirs?" Gavin asked, shocked.

"Yeah, we had a guest lecturer in a class last year, a retired Deputy from Texas. The topic was dealing with children and accidental shootings. He talked about a case he had back in the early 70s. He had lots of slides. The Great Zamphirs. A family of circus performers. Bob looks like the dad. He was shot in the leg by one of the kids and fell off the high wire."

"Deputy Bueford," Gavin growled.

"Wait! Really? He's actually…one of the kids?"

"He is. And there's that string we don't have time to unravel right now again," Gavin replied, starting to walk back to his office. Rudy noted the change in Gavin's mood. He had been harried and circumspect but friendly. Now, he seemed… annoyed. Gavin walked faster than before and didn't speak. When he got to his office, he walked in and dismissed Rudy.

"Don't you want to know what else I learned from the Webster girl's family?" Rudy asked.

"I do. Write up a report."

Then he shut the door, with Rudy standing on the outside of it. Crestfallen, Rudy started to walk away. Gavin was having flashes of an upside-down Humvee, of Horatio bleeding, of Evan Hondo coughing up blood. Those so-called "Christian" protestors at the funeral. The horrible things they'd shouted. Where the hell did that come from? He gasped.

Gavin wanted to punch something. What right did Bueford have to share Deb's family secrets like that? He paced his small office a few times, clenching and unclenching his fists. He leaned on his desk and took several deep breaths, controlling his temper. Evan's dad crying over a set of empty boots. He breathed. Just breathe, he thought, just breathe.

Once he regained his composure, he felt bad for the way he'd treated Vance. He made a mental note to apologize to his protégé. He glanced at the stack of messages from police headquarters in his "in" basket. He picked them up and shuffled through them. He needed to have a conversation with his mother. This was ridiculous. Then he found one, not from either of his parents. It made his skin crawl.

The caller identified himself as Riley King. The message was, "Did you like the welcome gift?" The time of the call was recorded as 7 am yesterday morning. Officer Andrea Grimes took the message.

"Son of a…" he screamed. He didn't even try to hold back. He punched a hole in his office wall.

At the sound of the ruckus, Rudy ran back to Gavin's office and flung open the door. Gavin was sitting at his desk, his knuckles scraped and bleeding. He looked up at the younger man. "He called me. The son of a bitch called me. He left a message." He tossed the message onto the desk.

Rudy stepped inside and picked up the sheet of paper. "How do you know it's him?"

"Riley King is B.B. King's real name."

He pulled a first aid kit from his desk drawer, cleaned up his knuckles, and bandaged his hand. "Go talk to Officer Grimes, Rudy. I'd do it, but right now, I have a class to teach. Oh, and do you know who I might call to fix that?" he asked, pointing to the hole in the wall.

"Sorry. No. But you should get a boxing bag. I saw some at the Ferry Farm Walmart yesterday," Rudy suggested.

"Not a bad idea, Rudy. Thanks."

CHAPTER 10

Gavin's class ended at 3:30. At 3:45, he pulled into the Ferry Farm Walmart parking lot. As he strode in, he caught sight of Chief Lindstrom, who clearly did not see him. The Chief was in a heated conversation with a skinny, scruffy-looking young man, maybe 25, in a Walmart vest. As he moved past them, unobserved, he heard the Walmart employee huff, "Whatever, Uncle Harry!" Gavin smiled. Nice to know even Chiefs had snarky relations.

Gavin headed straight back to sporting equipment. He found a boxing bag and gloves and loaded them into a cart. He winced using his hand. It was swelling. He stood in the checkout line, and just as he reached the front of the line, the checkout clerk logged off, and a new one logged in. Luck would have it; it was the Chief's nephew. Gavin stood and waited patiently, watching the shift change. It was 3:50.

It had been raining on and off all day. Gavin noticed the mud on the shoes of the new checkout clerk. Just a little, like he'd cleaned the mud off but couldn't get them completely clean. Still, it looked fresh. Fresh orange mud. That would drive him crazy.

The clerk rang up Gavin's stuff and told him the amount due. Gavin's phone rang. The clerk sighed and shifted impatiently. Gavin held up one finger, answering his phone despite the clerk's silent protestations. He pulled his card out of his wallet to pay as he spoke. "Mahoney. — Yes. — River Road? Um, yeah, that runs along the river below Chatham? — Okay, I happen to be on that side of the river. Be right there."

He inserted his card into the transponder.

"Do you need something to punch, Officer?" asked the Chief's nephew. He looked at Gavin's bandaged hand.

"I needed something to punch that I won't need to repair. The wall broke. My hand just has a few scrapes. Don't ever mistake a bandage for a sign of weakness, Marcus," Gavin answered, reading Marcus's nametag. "More often than not, it's nothing but a bandage." He was weary and in no mood to suffer any foolishness.

He took his receipt and punching bag and returned to the Charger. He loaded his purchase in the backseat, returned his cart, and drove away.

He found the police cruisers lining the low point on River Road quickly. The officers had taped off an area on the river side of the road. A woman, walking her dogs in the wooded area, had found a blood-covered laptop in the mucky undergrowth. The officers searched the area and also found several shotgun shells, blood evidence, and Yvette Marcon's basketball jersey, which showed the type of damage and blood splatter expected if that was what she had been wearing when she was shot. The laptop proved to be Jeff's. Yvette's shorts were not found. Nor was Jeff's missing shoe. But they were still looking.

There were tire tracks for a four-wheeler ATV and footprints, indicating the killer had brought the kids out to this area, and then the kids had run away. There were cigarettes next to the ATV tracks. So, he had given them a head start. Then he climbed back on the ATV and chased them down, shooting them within the same quarter-mile area of the road's lowest elevation.

They'd found the murder crime scene for both victims.

Gavin walked along the area down near the river.

Something caught his eye, stuck in a tree branch of a log halfway on shore and halfway in the river. He grabbed a stick to try and untangle it and fish it in. It turned, and a tiny hand revealed itself. Gavin's heart sank as he called for assistance. The debris was a baby. He wanted to throw up, but he didn't want to contaminate the scene, so he swallowed hard and took three big gulps of air, composing himself again.

They pulled the baby, a girl dressed in a tee shirt that read "Blue Jean Baby" and a tiny pair of jeans, from the Rappahannock. The coroner estimated her to be 6 months of age. She was a Caucasian female, and she'd been in the river for no more than an hour when Gavin found her. She was bruised and battered, but she did not appear to have been shot. A shotgun would have torn her apart, she was so tiny.

"Maybe it's unconnected," offered one of the officers as it started to rain.

"Get canvases up to help keep evidence from washing away!" Gavin called to the others. "No, it's connected."

"How do you know?"

"Blue Jean Baby," he replied.

He walked back to the Charger and sat behind the wheel. He sat there for several minutes as the rain began to fall with more intensity.

He called the office of the President of the University.

"President Marshall, please. — It's Gavin Mahoney. — It's an emergency." He waited a few seconds. "President Marshall. I just pulled a baby out of the river. Any faculty or staff who would have a six- to eight-month-old infant daughter? I need a list. Immediately, if not faster."

He climbed back out of the car. "Who found the laptop?" he asked the closest officer. The officer pointed to a squad car. Gavin walked over, oblivious to the rain.

"This the lady who found the laptop?" he asked the officer

standing beside the cruiser where a woman in her forties with two dogs was sheltering. His tone was stern and angry.

"Yessir," he replied.

"I want to talk to her."

"You want me to bring her back to headquarters?"

"No. I want to talk to her now. That baby hadn't been there for more than an hour. We were meant to find her."

"Yessir," the officer replied, opening the door.

Her name was Honeysuckle Rose. Her parents had been hippies. Gavin's eyes narrowed. She was an alumnus of UMW. She was a music teacher at Walker-Grant Middle School. Her brother had taught Music at UMW until two years ago, when he passed away. She said she walked her dogs here every day at the same time, indicating she lived just a mile away, up by Chatham. She said she did not own a shotgun and wouldn't know what to do with one if she did. Her answers rang as truthful, but at the very least, the killer intended for her to find the crime scene, given her name was that of an old song and her connection to UMW.

The list from the President's office proved more successful. Johnna Wesley, a TA in the English Department, had been busy all day and had not been to her office. Her daughter Christa was six and a half months old and in daycare. Only she wasn't. The daycare had received a bomb threat at noon. The building had been evacuated. Christa was supposedly accounted for when they evacuated but was missing when they re-entered the building at 2:24. The daycare had reported her missing to the police at 2:30. They had tried calling Johnna, but her phone battery had died at 2:00. She did not have a chance to charge it. She never saw the letter, which Gavin found unopened in her office after breaking her into a million pieces when he delivered the news and asked her to come identify the child who had been drowned in the river. Her mother had never seen the outfit she was wearing before.

The sheet music was "Tiny Dancer." The handwriting on the envelope matched that on the others. Again, the envelope had a no-lick seal, and the killer used a Forever stamp.

CHAPTER 11

It was after 8 pm when he unlocked his apartment door. Inside, it was warm and welcoming. Deb, Bob, and Jason were playing Candyland. Jason was bathed and in his favorite space pajamas.

"Hi, Honey," Deb laughed, "there's a sandwich in the fridge."

He tried to smile. But it wasn't in him. He closed his eyes. "I'm not hungry," he said, shaking his head. He walked to the bathroom, closed the door, and threw up.

Deb moved to stand. Uncle Bob grabbed her hand. "Let him get it out. He doesn't want to bring it home."

Sure enough, within a few minutes, he had washed up and brushed his teeth, and returned to the family he loved. He played a round of Candyland with them. He gave Jason a piggyback ride to bed. He read him a story. He tucked the child in and kissed him goodnight. He seemed normal. But Deb looked over at him as he sat silently watching television. She watched the single tear run down his cheek before he felt her eyes on him and hastily wiped it away.

"I'm going to bed," he said, suddenly, without explanation. Then, he simply walked out of the room.

Deb was perplexed and worried. She looked at her uncle, her brow furrowed. "Now, he needs you," Bob assured her.

She nodded, stood, kissed her uncle on the cheek, and followed Gavin.

He was sitting on the end of the bed, taking off his shoes. His lip quivered as he looked up at her, and he just started crying. She didn't say anything. She walked over and stood in front of him. She ran her fingers through his dark hair. He wrapped his arms around her waist, and she held him close until he stopped crying. He looked up at her worried face.

"I pulled a baby out of the river this afternoon. I had to tell the mother that a serial killer drowned her six-month-old. To him, this killer, it's a game. To her, it was her whole world."

He rubbed her stomach and pressed his ear to it, closing his eyes. "I think I'd just die."

She pushed his head back, making him look at her. "You'll catch him," she whispered.

"Yeah. I'll catch him. But I can't give Fiona Jeff back. I can't give Yvette her senior year. And I can't put that mother back together again. Sometimes…it hurts. Look at Dan. How he still lives with it."

"Dan came through it just fine," she sighed.

"No, he didn't. And you know it." He was quiet for a minute. "I've never experienced it the way you do. It sticks to me. The hurt I cause these people sticks to me."

"Don't be silly," she protested.

"Deb, you accused me of tackling you when Mark died, and you literally couldn't look at me when your mother…"

She gasped, horrified that she had hurt him so deeply. "Gavin, that had nothing to do with you. I was…I lashed out at you. But I swear, my hurt didn't stick to you. You didn't make me hurt. You helped me get through it. Don't you know that? You were there for me every single day. You are my best friend. You laugh with me. You cry with me. You make me…better. It's about time I get over myself and do the same for you. Before I met you, I was selfish and spoiled. I hurt Dan. Me. Not me telling him what somebody else did to hurt him. I can't believe how egocentric I was. I wasn't happy. So, that made it okay for me to disregard my marriage vows. You didn't break that mother, Honey. The man who killed her child did. Baby, I love you. I promise you, I give you all of me. I will cry with you. I will laugh with you. I will help you through your hurt. And I hope, in some small way, I can make you a better version of yourself, too. And forget what I said about forever. Forever isn't going to be long enough."

"Damn, Deb. That almost sounds like wedding vows," he said, shocked.

"I haven't had my nightmare about Mark in months. But I have been having a recurring dream. Mark comes to me and asks if I really love you. It ends with him telling me to be happy. You make me happy. I believe…I hope…I make you happy. I've been afraid, Gavin. Afraid I'd hurt you like I did Dan. But I'm not the same person I was then. I will never act that way again. Not just because it was wrong. But because I didn't like who I was. I like who I am now. And then, I've been afraid of losing you, the way I did Mark. All that did was tie you up in knots. You aren't Mark. I'd marry you in a second. In my heart, you are already my husband. I am already your wife."

"Are you asking me?" he sniffed, finally smiling.

"Do you want me to get on one knee?"

"A guy dreams of this moment all his life. Damn right. Make like Kaepernick, Baby."

She blushed and dropped to one knee, taking his hand into hers. "Gavin Mahoney, blue 32! Will you marry me? Hutt, Hutt!"

"Sacked!" he bellowed, lunging toward her and taking her to the floor. She laughed as he kissed her, lying on the floor. He pulled back and stared into her big blue eyes. "Yes. I will. I was always going to. I was just waiting to catch you at the bottom of the cliff."

"You promised I'd never hit the ground," she quipped, patting the floor.

"You didn't. You're one floor up from the ground." He lay there for a minute before he spoke again. "The thing is…"

"You don't want our engagement to be remembered as the day you pulled a baby out of the river."

"Yeah. That's the thing."

She sat up. "I can wait."

He reached out and took her hand.

"Oh my God, Gavin! What did you do to your hand?"

"I punched a wall."

"Drywall didn't do this!"

"No. Plaster and shiplap."

"Gavin, your hand is broken," she said, examining his hand.

"How do you know?" he asked, wincing.

"Well, that shouldn't hurt, for one. Put your shoes back on, Captain Caveman. We're going to the ER."

He picked up his shoe and stared at it. Fresh orange mud. "I'll be damned."

Deb looked at the shoes. "You want another pair? We can clean those when we get home."

CHAPTER 12

"Marcus Rose," Gavin said, placing his own bagged shoes on Chief Lindstrom's desk. Gavin noticed the spark of recognition at the mention of Marcus. It passed as quickly as it had appeared on the Chief's face.

"Who is Marcus Rose? And what happened to your hand?"

"I broke it. Three places. You know who Marcus is. He calls you Uncle Harry. At the moment, he is my number one person of interest. He is 25. He failed out of UMW after his cousin, Joe Rose, a professor of Music, suffered a massive stroke two years ago. He's undeniably smart and talented but underperforms. He's left-handed. He was in choir and an acapella group on campus. He exhibits encyclopedic knowledge about music. He lives alone in an apartment in the basement of his cousin's house a quarter of a mile from the crime scene on River Road. His cousin is Honeysuckle Rose. He works at Ferry Farm Walmart. I saw him yesterday. He had mud on his shoes, like this," he pointed out, indicating his own shoes. "I got mine muddy at the crime scene."

"Well, we need more than that. You're right, I know Marcus. I don't believe this is him," Chief Lindstrom replied.

"Okay. But I have to look at him. Anyway, I think we have until December 30th before our killer strikes again," Gavin suggested.

"Why December 30th?"

Gavin didn't flinch. "That's the next New Moon on Monday."

"It was a new moon on Monday?"

"Yes, Sir. At 9:55 p.m."

"And the New Moon ended last night?"

"This morning. A new moon lasts about 3 and a half days," Gavin explained.

"So why do you think there isn't a fourth victim during this new moon?"

"Because he gave us the crime scene and Christa."

"He did?"

"Yes, Sir. Honeysuckle walks her dogs there every day. She didn't find the laptop until yesterday, the third day. And he had just been there to kill Christa. He obviously intended for her to find the laptop."

"Okay. So, what song represents our crime scene?"

"'Down by the River,' by Neil Young," Gavin replied again without flinching. He took out his phone and played the song. When the song reached the chorus, Chief Lindstrom shook his head.

"That's demented," he said. Then, an idea occurred to him, and Gavin saw that spark of relief cross the Chief's face again. "Christa wasn't shot!"

Gavin handed him the M.E.'s report. "It turns out Christa had been shot with a pellet gun. It was non-lethal, but it suited his purpose."

"How exactly did he get Christa? I mean I can see his luring away Jeff and Yvette. But the baby? She just disappeared during a bomb scare!" the Chief asked. Was he actually crestfallen?

"A magic trick," Gavin suggested.

"What?"

"My girlfriend's uncles can get in and out of just about

anywhere without anybody seeing how they do it."

"Bullshit. Get someone on figuring that out."

"Okay," Gavin agreed, but he knew he was right.

CHAPTER 13

"Okay. What do I do next?" Deb asked her tablet.

Gabriella Mahoney, on the video call, said, "You put them in the oven for thirty minutes."

"And I did them right?"

"Yes, Mija. You did them exactly right."

Deb took the dish of enchiladas and put them in the oven, setting the timer.

"Whatcha cooking?" Gavin asked, suddenly appearing behind her.

"Ahhhh! Jesus! Gavin, where did you come from?" Deb yelped, nearly jumping out of her skin.

"Sorry, Babe. It was an experiment," he grinned, giving her a kiss. He turned to the tablet. "Hey, Mom."

"Hi, Sweetheart. What's with you punching walls?"

"Yeah. It was stupid. I bought a boxing bag. But I gotta wait for my hand to heal. This guacamole?" He pointed to a bowl on the counter.

"Uh…I hope so…" Deb replied, grimacing.

He grabbed a chip and dipped it in. He popped it in his mouth. "Hmmm. Not bad. Needs salt…and a little lime juice, but it's good."

"Really?" She grabbed a chip. He held up his hand. He

picked up the salt and added some. Then he got a lime, cut it in half, and squeezed the juice in. He stirred it in and motioned for her to go ahead. She dipped in her chip and popped it in her mouth. "Oh my God! It actually tastes like guacamole!"

"See. I told you I could teach you!" Gabriella said from the tablet.

Deb turned back to Gavin, but he wasn't there.

"Gavin? Great! Now you pop in and out!"

He opened the apartment door and came back in. "Magic."

"How'd you do that?" she laughed.

Uncle Bob was suddenly where Gavin had been. He put his index finger to his lips and said, "Shhhh."

"Jesus!" Deb jumped. "Stop that! Both of you."

"Misdirection. It's a trick. That's all. Now I just have to figure out how Marcus Rose did it at the daycare," Gavin said, shutting the door.

"And that's why I'm here, apparently," Bob said. "To help you do that. I knew when I left Chicago, there had to be a reason."

CHAPTER 14

Gavin headed back out. He had another class to teach, and he wanted to look at the crime scene again before going back to the University. Bob agreed to meet him at FPD headquarters later in the afternoon, and it would be too dark if he went after that meeting.

He parked along the road and got out. He found the ATV tracks and followed them back to John Lee Pratt Park. He took a trail and found himself looking at Chatham Heights. Two houses down from where the trail emerged was the home of Honeysuckle Rose. He looked over in that direction and locked eyes with Marcus Rose.

There was a good 200 feet separating them, but they might as well have been standing nose to nose. Gavin stared at him with an intensity that hung heavily in the air around them. Gavin could make out every detail of Marcus's face, his brown eyes, skinny neck, his narrow, drooping shoulders, and his long, dark, dirty hair. His olive complexion was sallow. Marcus scowled at Gavin and spit on the ground, looking anywhere but back at Gavin.

Gavin took a cleansing breath, as was his habit, to clear his mind and control his emotions. He stepped forward, closing the gap quickly.

"Good day, Mr. Rose," he said when he was directly in front of the younger man. Who maddeningly looked over Gavin's shoulder.

"Officer. You have a cast now." Marcus shifted his weight from foot to foot, clapping his hands together as he rocked his weight back and forth between his feet.

"Yeah, I broke it. I got your message."

"I didn't leave you a message," the boy said coldly, mechanically, still looking over Gavin's shoulder.

"You asked if I liked my welcome gift. No. No, I didn't," Gavin continued.

"I never said that."

"If you did, I'm going to prove it, Marcus," Gavin promised.

"Okay, but I didn't. Do you like music Detective? I have a song bouncing around in my head. Joe told me it was called an earworm. 'I Don't Remember' by Peter Gabriel. Do you know it?"

" Yeah. I know it," Gavin replied.

"With lyrics, sometimes a silver hammer is a hammer. Sometimes, the message is very clear. Other times, you have to filter out the noise to hear the real message," Marcus's eyes narrowed, and his mouth twisted into an odd grin.

"Is that what this is? Music education?" Gavin's eyes flashed. This kid was hitting awfully close to home. Ultimately, he'd chosen to write his thesis on investigative procedure, but he'd toyed with and heavily researched music, lyrics, and poetry effects on psychosis, inspired by his memories of his friend Dan Bradley's mother and sister, who were killed with a new hammer and while the refrains of "Maxwell's Silver Hammer" played that afternoon before the police cars came barreling down his street. He'd been 10, almost 11, at the time. Until he'd learned what had happened, he'd thought the unfamiliar song was funny. Later, he'd been horrified and frightened by what he remembered. He still hadn't told Dan.

CHAPTER 15

"The daycare had a bomb threat that day. Here just before the threat came in, Andrea Grimes is seen entering to drop off her son, Davison. It was a small device, but it was an actual bomb. She's the first uniformed officer on the scene because she was there when the device was found. She took charge of the evacuation until other officers arrived. She did well." He fast-forwarded. "There are the officers responding. That's Rudy Vance going in and Lieutenant Bryant directing the evacuation. The daycare claims Christa was accounted for when they evacuated the building. But she was gone when they reentered the building. No one approached them once they evacuated. They were within full view of the CCTV camera the entire time," Gavin explained, showing Bob the video from the daycare.

"No. He took her before they evacuated. Watch the employee in charge of the infants. She checks several of the other babies. But never the cart that supposedly held Christa."

"Yes, I noticed. And I agree. She knows Christa is gone. My guess is she handed Christa off inside the daycare during the evacuation. The trick is how did he get in and out while avoiding all the CCTV. And how did he get her to help him? Is she a dupe or an accomplice? I'll figure that out. I want you to prove that you can get in and out of that facility without getting caught by security or CCTV."

"I can do that in my sleep, Gavin. I think you could as well," Bob snickered.

"I'm an amateur, Bob. You've been doing this sort of thing for 50 years."

"That's true, but I don't think your killer has my resume, either."

"I know. But I just need to prove it can be done. And I have no doubt you can do it. Whereas, I am not so confident in my ability to do so," Gavin pleaded.

"Well, the easiest way, as you've learned, is the direct way. Just go in the front door, like your officers." Bob explained. "Be somebody you expect to see on the CCTV."

"I doubt this kid has that much finesse," Gavin replied.

"What's that?"

"The bomb disposal robot," Gavin replied. He fast-forwarded again.

"There. What's in those sacks the officers are bringing out?"

"Evidence. Letters, computers."

"A baby?"

Gavin turned back to the video. "Huh. Thanks, Bob."

"To you, I'm Uncle Bob. You're part of the family… whether you like it or not."

Gavin laughed. "Thank you, Uncle Bob. I am honored."

Rudy Vance knocked on Gavin's office door. "Detective Mahoney?" he asked, sticking his head in the door. "Mr. Zamphir. Hello again."

"Yes, Officer Vance, what can I do for you?" Gavin responded.

"Honeysuckle Rose just walked in and is asking to speak with you."

"Interrogation 1, Vance. I'll be right there." Gavin replied.

"Stay here, Uncle Bob. I mean it. No parlor tricks. Okay?"

"Scout's honor," Bob agreed, holding up two fingers.

"Yeah. That's a peace sign, Uncle Bob. The Boy Scout sign is three fingers together."

"You're an Eagle Scout, aren't you, Son?" Bob snickered, closing the gap between his fingers and lifting the third.

"Troop 72," Gavin affirmed as he walked out the door.

Gavin made his way to the interrogation room. He took a breath and opened the door. "Miss Rose, how can I help you?" he asked, entering the room.

Honeysuckle looked up. She had a busted lip and a black eye. "I don't know that you can help. I don't know that anyone can," she replied.

"What happened?" he asked, obvious concern in his voice.

"My cousin...Marcus. He hasn't paid his rent in three months. I need the money. His car was in the driveway, so I knocked on his apartment door. He lives in the apartment in my basement. He didn't answer. I tried the door. It was unlocked. So, I opened the door and called out to him. I stepped inside, and he jumped on me like a rabid dog. He punched me in the face several times and screamed at me to NEVER EVER come into his apartment. Then he told me to get out. And to be sure to come tell you...he specifically called you by name...to tell you that if you don't watch out, he just might have to teach you the deeper meaning of 'Dance Gypsy Dance' by Charlie Daniels. I don't know what that means, but I'm pretty sure he was serious and that if I didn't come tell you that, he might do me far worse than this," she cried.

Gavin went pale.

"Miss Rose, I want you to file an assault complaint against your cousin. Officer Vance will take your statement. I have to go home. Now."

With that, he rushed out of the room and ran to his car.

Bob was sitting in the passenger seat. "I'm sorry. But I had a feeling we should be leaving."

"A feeling? Or a warning from beyond?"

"You believe in ghosts, Gavin?"

"I'm starting to."

With that, he started the engine, put on the siren, and drove home as quickly as the Charger would carry them.

CHAPTER 16

Gavin bounded up the stairs. The apartment door had been bashed in. The door frame was splintered, and the chain hung uselessly attached to the toggle, which pulled free from the broken frame.

With his heart in his throat, he rushed inside. "Deb!" he called, in a panic. "Jason!"

Deb moaned. He turned to the sound. She was in the kitchen, behind the counter. She lay on the floor, semi-conscious. Like Honeysuckle, she'd been beaten, though far more severely.

"Oh my God!" Gavin exclaimed, dropping to his knees at her side. "Don't move, Sweetheart. Don't move." He looked up at Bob coming in the broken door. "Find Jason, Uncle Bob."

"I's here," came a small weak, tear-filled voice from the cabinet behind Deb under the sink.

"Jason! Are you hurt?" Gavin bellowed, pulling the child out of the cabinet and checking his extremities for injury.

"I's otay, Gabin. Mike told me to hide and stayed with me. Mike said you's was coming!" the boy cried.

Gavin hugged the child. "Thank you, Mike," Gavin said out loud to the room, tears falling. Mike was Jason's imaginary friend. He had gotten the name from Miranda Bradley's deceased brother. He released the boy, turning his full attention to Deb.

"Jason's okay, Sweetheart. I'm calling for an ambulance. I'm afraid to move you alone. I'm so sorry, my Love. I'm so sorry." He reached down and squeezed her hand. She opened her eyes and moaned again.

"Not your fault. Ga…vin…ba…by?" she whimpered.

"I don't know," he whispered. He reached over and called for assistance on his radio.

Bob picked Jason up and walked back to the bedroom with him. "Mommy! Mommy!" the child cried, kicking and reaching for his mother. Bob remained oblivious to the kicks and hugged the boy tighter.

"Dan…call Dan…Need Ja…son…to go…" Deb tried to speak.

"Shhhh. Don't try to talk, Sweetheart. I'll call him," Gavin whispered to her. He took out his phone. "Hey, Dan." His voice cracked. "Um. Deb's hurt bad. Please, just come here. I have to go. The ambulance is here." He disconnected as sirens blared and flashing lights filled the room from the window.

His phone rang. It was Dan calling him back. "Hold on, Dan. I can't talk. Talk to Uncle Bob. Bob reappeared behind him and took Gavin's phone from him, gliding silently back to Jason's room, where he had left the boy momentarily.

"Hello, Dan. Let me explain. Gavin is taking care of Deb right now. She's been attacked, Dan. — He thinks perhaps his suspect in the murders of these children he's working on. — Yes, Jason is fine. He hid. — Here, talk to Jason."

"Daddy!" Jason cried into the phone. "Mommy is on the floor and can't get up! And Uncle Bob won't let me help her! — Yes, Daddy. — I knows Uncle Bob wuvs me and Mommy. — But Mommy nees me! — Yes, Daddy. Gabin wuvs Mommy vewy much. — Yes. I pomise. I'll do what Uncle Bob says. — I wuv you, too, Daddy." The boy was sobbing uncontrollably as he handed the phone back to Bob.

Bob hugged the child lovingly as he returned to the call. "Dan. — Yes. — The EMTs are here. — She wants you to come get Jason. — Yes, I have him until you get here. — I'm going to follow the ambulance to the hospital. — Gavin isn't in a good place. He needs his friend. — She's pregnant, Dan. — Yes. — Great. We'll see you when you get here. — Thank you." Bob looked at Jason after he disconnected. "Come here, my nephew. Let's go follow Mommy." He picked the boy up and carried him out of the room.

The apartment was a hive of activity. Police had taken control of the crime scene. The EMTs lifted Deb to the gurney. Bob handed Gavin back his phone. Deb reached out and grabbed Gavin's hand.

"Thomp…son…knocked. Didn't unlatch…opened… crack…he busted door…"

"Okay, Baby. Okay. I promise. I'll get him. Okay? Right now, though, we're going to the hospital," he assured her.

Fear flooded her eyes. She started to hyperventilate. She held tighter on his hand.

"I'll stay with you. I won't leave you, my love," he replied to her unspoken request.

"Okay, we're going to move you now, Deb. Your husband can ride with you. Ready?"

With that, they lifted the gurney and rolled her out the broken door. Gavin followed them, and Bob, with Jason, followed him, grabbing Deb's purse on his way out.

Once they reached the parking lot, Fiona stepped forward, stopping Gavin. "What happened?" she asked, afraid for her friend.

"Deb was attacked. Probably by Jeff's killer," he reported.

"Are you sure? It's the same guy?"

"I'm not sure about anything. Fiona, who's Thompson?"

"Mildred Thompson, Unit 307," she replied, pointing to the next stairwell in their building. "She's lived here forever.

Why?"

"Officer! Apartment 307. Mildred Thompson. Deb says she knocked when her attacker busted down the door," Gavin called to the uniformed officer walking by. Rudy nodded and started moving toward the apartment Gavin indicated.

The EMTs loaded Deb in the back of the ambulance. Gavin climbed in beside her, taking her hand into his right, un-casted hand. The hand in the cast he rested on his knee.

Bob walked quietly to Deb's minivan and buckled Jason into his car seat in the back seat. He climbed into the driver's seat and followed the ambulance out of the apartment complex.

CHAPTER 17

It was after 9 pm when Dan and Miranda ran into the ER at Mary Washington Hospital. Behind them trailed Katelynn and Brandon Kaminski, Deb's sister and brother, and Dave and Gabriella Mahoney, Gavin's parents. They spotted Uncle Bob sitting calmly with a sleeping Jason on his lap. Dan rushed over. "Bob!" he barked. "How is she?"

Bob held his finger to his lips. "Shhhh. He just fell asleep. She's doing okay. She's a brave woman. She protected her abdomen. She has an orbital fracture, a broken nose, a broken jaw, a severe concussion, a broken left wrist, and a whole lot of bruises. But, for now, the baby appears to be fine. She's stable. They're admitting her. We're just waiting for them to take her up."

Dan took his sleeping child from Bob, hugging him tightly and kissing his face. "Hey Bud, I missed you," he said, wiping the hair from his son's eyes.

"Hi, Daddy," Jason yawned and buried his face into his father's shoulder, falling instantly back to sleep.

Miranda sat down beside Bob and took his hand. "How are you, Bob? Have you eaten?"

"Uh, yes, thank you, Miranda. Jason and I have eaten," he responded.

Katelynn sat down on his other side. "I don't understand what happened," she said meekly, staring at the floor.

"I'm afraid I was a little foggy on the details," Dan said.

Bob nodded. "Somebody broke into Gavin and Deb's apartment and attacked her."

"Was it a robbery? Or was somebody trying to kill Deb?" Brandon asked, towering over the rest of the group at 6'5" tall.

"Gavin says not. He thinks it may be connected to a serial killer case he's working on, but even if it is, he wasn't trying to kill her. His goal was to hurt her. Killing her would break his pattern."

"What's his pattern?"

"The three days of a new moon starting on a Monday," Gavin said, from the door behind them. "New Moon on Monday."

"Like the song?" asked Katelynn, the musician of the family.

"Yes. Like the song. They're taking her to her room now. 314." He sat down in the nearest chair and buried his face in his hands. "I'm going to kill him."

Dan handed Jason off to his wife and sat down next to his friend. "Trust me, I know exactly how you feel," he agreed, looking at Miranda. "But you're not going to do that. Just do your job, Gav. He'll pay for what he's done."

Gavin glared at his friend. "I'll kill him," he repeated. "You should see her, Dan! What he did to her!" His voice broke as he started to sob.

Gabriella had enough. She put her foot down. "Gavin Enrique Mahoney! You will do your job. You will get justice. And you will do it the right way. I have every confidence in you, Son."

He looked at his mother. His lip quivered. "She's in so much pain, Mom. She could still lose the baby from the stress and the pain." His shoulders shook, and his eyes filled with tears.

"If you love her, you'll do what's right," his mother added

confidently.

"I love her more than life itself," he replied, wiping a tear from his cheek.

"Yeah, I know how that feels, too," Dan smiled, still gazing lovingly at Miranda.

"What do I do now?" Gavin asked suddenly. "They won't let me stay with her because we're not married. They kicked me out."

"Go home. Rest," his father answered.

Gavin laughed sadly. "I don't have a door."

"Your mother, Brandon, and I will come with you. You rest. I'll fix the door," Dave suggested. Dave had a slight Irish brogue. He had lived in the US since he was a child, but he had been born in Dublin. His parents had actually moved back to Dublin when he was a young man, but he stayed.

"We're going to the beach house tonight. We'll take Jason with us. We're here as long as you need us, Gavin," Dan said, placing his hand on Gavin's shoulder.

Gavin nodded, wiping his eyes again. "I never knew my heart could hurt this much."

Katelynn stood up, walked over, and stood in front of him. Her shyness prevented her from looking at him, so she stared at the ground. "She loves you, too, you know?"

He looked at her. She was so petite he barely had to raise his eyes. "I know."

CHAPTER 18

"I can't help you on this one, Marcus. There are witnesses. Honeysuckle filed a complaint. Gavin Mahoney isn't going to let you get away with this. None of it!" Chief Lindstrom bellowed at the young man sitting in the interrogation room.

"I want to go home, Uncle Harry," Marcus replied, rocking in his seat.

"What have you done, Marcus? And I don't mean beating a pregnant woman half to death. We all know you did that. He thinks you did…unthinkable things, Marcus."

"'An Innocent Man.' By Billy Joel"

But Harry Lindstrom wasn't convinced, and the evidence was piling up. Gavin Mahoney was right. God damnit. He was right.

"I'm done, Marcus. I wash my hands of you."

"'Pontius Pilate's Dream' by Andrew Lloyd Webber," and he smiled again.

"A baby? What kind of monster are you, Marcus?"

"'Enter Sandman' by James Hetfield"

"I don't understand," Harry blundered back.

"'He'll Understand and Say Say Well Done' by Lucie Campbell," Marcus replied.

CHAPTER 19

The night passed. Not that Gavin slept. He lay in the bed, but he never closed his eyes. He listened to his father, Brandon, and Bob fix the door. He listened to his mother watch the late-night news and talk shows. He heard his family open the sleeper sofa. He heard his mother find the bedding. He even heard silent Bob, who never made a sound when he moved, climb into Jason's vacant bed. He barely grunted consent when Brandon asked if he could sleep on Deb's side of the bed. Then he listened to them all snore in different registers, except Bob, of course, who slept as silently as he moved.

When the sun rose, so did he. He showered and dressed. First, he called his TA at the University. He arranged for the TA to cover the classes for the next week. Then he called FPD headquarters, advising he'd be out of the office but available on his cell phone. Once he had cleared his schedule, he walked out the door, down the exterior stairs, over to the next set of stairs, and up two flights, where he pounded on Mildred Thompson's door. It was 6:30.

He heard her moving inside. He knew she was peering at him through the peephole. "Mrs. Thompson? I just want to talk to you," he said.

She unlatched the chain and opened her door. "I'm so very

sorry, Mr. Mahoney! I didn't know. He was always a good boy. I've never seen him act that way."

"Why didn't you call 911?"

"I…I…I was scared. He killed my Bonnie."

"Bonnie?" he asked.

"My cat. She followed us over to your door. And when he busted in the door, he looked at me, scooped up Bonnie, and wrung her neck!" Lie, he thought. She was crying by this point.

His anger began to abate as his professionalism kicked in. "That must have been terrible for you, Mrs. Thompson. I'm sorry for your loss." Then he remembered Deb's face when he'd found her. "So, you knew the man who broke down my door and beat the love of my life to within an inch of her life?" he asked snidely.

Mrs. Thompson swallowed hard. "Yes. I taught him. Algebra. It was Marcus Rose. I did tell this to the other officer." Lie, he thought again, perplexed.

"Yes, ma'am. I'm sure you did. I wanted to hear it for myself."

"He told me you and he was friends, and he was looking for your apartment. I said I'd show him. And then…" Mrs. Thompson looked down at her slippers. "I am so sorry. I hope Miss Bradley recovers quickly." All lies…except she did wish Deb a quick recovery.

He smiled and murmured, "Ms. She's divorced."

"I'm sorry, I couldn't hear you," Mrs. Thompson said.

"Oh, nothing. Thank you, Mrs. Thompson. I appreciate your talking to me after already talking to the officer yesterday. Have a good day, Mrs. Thompson." He turned away. She reached out and grabbed his arm. He turned back to her.

"I saw him here. Monday night." Lie, again.

"Who?"

"Who are we talking about? Marcus Rose. I saw him here Monday night," she mumbled.

"What time?"

"7:30 — 8:00. It was after Jeff Webster was dropped off by his idiot father but before it was dark out." Lies, all lies.

"What was he doing?"

"Just sitting in his car. He was watching…" Lying, bitch.

"Jeff?"

"Oh, no. Not at all. He was watching your apartment. When Jeff walked out and threw the trash in the dumpster next to where he was parked, he jumped. Had he been watching him, he'd have seen him before he threw the bag in. That's why I believed him when he said you were friends." Why are you lying?

"I never met the man before yesterday. And to my knowledge, I never laid eyes on him before Wednesday," Gavin replied, puzzled. "Why would he be watching…Wait, you said 7:30 or 8. We weren't home until after 8."

"Yes, your minivan was not in your parking space. He left right after you pulled into the spot."

"And Jeff?"

"Jeff had walked off with his laptop towards the Manager's office. I never saw him come back." She released his arm. Truth. Finally.

"Did you tell this to the other officer?"

She shook her head no. He sighed. "Okay, Mrs. Thompson. Thanks."

He jogged down the steps.

Chief Lindstrom was waiting at the bottom.

"Hello, Detective," he said, taking a sip of his coffee.

"Chief. What brings you here?"

"I wanted to check on your girlfriend…and you," he said.

"I'm fine. My girlfriend is…not," Gavin said, turning toward his side of the building.

"We picked up Marcus Rose last night. He had abrasions

on both hands. Your girl bit him. Hard. She fought back."

"Of course, she did. If he hadn't caught her off guard, she'd have gotten one of my guns and shot him. Unfortunately for Deb, he tricked an old woman into knocking on our door for him. Why was he watching me BEFORE I was offered the head detective job?" Gavin stared at the Chief, long and hard. Might as well use the lie.

"How would I know?" the Chief coughed.

"I don't know 'Uncle Harry.' How would you know?" Gavin shot back.

Chief Lindstrom took a deep breath. "I'm an honorary uncle, so to speak. His mother, Harmony Rose, was an old friend. His father... anybody's guess. Harmony, like her brother Greg, was a bit of a hippie. Greg is Honeysuckle Rose's father. Anyway, Harmony didn't believe in monogamy. Unfortunately, she wasn't always careful in her choice of partners. Marcus lived through some pretty terrible things. When I moved back here, I tried to help give Marcus a good male role model. I mostly failed. When Harmony passed away, he was only 17. He was completely lost. Honeysuckle let him live in her house, in the basement apartment. He just hasn't been...stable since he lost his mother. When Joe died, too, it just got worse."

"And, even though your head detective hadn't quit yet, you had my credentials on your desk?"

"Yes. I...Detective Miller was ineffectual in his post. I was looking to replace him before he quit unexpectedly. It really wasn't all that unexpected, I guess."

"Marcus knew I was a candidate?"

"You were the only candidate. I wanted you for the job," revealed the Chief.

"You're a father figure to him?" Gavin asked, perplexed.

"I guess. Yes."

"Where's Miller?" Gavin asked.

"I haven't seen him since before he quit. He left his letter of resignation on my desk Sunday night…Damn…I'll have an officer do a wellness check at his residence. You think someone manipulated things so you'd take the job?" Truth.

"I haven't a clue, and right now, I really don't care. I'm going to be with Deb. I'm going to stay by her side. And when I know she's okay, then I'm going to put whoever did this away for the rest of his life." Gavin proclaimed. "And anybody who has assisted him in the commission of his crimes with him." He started to walk away. He turned back to Harry. "There's a girl at the day care. She may have let our serial killer have Christa. Does she have any connection to Marcus?"

"I swear I don't know. I've never seen that girl before. Her name is Marlene Travis. She just moved to the area. We checked. But she's in the wind." Truth.

Gavin turned away again. "I'll have my phone on me."

With that, he climbed the stairs and entered his apartment.

Gavin didn't bother to wake his family. He grabbed his keys, pulled off the Charger key, leaving his personal vehicle's key for his family with a note for them to feel free to use it as needed, that he was going to the hospital. He walked down to the Charger. Bob was seated in the passenger seat.

"Can you take me to my car?" he asked. "We left it at police headquarters yesterday."

"Sure."

CHAPTER 20

Gavin entered the room quietly, in case she was sleeping. She was not. She turned to look at him, her one eye patched, both blackened. She sighed in relief.

"Hi, Baby," he said, stepping inside and to her bedside. "Did you sleep?"

She shook her head no. "Hur too mu…jaw wurre shu."

"Yeah, I know. He broke your jaw. It's wired shut, yes."

"Ayson?"

"He's with Dan and Miranda at the beach house. They got on that private jet and were here as fast as possible."

"Aylynn? Bannon?"

"They brought them with them. Mom and Dad, too."

She took his good hand into her good hand. "Ear er… Avin…see."

"No. Trust me. You're beautiful. You don't need to see what he did. Okay? Not right now."

"Ear er!"

"I don't have one, Honey," he replied, looking around.

"Urse." She pointed to her purse. Uncle Bob had had the presence of mind to grab it for her yesterday.

Gavin walked over and opened it, finding her makeup bag inside. He unzipped it and pulled out a small mirror, handing it to her reluctantly.

She looked into it and gasped.

"I told you not to look," he said, taking back the mirror.

She sobbed painfully and looked at him intently. "Ho me?" she implored.

He was hesitant. He was afraid he'd hurt her. She was so battered and fragile-looking.

"Hurr anway. Peas," she said, scooting to make room for him beside her, wincing as she moved.

He climbed up beside her and slipped his arm under her waist, pulling her gently to him, "Okay?" he asked. She nodded and laid her head against his chest, wrapping her arms around him. Within seconds, they were both sound asleep.

"I'm sorry. I need to check her vitals, and you're kinking her IV," the nurse said, touching him on the shoulder.

"Oh. I must have fallen asleep. Is she okay?" Gavin asked, starting awake at the sound of the nurse's voice and her touch, noticing the alarm beeping.

"Yeah, she's okay. Her IV is kinked, is all. This is the first she's slept. I hate to wake her, but I need her vitals. You're fine." She motioned that he did not need to move as he tried to untangle himself from Deb's embrace.

"No. I need to get some coffee, anyway." He gently kissed Deb's forehead, freeing himself and climbing off the hospital bed.

He paused by the door. "How's the baby?" he asked.

"So far, so good," the nurse answered. "No cramping. No bleeding. Her last pregnancy test a few hours ago was positive. You're the father, I take it. Given the…" she motioned to the bed and smiled.

"Yeah. I am."

"She's a tough cookie. She refused any pain meds because of the baby."

"What's that, then?" he inquired of the meds prepared by

the computer.

"Prenatal vitamins and calcium."

"Liquid?"

"Yeah. Well, her jaw is wired shut. She'll be on liquids for a good 6 to 8 weeks."

"Of course. Stupid question."

"No such thing," the nurse replied with a kind smile.

"Coffee?" he asked, pointing at the door.

"There's a coffee shop in the mezzanine. I'd recommend that over the cafeteria."

"Great. Thanks." He walked out and headed to the elevator.

CHAPTER 21

Gavin paid for his coffee and walked over to a table in the mezzanine. He sat down and pulled out his phone. Harmony Rose. When the Chief had said her name, he had struggled to not react. He knew Harmony Rose. Or at least a Harmony Rose. It couldn't possibly be the same Harmony Rose. Could it? Harmony Rose was the name of a music teacher at Challand Middle in Sterling when he was a kid, when he was 11, in fact. She'd also been a photographer in town and for the newspaper. He googled "Harmony Rose, son Marcus Rose." Her obituary came up in the Fredericksburg paper, *The Freelance Star*. There was a picture. She was older. But he was fairly certain that it was the same woman.

He called his sister. "Hey, Molly. — Yeah, she's okay. Relatively. — I need you to do something for me. Like Now. Please. — Go to Mom and Dad's house and find my 1998-99 Challand Middle School Yearbook. Find Ms. Rose, the music teacher. — Yes, it's important. — I think she's my serial killer's mother. — Yes. — Why would I ask for something trivial at a time like this? — For God's sake, Molly, please just do it. — Well, you take a picture of her picture in the yearbook and text it to me. — Molly! — Fine. Get one of the kids to do it. They know how to send a picture via text. God, how old are you? — Thank you! Geez. — Yeah, I'll give her your love. — Yes, I will. — I'm at the hospital right now. — I won't forget. — I love you, too." He let out a deep breath. He looked hard at the obituary photo again. What the hell was going on?

He looked up as Dan, Miranda, and Katelynn approached his table. Jason bounded over and jumped into his arms, kissing his cheek. "Hi, Gabin! We's here to visit Mommy!"

"She can't wait to see you!" Gavin assured the boy. "In fact, maybe Nana and Aunt Katie can go ahead and take you up right now. I need to talk to Daddy."

Dan raised an eyebrow. "What's up?"

"Um, I'm not quite sure, but...whatever it is, it's weird."

Dan sat down. "Go ahead, Honey. We'll be up soon."

Miranda took Jason in her arms, and she and Katelynn left Gavin and Dan to talk. When they had moved past the visitor's desk, having picked up visitor badges, Gavin said, "I've never really told you about what happened to me the day your mother died, why it affected me so much."

"You told me you never believed the official story was the whole story. We've proven that...a couple of times now."

"It's not that I didn't believe it. I knew it wasn't," Gavin said, looking away.

"Gavin? What?"

"I was there. I saw things. I heard things," Gavin admitted.

"What?"

"I was riding my bike around the neighborhood. I heard a song I'd never heard before playing over somebody's car speakers. It was the Beatles, 'Maxwell's Silver Hammer,' The car was in your driveway. It was a Mercedes. I stopped my bike to admire the car and listen to the funny song. This older man, like my Abuelo's age, yelled at me to get lost from your front door. Then I saw a younger man behind him, inside your house. I thought it was weird he was holding a hammer." Gavin stared at the table as he spoke.

Dan's voice cracked, "You…you saw them?" His mother and sister had been killed when he was 5. For years, the official story had been a vagrant had broken in, hoping to rob the house, killing Ellen and Carrie Bradley with a new hammer he'd found in the garage, then hung himself. Dan had proved that his biological father was the vagrant and that he had not killed either his mother or sister. His biological grandmother's husband and son had done the deed.

"There's more."

Dan took a deep breath. "Go on."

"As I climbed back on my bike, Joe Conti parked his beat-up car behind the Mercedes and started yelling for your mother. The old guy said, 'She's not going to answer you, Joe.' Then he screamed at me again, and I took off on my bike. Later, after we found out what had happened, I told my dad. We went down to the police station, and I told them I wanted to make a statement. They didn't believe me. They never took my statement. Dad yelled at them that I wasn't a liar, but it didn't help. They had their easy resolution. They weren't interested in what a kid on his bike claimed to see."

"Holy crap, Gavin! Why didn't you tell me before now?"

"I don't know. I thought it might change your opinion of me," Gavin shrugged.

"You and your white knight complex." Dan laughed. "Gavin, you were a kid. It's not like I expected you to rush them like you did Ivan Polaski when he held us at gunpoint. Nobody believed what I remembered about that day either." He sat there a moment, contemplating what he'd just been told. "So, why tell me now?"

"The kid who they arrested for this …he talked to me about silver hammers and music…" His phone beeped. His sister came through! He opened the picture. "Here. Look. This is Harmony Rose, my fifth-grade music teacher." He showed Dan the picture. "September, 1998." He opened the obituary again. "This is Harmony Rose, mother of Marcus Rose, my suspect. June, 2016. Is that the same woman?"

Dan sat back. "Yeah, I think so. What the fuck?"

"Dan, the kid. He looks a little…" Gavin said, lowering his voice.

Dan leaned in, "A little…?"

"A little like Katelynn." Katelynn was Deb's half-sister. Her father turned out to be Salvatore Geneli, really Andre Polaski, as it turned out, Dan's grandmother's husband.

CHAPTER 22

Deb was sitting up in her hospital room chair when Gavin and Dan entered. She had her "breakfast" in front of her, an unappetizing bowl of chicken broth and a fruit smoothie.

Knowing she'd have her jaw wired shut, Miranda brought her some metal straws that would hold up to the hot liquids better. Deb smiled at Gavin and held up the straw to show him, a glint of his devilish girl registering in the uncovered eye.

"Nice," he laughed. "Just what you've always wanted."

"Ha ha," Miranda retorted. "It's more practical than flowers."

Deb reached out, grasped Miranda's arm, and smiled warmly.

"You're welcome, Sweetheart," Miranda said. "I hope you never need it again after this."

Jason was sitting in the chair by his mother, playing with the tv/bed control. He pushed the call button. "Yes. Do you need something?" came the nurse's voice over the controller.

"Oh, no! Sorry, my son pushed the button," Dan answered, making a face at Jason that said, "Stop that."

Jason gingerly put down the controller, and Deb hugged him tightly. "Iz otay, Baby. Jus a assaden."

Jason giggled, "You's tawk funny, Mommy."

"Ye, I know. Boke ma jaw. Ta docor wayed i tageter. I will tawk funny fer a whi."

"I was so scared when you was hurt on the floor, Mommy!" the child exclaimed, hugging her back.

"Me, oo," she replied.

"Me, too," Gavin said quietly.

Dan laughed, "Yeah, Man. That was one hell of a phone call I got from you. 'Deb's hurt. Bye.' I was standing in line at Starbucks like, 'What the hell was that?'"

Gavin laughed. "Yeah, I may have been a bit... preoccupied."

"Ah. Ewe wuv me!" Deb teased.

"I sure the hell do."

"Mike tole me to hide. He ma fend. Will da bad man come back?" Jason asked.

"No, Honey. I'll make sure he doesn't, but you're going to Chicago with Daddy for a while, okay?" Gavin replied.

"But Mommy nees me!" the child protested.

"Mommy should..." Gavin started.

Deb glared at him and shook her head no.

"Need you," he corrected. "You're very important, but I promise I'll take good care of her."

Katelynn was sitting quietly across the room, working up the courage to overcome her shyness to speak. She suddenly blurted out, "Why couldn't you guys talk in front of Miranda and me?"

Everybody turned to look at her. She blushed bright red and looked at the ground.

Gavin walked over and squatted in front of her to look her in the eyes. "It's a fair question, Katelynn. I'm sorry if it hurt you. And you're right. It may very well concern you, but I'm not sure yet. Give me time to work it out. I promise I'll tell you, then. Okay?"

She looked up, staring him directly into his eyes, "It has to do with my father, doesn't it? It always comes back to him." Her eyes filled with tears.

"Yeah. It sure seems that way. He's a bad guy, Katelynn. But you're good."

She laughed a little maniacally. "Sometimes not."

"That's true of us all," Miranda interjected.

"What she said," Gavin agreed.

"Can I stay here with you?" she asked.

He looked back at Deb, who nodded her consent. "As long as you like."

She surprised him by throwing her arms around his neck and hugging him. He was nearly thrown off balance by the suddenness of her movement.

"We'll stick around over the weekend anyway," Miranda announced. "Because Jason's right: his mommy needs him."

CHAPTER 23

Deb's doctor came into the room. "Well, this looks like a party!" he joked.

"Yep! We're celebrating that you're going to tell Deb she can go home," Dan replied with a grin. "Miranda, Katelynn. Let's take Jason down to that giftshop we saw on the way in to buy his mom a gift."

"Oh boy!" Jason shouted, jumping up and running to his father.

The doctor waited for them to leave the room. Gavin sat down in the chair Katelynn had vacated and just tried to control his breathing.

"You're doing great, Deb. You don't seem to need surgery on your eye. The orbital fracture is minor. Your vision seems fine. It will take time to heal. Keep it patched to let the eye muscles rest. The main issue is your jaw. Because your pregnant, you're going to have to really push yourself to drink as many calories as you can. You're not going to be able to eat solids for anywhere between 6 to 8 weeks. You are concussed, but you're doing well. Just rest as much as you can. I know you are in pain. You can take Tylenol if you need to, but you've refused it so far, and you're managing. Your friend is right. I think we can have you out of here by this afternoon. But you're on bedrest. You need to follow up with your OBGYN before you come off bed rest. Understand? Also, follow up with an orthopedist about your wrist and your primary care physician. Good? Good."

Gavin realized he'd been holding his breath and let it out slowly.

"Take care of her, Dad," the doctor said with a wink. Then he stared suspiciously at Gavin's cast, looking back at Deb's face.

Deb laughed. "Don' werwee, Doc. He boke dat before dis appened. Avin has neber hur me. An neber wood."

Gavin looked at his hand, confused for a second. "Oh! God! No, I punched a wall like a moron. I bought a punching bag to work out my frustrations on in the future. I'd never…We arrested the guy who did this."

"Oh, you're a police officer. I see. It's here. Social Services already cleared it. Sorry." The doctor blushed.

"Don't be. Thanks for doing your job."

Deb pushed the tray in front of her out of the way and stood, holding her arms wide for a hug.

Gavin jumped up and ran to her, sweeping her off her feet and depositing her gently and gracefully on the bed. "BEDREST, DeBella Marie!" he bellowed.

She laughed, grabbing him and pulling him toward her. He kissed her forehead and sat on the side of the bed.

"Alrighty then," said the doctor, looking around the room. "Here's where I leave." He made a hasty exit.

She caressed Gavin's cheek with her good hand, tracing his cheek bone with her thumb. He smiled down at her. "I love you, Deb. With all my heart. I'm so sorry."

"Fo wha?" she asked.

"For being too late," he answered.

"Avin, sit appenz. Noh yo fau."

"Yeah, well, I'm still sorry."

"Otay. Now tiss me…denly,"

"Thought you'd never ask." He leaned down and gently kissed her lips.

"Tay ma name adin," she smiled.

He nuzzled her neck and whispered in her ear, "DeBella Marie. The beautiful Marie."

"Mmmm, ewe mayt tat soun so pri-ee"

Bob cleared his throat at the door.

Gavin grinned. "Hi, Uncle Bob."

Deb waved.

"Feeling better?" Bob snickered.

"Oing home!" Deb said, clapping.

"On bedrest!" Gavin warned.

"On beres," she agreed.

CHAPTER 24

Gavin grabbed Deb by one shoulder and Dan by the other. They lifted her rather unceremoniously, carrying her up the stairs. She laughed at their fake straining and groans. "Derks!"

The sound of Deb's laughter thrilled Gavin. At the top of the stairs, he swept her up in his arms in the bridal carry, kissed her lips, easily carrying her inside their apartment and straight back to the bedroom. He laid her on the bed, pointed his index finger at her, and warned her yet again, "Bedrest, DeBella."

She nodded. He looked around the room. "Yeah, this is awful. I'm going to go get a tv for in here, and a chair or loveseat or something."

"Noooo! Anda!"

"Right. Miranda!" he called.

"Yeah," she replied, sticking her head in the door.

"Uh, we need a TV and some seating in here. And the lady doesn't trust my decorating skills…wisely, I might add."

"Good call," Miranda said to Deb. "Got a tape measure?"

Deb pointed to the nightstand. Miranda walked over, pulled open the drawer, and dug through it. "Ah, here we go. Paper and pen, Gavin. Chop chop," she giggled. Then she saw the ring, a large silver spider with a ruby back. She picked it up. Hey, I remember this ring. I thought you said you gave it to…

Um, my mistake." She dropped it back into the drawer.

"Gave it to…who?" Gavin asked.

Miranda blushed. "You."

He huffed. "You know plenty."

"I may have been listening to a private conversation a few months back," she blushed.

"Well! Okay, then." He took a tablet and pen from his nightstand drawer.

"Sorry." Miranda gritted her teeth.

"It's not a secret, Red. It's all good. Imagine how Brandon feels. He put Candy up to the dare."

"Bannon di wha?" Deb asked, shocked.

"Yeah, he thought it was hysterical at the time." He smiled and held up the tablet and pen. "Ready?"

Miranda took several measurements, calling out the numbers. Gavin dutifully jotted them down. "Okay, let's go," she announced, returning the tape measure to where she'd gotten it. And slipping her arm through Gavin's.

"Go where?"

"U-Haul, first to get a truck. Then, Antique stores downtown. New furniture isn't going to be ready today. Antiques are available to take immediately. Especially with big, strong men to carry them." He looked nervously at Deb. "She's fine. Your Dad and Bob are here. You, Dan, and Brandon are on making-that-bedroom-inhabitable-for-an-extended-amount-of-time duty. Gabriella! Katelynn! Wanna go shopping?" Miranda called as she moved Gavin down the hall toward the door.

"I'd rather not," said Katelynn.

"Are you kidding? Where's my purse?" Gabriella responded.

"Oh great," sighed Dave.

"Sorry, Dad. I lost control somewhere back there," Gavin said, pointing back to the bedroom.

"Yeah, it was when you said, 'Miranda,'" Dan laughed. "I've made that mistake on occasion. Jason! Stay here with Uncle Bob, Dave, Katelynn, and your mommy. We'll be back soon."

Gavin looked at the size of the group for his simple shopping expedition. "Minivan," he sighed, grabbing Deb's keys.

CHAPTER 25

Miranda picked out two armchairs, a settee, a tea table, a dresser, a cedar chest, and a standing Tiffany lamp, along with several… what she called tchotchkes.

Gavin stared at the bill. "Um, Brandon, you got your platinum card? Mine's in a safety deposit box in Sterling."

Brandon reached for his wallet, but Dan interceded.

"I got you. Pay me when you can. Miranda has never really worried about the cost of things," Dan whispered.

"Thank God Melissa is happy with furniture from IKEA," Brandon joined in the whispering.

Miranda turned and smiled sweetly at them. The three of them smiled back and waved.

"I'll have the money for you Monday," Gavin whispered again. "Thanks."

"No problem. What are friends for?"

"Stop whispering, you three! I swear, you're like little kids," Gabriella said, pushing past them. "Miranda, Honey, what do you think?" She held up the treasures she'd unearthed, a silver hand mirror and what appeared to be a lace Christening gown.

"Oh! Beautiful. Chantilly lace. Good price. Good condition. The mirror is a reproduction. I'd leave that," Miranda offered.

Once they had paid and loaded the furniture in the truck,

Miranda, Gabriella, and Brandon headed back to the apartment in the U-Haul. Dan and Gavin took the minivan to Walmart.

Between the two of them, they picked out a television and surround sound system and headed to the electronics check-out counter. Gavin froze as he was walking toward the counter. Marcus Rose was working at the register.

"We'll take it to the front registers," Dan said, looking between his friend and the picture of a young Geno Geneli.

"Against store policy," Marcus said, mechanically. She'd put up a good fight. He had a black eye and a bruised cheek. His forearm was bandaged, presumably where she'd bit him.

"Fine," Gavin said, stepping forward. "I wondered how you could do that to a baby. I guess it's hereditary…the lack of conscience. Just like your father." Gavin watched for his reaction, but there was none. Gavin wanted him to answer so he could gauge whether he was lying or not.

He rang up Gavin's items. "$2456.98."

Gavin paid. "Come near her again, and you'll wish I'd killed you." He pushed again.

"What do you think of 'I Shot the Sheriff?' Do you think he did shoot the deputy?" Marcus said, looking at Dan. Nothing.

"Well, aren't you a peach?" Dan retorted, taking his friend by the arm and leading him out.

CHAPTER 26

Miranda arranged the bedroom beautifully. Gavin was surprised that all that furniture fit, but not only did it fit, it looked like it belonged there. Brandon, Dan, and Gavin installed the new tv and surround sound. Gabriella and Miranda made several pots of pureed soups and put them in the freezer.

As evening approached, Dan offered to get Gavin's parents and Brandon hotel rooms, but they refused, getting their own. Katelynn insisted on staying with Deb. And Gavin had told her she could stay. Bob said he was staying as well, but as the majority of their guests left, and Jason went with his father. The apartment felt like theirs again.

Deb drank some tomato soup and a nutrition shake and lay back in bed. She patted the bed beside her. Gavin was beyond exhausted, having only slept the twenty minutes or so while holding her. He climbed in beside her on top of the covers in his clothes, snuggled up against her, and fell immediately asleep.

"Lieutenant Mahoney!"

Gavin opened his eyes. "Detective or Professor now," he replied, confused. He was standing outside the burned-out condominium that Kathy, Deb's mother, had burned to the ground. A soldier was standing menacingly in front of him. There was snow on the ground, and he shivered in the cold. Why was there snow? Evan? Why is there snow?

"She can't come in. Deb disinvited her. But she told me to tell you to look in the box." But it wasn't Evan's voice. Mark?

"Who? What box?"

"Kathy. THE box."

The gunshot rang out. He saw a young police officer fall. Mark whispered, "Do you love her?" He saw Deb, Mark vanished, and reappeared behind him. "You love her!" Mark screamed. Then Mark shoved him hard. The gunshot rang out again.

Gavin was falling as more shots rang out, and there were distant screams. Then he was on top of Deb, lying in the snow. "Are you hit?"

Gavin startled awake and sat up. He jumped out of bed and went to the closet, digging past the Christmas decorations to find Kathy's box of "security." She'd acquired files over the years of working for and being mistress to Salvatore Geneli, anything she thought could have monetary value to Salvatore. He pulled it out of the closet and took it to the newly created seating area, turning on the Tiffany lamp before he sat down and started digging through it.

"Whaz za matta?" Deb asked, sitting up.

"Nothing, Baby. Go back to sleep."

"Wha ewe loo-in fo?" she insisted, groggily.

"I don't know. Mark told me to look."

"Wha?"

"I had a dream, is all," he explained.

"Ow tum ewe unerstan me, an obody elze tan?"

"What did you say?" he grinned.

"Ewe suck!" she laughed and threw a pillow at him.

"How do you read my mind half of the time?"

She shrugged.

"Same thing, I guess."

He looked through the box in silence. There it was: a Geneli file labeled "Harmony Rose." As with the file on Miranda, they'd found in the spring, it was a PI's report. There were pictures of Harmony and a Geneli, alright. Compromising pictures. But they weren't of Salvatore or Geno. It was Anthony. Anthony had been the least culpable of the Genelis. He had ultimately been convicted of conspiring to commit murder and the home invasion in which Miranda had been assaulted nearly a year ago. He had been an attorney with the State Attorney General's Office. He undeniably had the highest social standing between the three of them, and he had lost everything as a result. His wife had filed for divorce, he had been disbarred, his license had been revoked, he'd been fired, and Dan had inherited all his mother's fortune, leaving him deeply in debt. Oddly, Salvatore didn't order the report. Dominica did. Even odder still, she also signed the canceled check made out to Harmony for $45,000 that appeared by this report to have saved his reputation AFTER the murder of Dominica's daughter and granddaughter, Dan's mother and sister, the impetus for Dominica's revenge in the form of a will disinheriting her husband Salvatore and their sons, Tony and Geno. "What the hell?"

Deb watched him in silence. Finally, she sat up. "Ewe deam abou Mawk?"

He looked across the space between them, suddenly feeling it keenly. "I do sometimes."

"Wha do ewe deam?"

"The day he was killed. He yells at me because I love you and shoves me. Then the gunshot fires, and I'm on top of you asking if you've been hit?"

"I wuv ewe, Avin. Ewe don nee is pemisson."

"I wish I could have it, none-the-less." He stood and walked back to the bed and climbed on. He kissed her belly. "It's crazy to be jealous of a ghost, isn't it?"

She ran her fingers through his hair as he rested his chin

on her stomach. "Ee neber alled ee anyting bu Eb…or Ebbie," she confessed.

"How is that possible?"

"Ah awayz ated ma name."

"DeBella literally means 'the beautiful.' How can you hate that name? It describes you."

"Ah wuv when ewe zay it." She smiled and winced.

"Does it hurt to talk, Honey? Don't talk."

"Ah'm otay. Ma ead hurrs a widdle. An I zoun upid."

He laughed. "Would you like me to sleep on the settee thing Miranda picked out…Let you rest?"

She frowned and shook her head, wincing again. "No. Ah seep edder wit ewe ere." She patted his pillow.

"Okay. I'm going to get out of these clothes. I fell asleep still dressed earlier. Do you need anything?"

"No, jus ewe," she smiled.

CHAPTER 27

Gavin sat with his coffee, watching Deb sleep. She was beyond beautiful. When he'd met her not even a year ago, even though they'd been through so much that it seemed much longer, he'd thought she was the most beautiful woman he'd ever seen. She had a perfect creamy complexion, deep, ocean blue eyes, full naturally pink lips, and cascading golden blonde hair that he'd since learned came from a bottle. He had no clue what her natural hair color might be. Pictures of her through the years showed every possible hew known to man. But even with her face swollen and bruised, her beauty shone through. It wouldn't matter if Mark shoved him every night of his life. He'd suffer anything to be the man at her side. He'd pretty much decided that the day he'd tripped, knocking her to the ground amid a barrage of gunfire. He'd never admit that he tripped. She assumed he'd pushed her down to save her. And he would have if he hadn't started falling before the shots were fired. He left it at that.

He glanced down at the file on Harmony Rose. A spark of an idea had ignited in his brain last night as he slept. It was starting to burn.

He picked up his phone and placed a call. "Vance? — Yeah, she's doing okay. — I want Marcus Rose's file, including his mug shot. — Can you bring it to me? — Now, would be great.

— Vance! I want you to bring it. — Okay then, 9:30 am."

He stood, walked over to Deb, and gently shook her awake.

"Did you recognize him, the man who did this? Had you seen him before?"

"Di'n see im. Door fell on ee. Ah wuz knock unconsis," she replied.

Gavin took her hand, "This is important, Honey. The police report says you fought back, hit him, bit him."

She shook her head no. "Coul-n. Not consis."

The idea was a raging inferno now. He texted Dan, "Need to know exactly what Jason saw."

"Sure. On our way. You can talk to him when we get there," came the reply.

"Waz wong?" Deb asked, sitting up nervously.

"I saw what I was meant to see…a magic trick."

"Wha?"

"It's nothing, Sweetheart. I'm going to run out to Walmart and get you some of those nutrition shakes. I should have gotten them yesterday. But I guess I was distracted." He drank the rest of his coffee and kissed her. He woke Katelynn, asleep on the sofa, on his way out.

CHAPTER 28

Gavin leaned against the Charger, waiting. He'd already been inside the store and bought the shakes. It was ten minutes to 8 when Marcus emerged from the store. Gavin had purposely parked in a CCTV blind spot. He called out to Marcus. The young man approached, again looking past Gavin more than at him. Gavin again noted the rocking and clapping. Now he understood. He wasn't seeing psychosis. He was seeing a man on the autism spectrum.

"Who hit you, Marcus?" Gavin asked, kinder than he'd been previously.

"I'm hearing 'The Boxer,' by Simon and Garfunkel."

"I'm sorry, Marcus. I was wrong. I just about fell for the misdirection," Gavin said.

"That's okay," Marcus replied. He gave no indication if he understood or not. He simply accepted the apology. He reached out his hand.

Gavin laughed and grasped Marcus's hand in his, giving the younger man a hearty handshake. "I wish everyone were so forgiving, Marcus."

Marcus laughed mirthlessly back. "Me, too." He rocked with a little more energy.

Gavin was now completely convinced that Marcus was

not guilty of anything. He saw a course of action, but it could go badly for him. Still, he felt he owed the younger man. He had to prove his innocence, starting with the assault on Deb and working back to the murders.

"Can you come with me, Marcus? I need to prove you didn't do what you were arrested for."

"I don't want to go back to the police station," he replied, warily.

"No. Not there. I promise."

"Okay, then. Can I ride up front?" he asked.

Gavin laughed again. "Of course you can."

"Can we listen to the radio? Not the police radio. The real radio."

"That we can," Gavin affirmed.

"Will Uncle Harry stop being mad at me?" Marcus looked him in the eyes for the first time, for only a second. It was obvious the act felt horribly uncomfortable and unnatural to Marcus.

"I don't know. I hope so. Come on," he said, opening the passenger side door.

Marcus hesitated. "My mother always said I should be careful who I choose to be my friends. Are you my friend? Even after you solve your case?"

"Marcus, I am your friend. Even after I solve my case," Gavin promised.

CHAPTER 29

Gavin took Marcus to his office on Campus and texted Dan to come there…alone. He needed to talk to his friend first. Dan knocked on Gavin's office door at 8:45. Gavin called out for him to come in.

Dan jumped and grabbed for his weapon when he saw Marcus sitting there across from Gavin. Gavin jumped up and held out both hands, waving Dan off. "No! It's okay. Come in. Sit down."

Dan slowly entered and took a seat next to Marcus across from Gavin. He was perplexed, but Gavin seemed fine, so he did as his friend commanded.

"Dan, this is Marcus Rose," Gavin said, motioning toward the younger man.

"Yeah, we've met," Dan replied.

"Have you? Really?" Gavin gave Dan a quizzical look. Dan was still confused, but daylight was starting to dawn on him. Gavin had changed his mind about this kid. Dan trusted Gavin's instincts more than any other man's. He turned and looked at Marcus.

Marcus rocked back and forth at the waist in his chair. He flapped his hands briefly. He looked past Gavin, not at him. He smiled awkwardly and said, "'Why Can't We Be Friends?' by

War."

"Huh," said Dan, sitting back. "I guess not. Hello, Marcus. I'm Dan Bradley. Nice to meet you." He then leaned forward again and extended his hand.

Marcus turned toward Dan, looking at his hand. He gave an odd little whoop and then shook Dan's hand. "'Nice to Meet You' by Niall Horan."

Dan looked at Gavin with his mouth slightly open, the question in his eyes still unformed on his lips.

"Marcus likes music, " Gavin explained, clearly amused.

"Ah. What's going on, Gav?"

"Marcus is your cousin, Dan." Gavin tossed the file from Kathy's box.

"Sure, you told me you suspected that much," Dan replied, picking up the file. His eyes got big and he gave a whistle as he flipped through it. "She knew?"

"As far as I can tell, she supported Ms. Rose and Marcus. At first, I thought she might have paid Ms. Rose off to save face for Tony, but given their rather strained relationship, that hardly seemed likely. At some point last night, I began to wonder if that was the only check. I called Judy. I hope you don't mind."

"Of course not, Sherlock," Dan joked. "What did my grandmother's personal secretary have to say?"

"That Dominica sent $45,000 every three months for the last 25 years of her life, that you told her to continue to cover the personal accounts as usual, so you have sent the money over the last year, three times so far," Gavin laughed.

"I have?" He looked Marcus up and down, noting his frayed hems, worn sleeves, and sallow complexion. "Where'd the money go?"

"My guess, Honeysuckle Rose took it," Gavin offered.

"She's the one who 'delivered the message' to you, claimed he'd beaten her, right? Why would she suddenly try to frame him for something like this?"

"Ah. Judy sent Marcus a personal note with the last check. She's retiring. Sorry, Man."

"Oh, I see, so Honeysuckle needs him declared dangerous and psychotic, so anything he says about what happened to the money is discounted before I get wise. That's nuts," Dan guffawed incredulously.

Marcus laughed and covered his mouth. "That's a naughty song," he snickered.

"What? 'Nuts?' I bet," Gavin winked.

"So, who is your serial killer? Surely not Honeysuckle Rose?" Dan smiled, changing the subject back to the topic at hand.

"Of course not. I'm still working on that," answered Gavin, looking at his watch. "I need to get home. Marcus, can we get you some decent clothes and some real food? And where do you get your prescriptions? Walmart, where you work?"

"'Yes Indeed' by Drake," Marcus replied, still rocking.

"I think the song titles are a kind of echolalia triggered by his anxiety. He can communicate. I've heard him. But if someone took his meds…maybe he'd regress enough that he'd rely on the songs to communicate, especially if he's stressed… you know… charged with a crime…that sort of thing," Gavin suggested quietly to Dan. Dan nodded.

"Marcus, do you want to leave Honeysuckle's house? Live somewhere else?" Dan asked.

Marcus laughed and gave the strange whoop. "Yes, thank you."

"Okay, let's go get you an apartment." Dan looked at Gavin. "We'll meet you back at your place later, Gav. We're going to extricate Marcus from the care of Honeysuckle Rose." He pulled out his phone and made a call. "Sam, hey. I need an emergency order for guardianship for my cousin. — Yeah, another one." He grinned. "This one is on spectrum, and I have reason to believe he's being abused. — Gavin found him." Then he laughed. The man on the other end could be heard laughing as well. Marcus smiled as he rocked.

CHAPTER 30

Gavin returned home to find Bob in the kitchen, heating up broth for Deb. Dan smiled and held up the case of shakes. "They're probably best cold. Think there's room in the fridge for the case?"

"Sure. And if not, I'll make room," the older man replied, though he didn't look older. Bob and his brother Frank seemed to be ageless. "I think she's reaching maximum boredom, Son. I'll put this stuff away. Go entertain her before she loses it."

"Where's everybody?"

"They went out to breakfast. They didn't want to eat in front of her."

Gavin nodded and headed down the hall to the bedroom. He paused at the door and leaned against the frame. She was punching a pillow. "Bedrest, DeBella," he said with a good-natured snort.

She huffed and lay back on the bed in frustration. "I'm soooo ored," she complained. "Enerain me."

He couldn't help himself. He laughed. She lifted her head and glared daggers at him.

"I love you, Deb," he announced.

"Funny vay oo sew id," she pouted.

"What do you want me to do?"

She got an evil glint in her uncovered eye, "Ance."

"Uh, no." he laughed. "But I'll watch a movie about dancing." He shuddered at the thought.

"Ed Astaire an Iner Ogers," she demanded and patted the bed beside her. "Ole oovie."

"Okay," he agreed. He walked over and arranged the pillows behind her. She clapped. He walked around to his side of the bed and arranged his pillows, and jumped up beside her.

She handed him the remote. "Ell id 'Sall ee ance?' Id oesin unwesan ee."

He took the remote, pushed the voice control button, and said, "Shall We Dance?"

Bob brought in her broth and her metal straw, looked at the TV, and quickly retreated.

"Coward!" Gavin called after him.

"Yep," he said, waving over his shoulder as he exited.

They had just started watching when there was a knock at the apartment door. "That'll be Rudy Vance. I promise. I'll just be a minute." Gavin said, pausing the movie.

'Uggggg," she groaned.

"I promise." He kissed the top of her golden head.

He emerged from the bedroom as Bob opened the door.

"Hello, Mr. Zamphir, Gavin," Rudy said, holding out a file. "Not a lot here. Other than Honeysuckle's complaint and your girlfriend's, of course, he's pretty clean. He did have an altercation with a professor at UMW before he failed out after Joe Rose passed away, but other than being a little odd, there's nothing here to cause alarm. Think he went off his meds or something?"

"Or something," Gavin replied, looking through the file. "Thanks, Rudy. I don't think he's our guy. This pretty much confirms what I was expecting."

"But Mrs. Thompson's testimony?"

"Yeah. She's lying." Gavin looked at his protégé. Rudy

didn't look surprised. He barely reacted at all.

"I trust your experience, Detective. But that leaves us nowhere on the serial killer," Rudy stated matter-of-factly.

"I'm aware."

As Rudy took his leave, Bob said, "He seems like a nice guy."

"Yeah, he does," Gavin agreed. He turned and walked back to the bedroom, climbed back on the bed, and took the movie off pause. He never said a word.

Deb took the remote from him and hit pause again. She stared at him. "Waz wong?" she asked.

He shook his head.

"Avin?"

"I think Rudy may be a sociopath. His reactions and body language…they read as purposeful." She looked at him, clearly not understanding his meaning. "He reacts as he thinks he is expected to react… on purpose. He has to think about it."

"Wha oes dat ean?" she asked, concerned.

"Nothing, really. Most sociopaths live perfectly normal, law-abiding lives."

"An dose dat don?"

"Well, they don't," he replied cryptically.

Deb swallowed hard. She remembered this: the panic, the fear. This was what he had been trying to spare her by taking the job at the University of Mary Washington, but he was calm, collected.

He reached over and patted her leg, "Don't worry, Sweetheart. I'll be fine." He only hoped he could keep everyone else in his life safe. He'd failed miserably on that front lately. He'd fallen for the magic trick. It wasn't the first time. Evan. Horatio.

But he'd never loved this way before. He'd dated, sure. He'd even lived with Shannon for a few years, and he'd cared for her, but this… he'd never felt this. He'd been missing out. He knew the first time he'd seen her temper rise, if she'd give him the time of day, he'd be hers forever. And here they were.

She glared at him. "Di dat wor on Sannon?"

As usual, she read his mind. He really didn't know how she did that.

"Stop clenching your jaw, Darling. It's broken. That has to hurt," he said, trying not to laugh. He'd blame it on her gypsy blood, but she'd just tell him gypsy was rude and that it was Romani.

"It is Omani," she said, smacking his hand and crossing her arms.

"Damn. I didn't say that out loud, Deb," he replied, amazed.

"Ou thin oudly," she replied, hitting play on the remote.

"How does someone 'think loudly?'"

"Ah on't know. Ou are da un tinking oudly," she snarked. He didn't hold back. He laughed. He grabbed her and hugged her. He felt her relax in his embrace.

"Shannon is happily married with a kid, a dog, a cat, and a mortgage in Green Bay, Wisconsin. Four years, now. She's ancient history," he whispered in her ear.

She turned to face him. "If ou an be ealous of ghost, Ah an be ealous of a iving, beathing woman, even if see is mawweed an in Isconsin."

"Fair enough," he acquiesced, kissing her softly so as not to hurt her, as Fred and Ginger whirled around the screen.

CHAPTER 31

A call to Judy Travers, who had been Dominica's private secretary and was now Dan's, as the sole heir to her estate, provided Sam with all the information he needed to get Dan replacement medications for Marcus and an order prepared for a judge to award Dan temporary emergency guardianship, pending a hearing to determine permanent guardianship. Marcus had been diagnosed with ASD at three. After his mother had died, Dominica had, in fact, shared guardianship with Joe Rose, his mother's cousin. Joe had loved the boy. He had worked tirelessly to help Marcus get an education and live a good quality life. No determination of guardianship had been filed or awarded since either Joe or Dominica's deaths. Honeysuckle had simply assumed the role. Since Joe's death, Marcus had failed out of his classes at UMW, regressed visibly in his communication skills, appeared malnourished, and, despite the $130,000 sent to him by Judy in the last year, his accounts were in the red. The judge signed the emergency order over his lunch with Dan Bradley.

Honeysuckle Rose was playing with her dogs in the backyard of her recently paid-off home, when the Escalade pulled into her driveway. A FPD cruiser pulled in behind it. The officers approached with the guardianship order. Dan stepped out of the vehicle, motioning for Marcus to do the same.

"You can't just take him!" she screamed across the yard.

"I can. What's more, I am having a trust set up for him. You'll not be receiving any more checks."

Her face fell. "I don't know what you're talking about," she stammered.

"Well, since my secretary sends the checks, I can and have stopped their being sent. Further, I've the information showing you deposited those checks into your account and paid off your mortgage with them. I'll be filing a civil suit to recoup those funds on his behalf. And since you lied in your complaint, stating he owed you unpaid rent, it calls into question the entire assault complaint, which has been dropped."

"But…but the detective's girlfriend?"

"Never saw him. So no charges are being filed on that," Dan advised her. "In fact, she says she was knocked unconscious and was unable to fight back, so the police are now investigating how Marcus ended up with all these bruises. Once his meds have a chance to kick in, maybe he'll be in a better position to explain that."

She read the threat in his green eyes. She'd taken a shot and missed. She could lose everything now. She sat down on the ground and cried as they removed all of Marcus's things, not that he had much. She'd taken anything of value ages ago.

CHAPTER 32

The next few days passed quickly. Dan found a placement in a private group home for Marcus. He seemed happier and healthier quickly. He was eventually able to relate that Honeysuckle had controlled his finances and medications. For some reason, she burst into his apartment that day with her boyfriend, Jerry Boniface. Jerry had struck him several times. Then he'd hit Honeysuckle at her insistence.

Jerry "Bonnie" Boniface was a biker. Big. Strong. He wasn't thrilled with the plan that included beating up a strange woman, but he'd helped spend the money. He felt obligated to help his girl out of this jam. He'd intimidated Mrs. Thompson, who had indeed been his algebra teacher, telling her who to blame. But the old woman had still hinted at his involvement.

Dan and Miranda, along with the entourage they'd arrived with, left with Jason. Katelynn decided to head home, to, having her own college career to focus on. Bob stayed.

Monday morning found Gavin sitting in the OBGYN's office beside Deb. It was the first appointment of the day. She'd dropped 6 pounds but was otherwise healthy. She was at 10 weeks gestation. She had not experienced any real nausea. But the shakes and soups were hard to get down. Still, she was advised to drink at least 6 of the shakes in addition to the broths and soups.

"You're healthy and recovering quickly. I see no reason you need to remain on strict bed rest. Just take it easy. Don't push yourself," her doctor suggested.

She sat forward, excitedly, "Ex?"

Gavin blushed.

The doctor laughed. "Sex should be fine. Just don't get too wild."

Her other appointments were equally encouraging. Her eye was okay. Her jaw was already showing signs of healing. Her MRI was normal. She just needed to take it easy. She'd been very lucky.

Deb nearly skipped out of the clinic. In the parking lot, Gavin grabbed her hand and twirled her toward him. He placed his left casted hand at her waist and danced with her.

"Ou sai ou couldn' ance," she giggled.

"No. I said I wouldn't," he replied.

Her phone rang. The caller ID read "S. Magill, Green Bay, WI." She showed Dan, feeling confused and a little hurt.

He took the phone and answered it. "Hello?"

"Gavin?" came Shannon's voice from out of the past. "What the hell?"

"My sentiments exactly, Shannon. How'd you get this number?" he asked.

"Me? You've been calling me every five minutes for the last two hours and hanging up after playing a snippet of some song!" she screeched.

"No, I haven't. We've actually been in doctors' appointments for the last two hours. No one made a call," he replied. "What song?"

"Who's 'we?' What difference does the song make? What's going on? I'm happily married, Gavin."

"Great. Happy for you. What damn song, Shannon?" he

snapped, irritated by her as he usually was whenever she started in on him, her presuming she knew things she was clueless about.

"Some stupid thing about an old flame!" she yelled, "Now, why are you calling me?"

"I told you, I'm not. My girlfriend's phone has apparently been cloned, and someone is messing with me."

"Messing with you? I'm the one getting the calls!" Shannon bellowed into the phone.

"Yes, I understand, and I'm sorry. But I promise you, neither Deb nor I have been calling you. We literally just walked out of the clinic after visiting 20 million doctors this morning."

"Well, that doesn't make any sense, does it? I mean, how would some rando know to call me to mess with you?" Shannon demanded.

"I don't know. They must know me." The words echoed in his head.

Shannon calmed down a little. "So you have a girlfriend, finally? Good. What's her name?"

"Her name is Deb Bradley," he answered.

"Is she sick or something?" Shannon asked, sounding annoyed.

"No. She was in an accident of sorts. Actually, she was attacked. I thought it was in relation to a serial killer case I'm working on, but it wasn't. But I'm not sure this phone call thing isn't. Tell Barry to call the Fredericksburg Police Department, Shannon. I'll text the number. I'll be there later today."

Deb looked at him, confused. "Bawwy?" she asked.

"Barry Magill, Shannon's husband. He was my Abnormal Psychology professor and dissertation advisor," Gavin explained. "He's also a profiler for the FBI."

"Ewe could tawk oo Uncle Om," Deb suggested, reading his distaste at the thought of speaking to the man.

"No. They called Shannon for a reason."

Deb grabbed Gavin's hand, "Avin, he's stawkin' ewe, isn' ee?"

Gavin didn't answer her.

Shannon's voice came back over the phone, "Gavin? Gavin Mahoney?"

He turned back to the phone, "Yeah, Shannon?"

"Are you okay?"

"Yeah. Just have Barry call the number I'm texting. Sorry, you got those annoying calls."

He disconnected, never dropping eye contact with Deb. "I'm fine, Honey. I'll be fine."

"It's ma faut! Ah made ewe ake da ob!" she said, starting to cry.

"No. It's not your fault. Jeff…was selected to draw me in. It's always been about me."

"Why?"

"I have no idea." He shrugged.

She rushed at him, hugging his neck. "On't eave ee!" she cried.

"I'm not going to leave you," he promised.

"Taday! Ake ee wid ewe. Peas."

"Okay. You can come with me to FPD headquarters today. But I do have two jobs, and tomorrow I have to get back to both of them," he admonished her.

She pushed him away and walked away from him.

He huffed, "Deb! I didn't mean that the way it sounded. Deb!"

She stopped and turned back to him. "Ah get dat ewe don wan oo live on An's oney. Ut it'z ma oney!"

"I know it's your money, Deb. I swear that isn't what I meant by that!" he pleaded. "I just meant that I have responsibilities to the Police Department and the University. I made commitments that I need to keep. I really didn't mean anything about you.

Honey, please. I'm sorry."

"Why id ee ave to call er?" Deb asked, opening the passenger side car door and getting in the car.

CHAPTER 33

Carl's Ice Cream was a slice of Americana on Princess Anne Street, emblazoned in neon with an oversized ice cream cone crowning the stand over its walk-up ordering window. Gavin pulled into the parking space and turned to look at Deb, who stared straight ahead.

"What flavor shake do you want?" he asked after several seconds of strained silence.

"Stawbewwy," she answered, falling silent again.

Gavin sighed and exited the vehicle. He walked up to the window. She watched him order and pay. Her chin started to quiver, and the tears spilled down her cheeks. They hardly ever fought. That they did so on what should have been a happy day devastated her, crushed her, in fact. Gavin was heading back to the car with two milkshakes. She lowered the visor and checked her face in the mirror.

That was a mistake. Her nose was still swollen, and both eyes were still black, though only the right one was visible as a patch covered the other. Her jaw below the patch was bright purple, and her lips were a navy blue on the left half of her mouth. She looked like she'd been hit by a truck. She imagined Shannon Gibbons Magill didn't look like she'd been hit by a truck.

He opened his door and handed her her shake before

climbing behind the wheel. He looked at her again. He pulled his handkerchief from his pocket and gently wiped away her tears. "Please don't cry, Sweetheart."

"Wha appened wid Sannon?" she asked.

He was confused. "We broke up," he answered, thinking that was actually an answer.

"Avin! No duh! Weally? Why? How?"

"Is that what's bothering you?" he asked. "Why didn't you just ask?"

"Ahhhh!" she gasped, frustrated.

"We had lived together for four years. She was expecting an engagement ring for her birthday. I bought her a camera. We had an argument. She stormed out. She was a social worker at the battered women's shelter. She went to work. A few hours later, I decided to go talk to her, resolve the fight. I went to the shelter. She acted like she was afraid of me in front of a room full of people. Someone called the police. I told them I was just trying to talk to my girlfriend. They said I should leave peacefully. I looked over at her. I swear she looked…smug. So I left. I went home. I packed my stuff, and I left."

"Ewe boke up ober a cama?" Deb asked.

"No. We broke up over her letting people believe that I would hit her. We broke up because she is a massive, manipulative bitch."

Deb's reaction was unexpected. She started laughing.

He stared at her, flabbergasted.

Finally, she said, "Oh, ma God! Ah imadined see was da lon lost love of or life."

"Well, that's ridiculous, Deb. You're the love of my life. She's someone I thought I cared about, whom it turns out I don't even like very much."

"Why don ewe ike er usband?"

"I don't dislike him. He was my friend, my advisor. She

showed back up two years later. She made a move to get back with me. I wasn't interested, so she moved on to Barry. She convinced him I was a violent man and that I beat her. Less than a month after she came back to Dekalb, he moved in with her. It hurt that he thought I would ever…physically hurt her. He asked to have me reassigned to a different advisor. It set me back. I don't need people like that in my life."

"Why don ewe ever tawk abou er?"

"Because I don't care about her enough to talk about her," he replied. "But if I knew this was bothering you, I'd have told you anything you wanted to know. No one holds a candle to you, Vida. No one." He smiled that dazzling smile of his. "I'm a little in my own head sometimes, Honey. Please don't ever be afraid to ask me anything you want to know. About anything."

She nodded. "Id ewe pay An back fir da furniture?"

This time, he laughed. "Yes. I Venmo'ed it this morning after rearranging some things. The furniture is my gift, Deb. I want to pay for it. And you don't need to worry about money. I'm not. I have money."

"Will ewe ever see ma money as our money?" She asked the hard question.

"It's not that. You can spend your money however you like. I just don't need your money. I have plenty. Is that okay?"

"Yas. I know dat. I'm sowwy. Homones. I'm a weepin ess ooday."

"Drink your shake before it melts," he instructed, giving her a kiss.

She took a sip through the straw. "MMMM! Dat's way bedder dan bwoth!" she laughed. "How mutt?" she asked suddenly.

"How much what?" he asked.

"Montey? Ewe jus said modewatly rict; not how mutt."

"Oh, I have no idea. My grandfather put it in trust from

his business."

"Twus…between eigh kis and 33 gankis?"

"Yes."

"Uh-huh."

"Debbie, I have more than enough money!"

She started to laugh.

"You're making fun of me!" he blushed.

"A widdle bid," she said, smiling.

She took another sip of milkshake. Then she looked at him again. "Di Sannon know dis?"

"Hell, no."

"How do ewe lib wid somun fir four ears an dey nah know ou're wich?"

He blushed. "Because, on the advice of counsel, I hid it from her. She's why my platinum card is in a safety deposit box, and I needed to borrow the money to cover the furniture. I'm used to living on my salary at this point."

CHAPTER 34

Deb and Gavin walked arm in arm into police headquarters. Gavin greeted Andrea Grimes at the front desk and introduced Deb. They signed her in as a guest, and he showed her around. Noticing her step slowed, he took her to his office and had her put her feet up on a sofa against the far wall while he worked through a pile in his inbox.

Chief Lindstrom knocked at his door.

"Hello, Chief," he greeted his superior, opening the door.

Deb moved to put her feet down, but the Chief waved her off. "Stay as you are, Ma'am. We're all happy to see you up and about."

She smiled, "Tank ewe, Chief."

Turning to Gavin, he said, "I checked on Maurice Miller, personally. He's fine. Enjoying some time off before he starts his new job at a private security firm next month."

"His name is Maurice Miller?" Gavin asked.

"Yeah, why?" the Chief asked.

"How old is he?" Gavin continued, ignoring the Chief's question.

"Forty-five-ish, What?"

"It's nothing. We had a Maurice Miller as head detective in my hometown when I was a kid. My dad worked under him. But he'd be much older than 45," Gavin replied, having a haughty chuckle at his suspicious mind.

The Chief gave a short laugh. "Yeah, this would be a different Maurice Miller. On a different topic, I understand you had a hand in clearing Marcus. I have to admit, even I was getting suspicious. Honeysuckle had us all duped. Looks like you are absolutely the best man for this job. Good due diligence, Mahoney. Especially given your personal connection to the case. Most guys would have just let the jail crumble on top of him."

Gavin blushed. "Her mistake was taking the meds away completely. With his anxiety under control, his ASD was nearly invisible. Without it, he showed all the classic telltale symptoms. Simple facts are he was, is, statistically, more likely to be the victim of violent crime than the perpetrator." He looked over at Deb. She was looking at her phone. "Speaking of that, Jerry Boniface, Honeysuckle's boyfriend, cut a deal. He's a piece of work. The neighbor told me Marcus killed her cat, Bonnie. She made certain to tell me that."

"Her cat? So?"

"We aren't allowed to have pets. Apparently, people call Jerry Boniface 'Bonnie.' I think she was trying to tell me something while sticking to the lie our perp told her to tell," Gavin whispered.

"Let me ask: Did you know she was lying when you talked to her that morning?"

"Ehhh. I was fairly certain. The story sounded rehearsed. Her body language was…off. It's not an exact science…reading body language, facial expressions, and voice control…but I'm more right than wrong most of the time." Gavin winked.

His office phone rang, and he picked it up. "Mahoney. Oh, yeah — Put him through, Andrea. — Barry, hi. — One second." He looked up at Chief Lindstrom. "I need to take this. A profiler I know. You want to listen in?"

"Oh, no. I trust your judgment. Ma'am, I hope you're feeling better real soon," he replied, leaving the office.

"Hey, Barry. I'm back," Gavin said. "I take it Shannon filled you in on what she thinks is happening. — Yeah, no. Neither Deb nor I could have made those calls. She had doctors' appointments all morning. I was with her. The phone never came out. — Not important and really none of your business. Suffice it to say, she's fine. — Yeah, I'm working on a serial killer case, in which the killer sent the families sheet music he used to stage the body dumps…so you see why the music playing is significant? — Yeah, I can send you the details. — Full profile — What's your email? — Yeah. I got it. — What? — Yeah, I got that after he left me a message after the first victim. — I'll be fine — Barry, thanks."

"How wong have ewe known ewe're da guy's target?" Deb asked from the sofa.

"Since Wednesday," he answered.

"Oo dey know?" She motioned to the office around them.

"I believe at least one of them does," he replied honestly.

Deb gasped.

"It's okay, Baby. I promise." He sat down and opened his case file on the Songster, as he had been nicknamed, and emailed it to Barry Magill. He shut down his computer, stood, walked over to the sofa, and held out his hand. "Let's go home, DeBella."

CHAPTER 35

After they'd returned home, he'd gotten Deb some tomato soup his mom had made from the freezer and one of the nutrition shakes. She'd forced them down and taken a nap while he went for a run. He was craving the physical activity. He ran hard, letting his muscles work out all the stress and worry he was feeling.

He came home to find Bob watching afternoon talk shows and Deb still sleeping. He drank some water and went to shower, leaving Deb's uncle sitting there when the older man merely laughed and waved him off after he'd announced his intention.

He turned on the shower to let the water get hot as he pulled off his workout clothes and threw them into the hamper. As the room filled with steam, he checked his facial stubble in the quickly fogging mirror. He'd shave once he'd showered.

He took a deep breath.

Why did it have to be Shannon? For whatever reason, Shannon was the sore point between him and Deb. He meant it when he told Deb that Shannon was ancient history, but she could never seem to accept him at his word. It is true Shannon had been the only other significant relationship in his life, but he'd thought himself lucky to have escaped the relationship before he'd ended up married to that harpy. He'd ignored the telltale signs until he couldn't, and then he'd broken it off clean. But the fact that he so completely disliked the woman now seemed to fuel Deb's insecurities about her. Deb argued that he must have loved her deeply to hate her so completely now. He hadn't. At the time, he'd thought he had, but then he met Deb. What he felt for her was so…overwhelming. It dwarfed any other emotion he'd ever felt in his life. It killed him to see her cry, especially over Shannon. Shannon wasn't worth the tears.

Of course, he could understand how Deb felt, even if he couldn't understand why it was Shannon that made her feel that way. He had similar pangs over Mark Redmond. Dan… he had a grasp on their relationship…and its inevitable demise. They were great as friends. They just really never should have gotten married. He didn't have the benefit of that kind of closure between Deb and Mark. With Mark, he was trying to compete with a ghost. How could he possibly live up to a man she'd loved deeply enough to leave her husband for. She'd been willing to sacrifice everything for Mark. And the only reason she wasn't married to him now was he'd been shot and killed by a sniper. Gavin wanted to believe Deb would choose him, but the ghost haunted his dreams…literally. What's worse, he haunted hers.

He stuck his cast in a plastic baggy and used a rubber band to "waterproof" it. He pulled back the shower curtain and stepped into the tub, letting the hot water cascade in his face. Then he leaned forward and grabbed the body wash Deb had bought. He gave it a sniff, shrugged, and poured it out on a washcloth. He was good and sudsy when he heard her knock on the door.

"Yeah?" he called.

"An Ah ome in?" she asked from outside the door.

"Uh, yeah," he answered. "You okay?"

She slipped inside the door, closing it behind her. "Yeah, I'm okay." She locked the door and pulled off her pajamas, sticking her own cast in a plastic baggy as he had just done and stepping into the tub with him.

"Oh," he said, with a slight smile, as he pulled her to him. She pulled back her hair and exposed her throat.

He leaned in, brushing his stubble against her skin. He nibbled on her neck and turned her, pinning her to the wall of the shower. She smiled and wrapped her arms around his neck.

"You are so beautiful," he whispered.

"Ewe too," she replied.

CHAPTER 36

It was 2 am when the first wave of nausea for this pregnancy hit Deb. She'd been lying awake for half an hour or so. Gavin, like most men, found sleep easy after…Deb wasn't as lucky. She felt more at ease about Shannon after they had talked. She realized she simply should have asked. And while, yes, she could on occasion read his thoughts, she couldn't possibly know things if he wasn't even thinking about them, and talking was still far more reliable than clairvoyance as a mode of communication anyway. The wave hit her, and she was terrified. Her jaw was wired shut. How was she supposed to throw up, which she increasingly felt the need to do?

She smacked Gavin three times as she retched.

"What?" he exclaimed, jumping awake at the abruptness of her method of rousing him. He quickly realized she was retching and jumped out of the bed. He grabbed the trashcan and moved around to her side of the bed.

"Okay, Honey. You need to lie on your side so you don't aspirate," he explained.

She looked at him like he was speaking Greek.

"So you don't breathe vomit into your lungs," he said, trying again.

She turned and lay on her side, hanging her head just over

the trashcan he held beside the bed.

"Luckily, it's just liquids, but let it come out in your cheeks…and through your nose."

Her eyes grew wide with fear.

"Yeah, it sounds gross, but better out than in. Trust me."

She retched again and couldn't fight it anymore.

He sat the trashcan on the floor under the stream and pulled her hair back out of the way, kneeling beside the bed. He gently rubbed her back until she had finished. "Done?" he asked softly.

"Fir now," she answered.

He took the trash bag out of the can and ran it out to the dumpster. He grabbed a new bag and stopped in the bathroom for a hot, soapy washcloth. She had sat back up. He handed her the washcloth as he replaced the trash bag in the trash can. She wiped her mouth and nose. She looked thoroughly disgusted and a little green. He smiled and took the washcloth back, gently cleaning her face.

"Dat waz igusting," she complained, screwing her face to show her disgust.

He laughed and kissed her neck. "Yeah. Real Exorcist vibe there, Babe!" he joked. "I don't care how gross it is. Promise me that's how you'll do it. Don't try to do it the usual way. Okay?"

"Otay. But, fir da recor…Uk! Ewe'll neber see ee as exy agin."

He laughed. "Ah, Honey. I've never seen anyone any sexier. Well, maybe not while you were hurling…but right now."

"Wiar!" she laughed back.

After he had returned to bed, she lay there beside him, staring at the scar on his shoulder. He felt her eyes on him and opened his eyes. "You okay, Sweetheart?" he asked sleepily.

"Hmmm. Yas. I ust wondah ow someun as smar as ewe ends up wid ee."

"My Love, you underestimate yourself and give me way more credit than I deserve," he replied, pulling her into his arms and kissing the top of her head.

"Ewe have a octorate. I only ave a high school iploma," she reiterated.

"By your own choice. Nothing is stopping you from going to college. Nothing ever has. If it bothers you, go to college."

"Wha abou Ason and da aby?"

"How are they stopping you? Is there really an insurmountable issue that we can't resolve regarding the children that will keep you from going to school if you want to?" he asked.

"Huh. I guess nah," she replied, surprised. "Ah'm a hoh ess, ahn't ah?"

He smiled lovingly at her. "You're wonderful. You should see what I see."

She fell silent and lay listening to his heartbeat. Soon, his breathing became deep and even, and she realized he'd fallen back to sleep. He was right, she realized. Nothing was stopping her from going to college. She had been accepted at Notre Dame when she had graduated high school. Her mother had convinced her they couldn't afford the tuition. She'd happily gone to work to help pay the bills and to assure Katelynn would be able to go to college. Somewhere through the ensuing years, she'd convinced herself she wasn't meant for academia, but she'd been a good student. Why had she thought that way? Why couldn't she go to college? For the life of her, she couldn't come up with one good reason.

She woke in the morning and felt like a weight had lifted. She rose before Gavin's alarm went off. She put in her earbuds, put some music on her phone, and danced her way to the kitchen, where she grabbed a broth and a shake, where she sang "Shake it Off" as she shook the shake and her hips.

As she heated the broth, she danced. She shook the shake

and poured it in a glass, and drank it through a straw.

"You're in a good mood," Gavin said, emerging from the bedroom.

She smiled, put down her glass, and jumped into his arms. "Ah'm goin to ollege," she said, kissing his cheek.

"Cool. Stay away from the frat boys, though. I'm too old to be fighting 20-year-olds for my girl."

"Ha! Ewe'd kick dere asses!"

He laughed and hugged her tight.

CHAPTER 37

Deb and Gavin had missed Jeff's funeral since Deb had been in the hospital that day. Uncle Bob had, without saying a word, attended in their stead and sent flowers. Fiona's mother, Barbara, asked her daughter about the quiet man at the back of the room with the mustache.

Bob was 5'7" on his optimistic days. But he carried himself with confidence. He was blessed with a strong physique and youthful features. He was 59 now, but he had always looked much younger than he was. His hair was still dark and plentiful. He was extremely pale.

He was an odd little man. He knew it. He relished in his own oddity. When people were creeped out by him, he found it amusing. He hadn't always operated within the constraints of legalities, but he'd never hurt anyone. He'd seen enough hurt in his life without inflicting any of it. And for many years now, he'd played it straight. He and his wife, Mary Beth, had owned and operated a family restaurant in Modesto. When she'd been diagnosed with breast cancer, they'd sold the business. He hadn't made a fortune, but they'd come out okay. He had been 43 when Mary Beth passed away, leaving him with 3 teenage boys. At first, he'd simply focused on his kids, but he'd found they needed his attention less and less as they grew older. He bought a furniture store near the restaurant he'd owned with his wife. By the time he was 50, he owned 5 stores. A few years ago, he'd expanded again, buying a store in Seattle and another in Santa Fe. Two of his sons worked in the business. The third, the youngest, was a resident at Boston Children's Hospital. Bob Zamphir was independently wealthy. He just didn't brag about it.

Barbara Ulrich was thrice divorced but still hopeful. She enjoyed life. She was 5′ tall out of the shower, 5′7″, once she'd done her hair. She was curvy but trim. She was very tan.

Her personality was bright and bubbly, a direct contrast to Bob's rather gloomy appearance. Where Bob moved, no, glided silently, Barb actually jingled because of all the jewelry. Bob dressed like a man from a different era in slacks, with a dress shirt and a waistcoat, a tie, and a pocket watch on a gold chain. He wore a bowler hat. Barb dressed like a divorcee from Florida, which is exactly what she was.

Neither of them expected to find the other at her grandson's funeral, of all places. And yet, there they were, spending every free moment with each other in every day since. Fiona was baffled at the obvious mutual attraction. Bob was not her mother's usual type. But whatever. He was nice enough, if a little morose. The strangest thing about the budding romance to Deb was that she hadn't even noticed. When Uncle Bob answered her knock at Fiona's door, she had to look around to check where she was.

"Uncle Ob? I was ondering where ewe 'ere," she said, obviously bewildered by his presence in her friend's apartment.

He smiled knowingly, "It's okay, my sweet. You've had a lot going on. Mrs. Ulrich and I were just about to go out for lunch. Would you care to join us?"

She walked past him into the apartment. Fiona, sitting in an armchair, shrugged in response to Deb's stunned expression. "They're taking Mavis and Christian if that helps you decline the invitation," Fiona snickered, her voice still tinged in sadness and grief.

"Ah an't ea anyway," she replied to her uncle.

He nodded and grabbed his bowler hat off the hat rack by the door. "Very well. Come, my dear, children. Our chariot awaits!" He took Barb's arm, and the kids bounded out in front of them. He closed the door behind them.

Deb looked at Fiona. Again, Fiona shrugged. "Turns out my kids love riding around in that hearse."

"Where ave Ah been?" Deb marveled.

"Well, obviously, you've been a little preoccupied. How are you, Deb? Does it hurt? I mean, obviously, it hurts. I mean…I don't know what I mean." Fiona said, shaking her head and sobbing.

"Eh hurs. But nah as baa as osing a chile," Deb said, hugging her friend.

CHAPTER 38

Barry Magill, like Gavin, recognized hints of Gavin's research from early drafts of an unsubmitted thesis for his dissertation in the pattern of this serial killer. It was disturbing. Firstly, the thesis had never seen the light of day, the keyword being "unsubmitted." Gavin had found the topic interesting but…flaky. He ultimately didn't put much stock in the theories and found the studies inconclusive in practical applications to law enforcement, at least on a scale large enough to make a real impact. Barry had agreed with Gavin's conclusions. To see them applied, as if by design, in an actual case was beyond frightening. Mainly because they did appear to be by design. The case was tailor-made for Gavin Mahoney. And with any serial killer, that kind of entanglement with any one person was a dangerous situation. Secondly, his wife had been drawn into this mess. It didn't take a profiler to see the danger that presented.

Gavin was very good at his job. His profile actually worked up pretty closely to the one Barry did. Barry placed the killer as a little older, in the 35-50 age range, but Gavin was definitely on the right track.

The fact that this was all taking place in Virginia instead of Illinois was baffling. Gavin had no real connection to Virginia other than a situation 5 months prior when he'd become entangled in a murder case in Colonial Beach, Virginia, which, as far as Barry could tell, was incidental and not related to these murders in any way. These appeared to reach back into Gavin's childhood. It crossed his mind that Gavin fit the profile.

It was at that point he decided he and his wife and daughter were going to Fredericksburg. According to Shannon, Gavin was a narcissist with very violent tendencies. And she'd certainly know.

He faxed his profile and booked a hotel and a flight.

"Shannon!" he called.

"Yeah, Hon," she said, bounding into his office as if she'd been waiting for him to call her. He wouldn't be surprised if she had been. Her breakup with Gavin had been acrimonious. She maintained a strong dislike for him, putting her feelings for Gavin in polite terms, which she rarely did. It didn't help that Gavin refused to acknowledge certain responsibilities he had as regarded to Shannon.

"You, me, and Olivia are going to Virginia. Either Gavin is in a world of hurt, or he's causing it. I need to go see which, and based on this, I'm not letting either of you out of my sight."

"Ugh. Gavin!" she groaned. But secretly, she was excited to rub her successful marriage in his stupid face. It would be nice to see him taken down a few pegs, which is all she ever wanted. Of course, it would mean she'd need to hide her lies from both men simultaneously, but she was certain she could control the situation.

CHAPTER 39

Gavin spent the morning at police headquarters, catching up on the work he'd fallen behind on. He received Barry's profile. Noted the difference in age and agreed with that assessment. He posted it to the detectives under him and proceeded to work on other cases.

At 11:30, he left for the university.

He found maintenance leaving his office, having just repaired the hole in his wall. "Thanks. Sorry about that," he said to the man, who laughed as he walked out.

He looked through the work in his inbox. His TA had actually already graded everything. He just needed to sign off on it.

At 11:54, his cell phone rang. It was his father. He answered. "Hey, Dad."

"Gav! My son! You are alive!" Dave joked.

"Ha! Yeah, sorry, Dad. We've been busy."

"How's Deb?"

"She's okay. She's in pain but healing. The doctor let her off bedrest, so that's good."

"And you've been busy, huh?" Dave chuckled.

"Jesus, Dad, you're as bad as Deb," Gavin laughed.

"She's not shy about sex, Son," Dave said, his faint brogue

becoming more prevalent.

"Um, no. No, she's not," he agreed.

He shuffled through some papers on his desk. Rudy Vance had left him notes on his interview with his predecessor, nothing the Chief hadn't already told him. "Hey, Dad, does Maurice Miller have any relatives in Virginia?"

"My old boss? Why?"

"Coincidently, the last guy in my job here at the FPD is named Maurice Miller. Not the same guy, obviously. Just curious."

"Yeah, well, my Maurice Miller was a… well, not nice. You know that. They lived next door for years. His son was a huge dick. Always yellin' about ya making noise, playing ball, the like," Dave said.

"Yeah, I remember. That and more," Gavin sighed. Mason Miller had always fostered a strong dislike for Gavin. It was strange, given Mason was 10 years his senior. He seemed jealous. Even over Mrs. Bradley. Maybe especially over Mrs. Bradley. Ellen Bradley was a beauty. She had showered the neighbor kid with affection and avoided the bullying young police officer, Mason, like the plague. Mason had made Ellen feel…uncomfortable.

"What more?"

"It doesn't matter anymore, Dad."

"He's the cocksucker who said ya were lyin' about what ya saw that day."

"Yeah, and the cocksucker who knew damn well I wasn't lying."

"What do ya mean?" Dave asked, concerned.

"Nothing," Gavin said. "Don't worry about it, Dad. It's ancient history."

After his class, he headed over to the Dean's office. As he had begun to suspect, the other candidate for his job had been Maurice Miller, the younger one in Fredericksburg, not his dad's former boss.

He wanted to meet this guy.

He left campus at 3:00 and drove out to Chatham Heights. He found Miller's address and pulled into the driveway, taking note that he was just left of the trail he'd followed to Honeysuckle Rose's house.

Gavin exited his vehicle and walked up to the door. As he reached up to ring the bell, a voice came from around the side of the house. "Hello, Dr. Mahoney."

Gavin turned to face the man. He was a big man, 6'3" tall, at least. He had arms like tree trunks. He was in a tee shirt and jeans. The Virginia weather was more like summer than fall at this time of year, very different from Illinois. Gavin stared at the tattoo. He hated that tattoo. Mason Miller had terrorized him as a child…well, he had been a child. Mason was supposed to be an adult. When Gavin was 8, Mason had come home sporting that ugly thing, two snakes intertwined in a Celtic knot, eating each other's tales, on his right forearm.

"Mason Miller. Well, well, well. Color me…surprised."

"You didn't think it was my father, did you? He died."

"I hadn't heard that. I'm sorry. Doesn't explain why you're using his name and credentials."

"I was as good a cop as he ever was," Mason proclaimed.

"Maybe, but you didn't earn his rank or his degrees," Gavin pointed out.

"Gonna run me in?" Mason laughed.

"Yeah. I am. For that and other things."

Gavin removed his handcuffs from his belt and walked over, and arrested the bogus Maurice Miller.

CHAPTER 40

As Mason was being processed, Gavin headed back to his office to find Dan and Sam waiting for him. They had come to appear in court regarding the permanent guardianship of Marcus.

"Hey!" he greeted them. "How'd it go?"

"All good. Honeysuckle Rose can't do any more damage," Sam replied, shaking hands with Gavin. "How's Deb doing? We were worried."

"She's okay, Sam, thanks. I told her about the trust, by the way."

Sam nodded. "I don't have a problem with that, Gavin. She's not a manipulative shrew."

Dan was confused. "Huh?"

"Attorney/client privilege, Dan. I can't elaborate," Sam replied.

"You're Gavin's attorney?"

"Yeah, he is. He's also my grandfather's attorney," Gavin explained.

"Oh. Okay," Dan said, not really feeling enlightened.

"I need you to change the provisional power of attorney to Dan anyway. We can talk in front of him. Oh, and I want the contents of my safety deposit box back." Gavin said, looking through his messages.

"Sure. Do you want a prenup drawn up?"

"Nope. What's mine is hers," he said without looking up.

Sam chuckled. Dan seemed to catch on finally. "Who's your grandfather, Gavin?"

"Enrique Fuentes," Gavin answered.

"Fuentes International. The Tool company headquartered in Sterling. Gotcha. Wait. Prenup?" Dan said.

"There's a ring in the safety deposit box," Sam said, having been given permission to talk.

"No shit!" Dan beamed and slapped Gavin on the back.

Gavin frowned as he saw Chief Lindstrom approaching with Barry Magill…and Shannon through the window of his office overlooking the Detectives' floor. "Fuck," he muttered under his breath.

Sam released his hand and turned, following Gavin's gaze. "Who is it?"

"Barry Magill, FBI profiler, and his wife Shannon."

"Ugh. What's she doing here?" Sam asked Gavin, giving him the side-eye.

"Apparently, her crystal ball revealed I was happy for five fucking seconds," Gavin muttered.

Chief Lindstrom knocked on Gavin's door and stuck his head in. "Can we have a minute?"

"Sure, come on in," Gavin said. "This is my friend, Dan Bradley, and my lawyer, Sam Davis."

"Um…okay. Why is Maurice Miller being processed?" Chief Lindstrom asked.

"Because his name is Mason Miller," Gavin replied coolly. "Maurice was his father. The credentials he presented to get his job here were forged from his father's. He doctored the dates, obviously."

"How'd you learn that?" Chief Lindstrom gasped.

Gavin sighed. "I went to his house and looked at him.

His father was my father's boss. He worked in my hometown's police department for years. His dad was a detective. He was a beat cop. A bully with a badge… and they lived next door to us. Trust me. His name is Mason. Mason Rupert Miller. He was an ass then. He's an ass now."

"You know him? He knows you?" The Chief glared at Barry, who appeared visibly relieved, while Shannon looked almost disappointed.

"My entire life."

"And he fits the profile," the Chief said.

"Sure, but so do I. I've got him on fraud. That's all right now." Gavin watched Barry and Shannon as he spoke. So did Sam. They both knew Gavin had read them correctly.

"Good work again, Detective," the Chief said, taking his leave. Barry and Shannon followed him out. Gavin shut the door behind them. "Psycho bitch," he muttered again.

"Jesus," Dan muttered, shaking his head. "They really came here to point a finger at you?"

"According to Shannon, I'm a narcissist with violent tendencies," Gavin explained.

"Toward whom?" Sam asked incredulously.

"Her, in her version of things. Even though I never… would never…lay a finger on her," Gavin sighed. "But for some reason, she keeps trying to convince Barry that I did. It's like she wants him to fight me or something."

"She'd tell him you're a serial killer over petty shit?" Dan huffed.

"Yeah, and for some reason, he always believes her."

CHAPTER 41

Gavin went home to get Deb.

"Ah ahn't ea. Why ah ee goin ou?" she complained.

"Ah, come on, Baby. We'll go to Carl's," he teased, snuggling up to her on the sofa.

She giggled and gave in.

At Carl's, she waved to Dan and Sam, who had claimed a picnic table, as she and Gavin approached from across the parking lot. Dan rose and kissed her unblemished cheek. Sam did the same. Gavin laughed and made his way to the window to get their ice cream.

From the passenger seat of their rental, Shannon grinned an evil little grin. "Barry," she said, pointing. "Look."

He turned his gaze to where his wife indicated. "Son of a…" he roared. "Stay here."

"Like hell," she replied, jumping out and grabbing Olivia from her car seat. She jogged behind her husband, who strode angrily toward the picnic table.

They arrived just as Gavin handed Deb her strawberry milkshake.

"I'm sorry, but you don't have to live like this, Dear," Barry said, placing a hand on Deb's shoulder.

"Essuse ee? Wha?" Deb asked. "Who ah ewe?"

"Deb, this is Barry Magill. He's unaware of the giant ass he's making of himself. THAT is Shannon. She's perfectly aware," Gavin said. "Barry, remove your hand."

"What are you going to do, big man?" Barry screeched.

Deb grabbed his hand and twisted it behind his back, bending his thumb backwards.

"Nothing. But she's going to break your damn thumb," Gavin responded, sitting down and taking a sip of his shake through his straw.

"Let go!" Shannon yelled, stepping forward, Olivia on her hip.

Deb let go. "'On't ouch ee."

"What?" Barry said, rubbing his thumb.

"She said don't touch her," Gavin said nonchalantly.

"My husband was just trying to help you! It's obvious Gavin lost his temper and nearly killed you!" Shannon said, her eyes gleaming triumphantly, glaring directly at Gavin with an evil grin.

"Avin wouldn't eber hur ee!"

"But his hand…" Barry exclaimed in exacerbation.

"I think you ARE the serial killer," Shannon spat between gritted teeth.

Deb's eyes got huge, "What? she asked. "Ohhhhh. Ewe're sooo ucky ewe ah oldin dat aby!"

"You listen to me, Gavin Mahoney. I'm going to push for them to investigate you. They'll listen to Barry. No one leaves me," she whispered to Gavin, leaning in close.

"Honestly, Shannon, I don't care what you do. You know as well as I do that I never laid a finger on you, that I'd never hurt a child, let alone three, and that I am not a narcissist with violent tendencies. Grow up. But if you can't do that, go away."

"Ahhh!" gasped Deb. "Ewe're wight, Oney. See's a psycho itch." She kissed him hard and then said, "Ow." She rubbed her lip.

"Don't do that, Goofy," he laughed.

Meanwhile, Dan and Sam sat there in amused silence.

Shannon handed Olivia off to Barry.

"Before we broke up, I was afraid for my life!" Shannon proclaimed.

Deb pulled the lid off her shake. She stood up. She dumped her shake on Shannon's head. "Ex ime, eep da aby." And she sat back down.

Barry stared hard at his wife. There was something about the way she was acting that didn't gel with her words. She acted more like she wanted Gavin than anything else. Gavin's cold responses enraged her. She wasn't a woman afraid of a man who beat her. While it was true battered women often returned to their abusers, proclaiming their undying love, that wasn't what he was witnessing. His wife was acting…more like the abuser.

CHAPTER 42

It only took 24 hours for Mason Miller to make bail.

He walked out of the city jail at 3:30 pm the next afternoon and onto the UMW campus at 3:41. He made his way to Gavin Mahoney's office unmolested but closely watched by Campus Police, who had been informed of his status as a person of interest in the recent murders of faculty members' children.

He knocked on Gavin's office door. Only Gavin didn't answer from behind the door. Instead, he appeared silently behind Mason. Mason didn't know where Gavin had come from. The hall had been empty when he'd entered. It made him do a double take.

"I'm not in there," Gavin said, leaning casually against the wall behind Mason's back.

"How? Where'd you come from?" Mason stammered.

"Sterling, Illinois, same as you," Gavin replied.

"Funny man."

"It's an irrelevant question, Mason," Gavin sighed. "What do you want?"

"You've got me all wrong."

"Have I?"

Mason grimaced. Gavin wasn't playing to the script. He remembered a child, but Gavin had long since left childhood behind. Gavin wasn't playing fair.

"Whatever! You are still just a kid with a bike!" Mason declared oddly.

"Um. No. I'm not," Gavin replied, baffled by the statement.

"You're not better than me, kid!" Mason said, poking Gavin in the chest and walking away.

It wasn't the first time he'd heard Mason Miller say those exact words in that exact intonation. It was…eerie.

When he'd seen Geno and Salvatore…as Joe Conti had arrived… Gavin, at 10, had scrambled to get on his bike and ride away. Mason, who'd been 21 but still living at home, which was the first of two houses between Gavin's parents' house and Keith and Ellen Bradley's, had emerged from his garage. He'd looked across the yard of the Ramirez's house, the other house between the Mahoney's and the Bradley's, pointed, and yelled, "Hey!" At the time, Gavin had thought he'd been yelling at the strange men. But later, at the police station, he'd called Gavin a liar. Then as Gavin and Dave left, he'd pointed at Gavin and said those very same words.

CHAPTER 43

There was very little Gavin could do but watch and wait. So Mason matched the profile. It wasn't enough. As a member of the police force Mason had learned how to manipulate forensics to hide his presence. There was nothing.

There was also nothing to indicate who was his accomplice in the department. Rudy Vance and Chief Lindstrom were on Gavin's shortlist, but without more evidence, he couldn't eliminate anyone.

So he let time pass.

Jerry Boniface confessed to attacking Deb in accordance with his deal. Mrs. Thompson changed her testimony to admit she'd been intimidated by the biker and his friends into accusing Marcus Rose. Honeysuckle and Jerry were arraigned and awaiting trial.

Dan had brought Jason back after a week. He'd have kept the boy as long as Deb wanted, of course, but she had missed her son and couldn't wait to have him home.

Uncle Bob had followed Barb Ulrich back to Florida two days after Jason returned home, investing in a ton of sunscreen before he left.

Fiona and Deb became fast friends. Gavin was pleased Deb was feeling less isolated. Their life together fell into an easy routine.

Just before Halloween, Deb had her wire and cast removed, his cast coming off at the same time. She had struggled with gaining weight between the wire and the morning sickness. They wanted to celebrate.

Fiona had started dating a security guard at GEICO. He had always had a bit of a crush on her since starting work there. In the weeks following her son's murder, he'd been sweet, kind, understanding, and a friend. Admittedly, Fiona fell fast and often, but she had a good feeling about this one. She wanted a second opinion, so she enthusiastically suggested the four of them leave the kids with Nancy, her babysitter, and go out to dinner. Gavin would personally have rather walked on hot lava barefoot, but Deb was excited, so he agreed.

At 5:00 pm on October 28th, Gavin and Deb met Fiona and her date, Ted Foster, at The Colonial Tavern on Lafayette Blvd.

Gavin warned Deb to order small, this being her first solid meal in almost two months. She had her own mind and ordered a shepherd's pie. She made it about halfway through when her stomach revolted. She bolted to the lady's room. Fiona quickly ran after her.

Gavin and Ted stared at each other silently for a minute.

Ted was perhaps 35 years old, a little on the lanky side, thin, well mannered. He was slightly balding with dirty blond hair and clean-shaven. He looked a little like Prince William, Gavin noted.

"So…office security?" Gavin said, breaking the awkward silence with an awkward question.

"Oh, yes, well. It's a job," Ted replied.

Gavin laughed, feeling more at ease, realizing his companion was as equally as uncomfortable as he. "It is at that. How long have you been in that line of work?" he asked, taking a sip of his Guinness.

"Oh, only about 2 years. I was a bank teller before that… for most of my adult life, actually. My bank was robbed, and…I just couldn't do it anymore. But I couldn't stand being afraid either. So, I started taking self-defense classes. That's how I met Ralph Bowers. He worked at the security company. He told me they were hiring, so I applied, and I got the job."

"You were afraid as a teller, so you became a guard?" Gavin asked, trying to hide his amusement.

"It's okay, Detective Mahoney. I, too, see the irony." Ted laughed.

"Oh. Good." Having permission, Gavin laughed.

"Of course, it's nothing like being a real police officer. Most of the guys I work with are…wannabees."

"Do you want to be?"

"Good Lord, no. I don't even want to be a guard. But I'm afraid I don't know what I DO want to be. Well…maybe I do, but I don't see an easy path to it."

"What's that?"

He blushed. "I'd really like to be my own boss, own a store of some kind."

"That isn't out of reach, Ted. I have a good friend, Miranda Bradley. She used to own an antique store. I'm sure she could offer some advice."

Ted's face lit up. "Really? That would be amazing."

Gavin's face fell, and he cursed, "Oh, fuck."

"I'm sorry?" Ted said.

Shannon Magill sauntered over and sat in Deb's empty chair.

"Hello, Gavin," she said, smiling sweetly and putting her hand on his thigh.

He grabbed her hand and removed it, placing it firmly on the table.

"That seat's taken," he said.

"So's the man!" came the rather loud retort from behind him. Deb stood there, arms crossed in front of her, tapping her left foot.

"Ah," said Ted, catching up.

"Oh, please, Sweetie. I've seen your war wounds. You wouldn't stand a chance," Shannon crowed.

Gavin guffawed. "That was against a biker and a door, by surprise. She put the last woman she fought in the hospital for two weeks."

"I threw hot chicken marsala in her face and beat her unconscious with the skillet," Deb said, leaning forward and speaking through gritted teeth.

"Damn, Deb," said Fiona, impressed.

"Well, aren't you just the match made in heaven, then?" Shannon replied. "Whatever. I just wanted to say hello. Let you know, I'm living here now. I left Barry."

"Like you left me?"

"Huh?" said Ted.

"*I* moved out," Gavin explained with a wink.

"Ah. I see."

"Whatever. We're no longer together," Shannon said, shimmying in Deb's seat.

"Good for Barry. Get out of my chair," Deb said.

"Bye," said Gavin.

Shannon smiled, stood, and walked away, but she looked back over her shoulder and winked at Gavin. Deb lunged. Gavin reached out and grabbed her hand. "Not worth the energy, Babe."

Deb sat down. "Wonder if she ate her baby?" she huffed.

Gavin laughed and kissed her.

CHAPTER 44

At 6:30, the group of four joined the walking ghost tour of downtown that Fiona had made reservations for. Gavin put on a smile and hooked his arm for Deb to take. Ghosts were bullshit. At least the ghosts on the tour. He was less able to dismiss the one haunting his dreams, but he was more concerned with the living. Shannon was just a pain in the ass. Mason was actually dangerous. Mark and long-dead Civil War soldiers were nothing in comparison. Still, it was Mark he thought about walking arm in arm with Deb.

Maybe it was the Civil War era bullets embedded in the brick of the bank's exterior wall, where the soldiers had scratched their names so they could be identified even if their dog tags were stolen, that started it. His head began to pound. Evan never got that opportunity. They never found his dog tags. Mark hadn't had time to scratch so much as a line, let alone his name, either. Which was worse? Knowing if the bullet was coming or not? His nightmare flashed through his thoughts. Evan condemned him to relive one day over and over. Mark condemned him to relive another, and somehow, those two days kept getting mixed up together.

It wasn't bad enough he'd tripped and fallen. Mark had to shove him night after night just to remind him.

Dan often teased him that he had a white knight complex. It was true, he realized. It was also a case of the pot calling the kettle black. But that was beside the point. He was thankful that he'd taken Deb to the ground during the gunfire, but it killed him that it had not been an intentional act. When the gunfire had started, he'd moved toward Collins, the first victim to fall, to administer aid. But Mark was between them. When Mark fell, Gavin had tried to maneuver so as not to fall on Mark. His feet got tangled, and he'd lost his balance, taking Deb down with him.

I'll never let you sleep peacefully until you tell her, Mark's voice heckled him in his thoughts. And night after night, Mark screamed at him for loving her and shoved him violently so that he fell, taking her down like he had that day.

Gavin pulled Deb closer and kissed her on the side of her head as they walked. "I love you, Deb."

"I love you, too," she answered, unaware.

"Wanna get married?" he asked.

"What?" she replied, stopping, letting the group move away from them.

He pulled a ring box from his pocket. "I've been carrying this around," he announced.

"Nope. Make like Kaepernick, Baby," she interjected, pointing at the ground.

He laughed. And knelt on one knee. The group stopped and turned to watch.

"DeBella Marie, will you marry me?" He opened the box, revealing a beautiful princess-cut diamond in an antique setting. With two princess-cut sapphires, one on each side of the diamond, and a series of smaller alternating sapphires and diamonds wound around the white gold band.

"Oh, wow!" Deb said, looking at it. "It's beautiful."

"My abuela's," he said.

She smiled and leaned over, taking his face in her hands.

"Yes, I will," she said, kissing him.

He stood, slipped the ring on her finger, and kissed her again.

The walking tour group applauded.

Fiona rushed over, grabbing her friend's fingers to look at the ring. "Congratulations!" she exclaimed. "Wow, is right!"

Ted shook Gavin's hand.

You'll never sleep peacefully until you tell her, the voice echoed again.

CHAPTER 45

"I don't really need a big wedding. Been there, done that," Deb proclaimed on the ride home after they picked up a sleeping Jason. "But if you want it…"

"Vegas works for me, Babe," he replied.

"Oh, that's perfect! Our friends and family can be there virtually. Oh! We can do it on Thanksgiving. Then Thanksgiving dinner will be like a big reception dinner," she laughed.

"Sure, sounds great. But my mother is going to want an in-person dinner. How about we do it the day before and host Thanksgiving dinner. They can watch it from here. We can ask Dan and Miranda to go with us as our witnesses and use his plane, get married, come back, and have dinner with my family. I can't spare a lot of time out of town, so a quick in and out would be great."

"I can't cook," Deb yelped, horrified at the prospect.

"No. Mom can cook. Not on your wedding day, my love," he laughed.

"Are you really okay with that?" she asked. "You've never been married. Will you miss the big wedding?"

"All I need is you, Deb." He drove for a minute without speaking. "And for your ex-husband to pony up his private jet because I don't happen to have one."

She teased. "You know he will. Regardless of our failed marriage, he loves YOU."

"He loves you, too." He fell silent again.

"Penny for your thoughts," she said finally as he pulled into their parking space at their complex.

He turned off the engine and turned to face her. "I'm a fraud," he announced.

"What?" she asked, stunned.

"The day we met. I…"

"Tripped." She giggled.

"You know?"

"I was there, Dummy." She laughed and covered her mouth with her hand, the ring sparkling in the moonlight. "I mean, it wasn't like the center of my focus at the time, but it was pretty obvious."

"Why didn't you say anything?"

"About what? You were clearly embarrassed. I didn't care that you pulled me down by accident. You pulled me down. And other than getting your own feet tangled together in a moment of pure chaos, you were nothing but courageous and professional." She leaned across the center console and kissed him on the end of his nose.

"Feel better?" she asked. "Can we talk about our wedding plans without your freaking out?"

He laughed, putting his hand over his eyes and shaking his head. "I've been tied up in knots for months."

"Huh. Maybe you should have asked me about it," she said smugly, turning his words to her about Shannon back on him.

"Well, Shannon was right about one thing tonight: We are a match made in heaven."

Hahaha! Gotcha! laughed Mark's ghost in his head.

CHAPTER 46

Gavin was in an incredibly good mood. He hummed as he walked through the Walmart aisles, trailing behind Deb, holding Jason's hand. "Pretty Woman" started to play over the store's sound system. He started to sing.

Deb smiled. She hadn't really heard him sing before. She'd heard him mumble lyrics under his breath in the car but never sing. Out loud for everybody to hear.

A few bars in, she realized he was good. She stopped pushing the cart and turned to watch him serenade her. He hammed it up. Then he did something she hadn't seen coming. He sang along, but in Spanish, taking her hand and pulling her to him in a salsa dance move. Jason burst out laughing. Something about his mellifluous singing voice, his handsome face, his well-maintained physique, and the Spanish was a deadly concoction. She actually felt her brain turn to mush. This man was dead sexy. He spun her around and dipped her, pulled her back up, and into his embrace as the song ended. He kissed her nose and let go. She grabbed the cart to keep from falling.

"Lucky girl," muttered the little old lady shuffling past her.

"You dance, and you sing," she said breathlessly. "Do you play an instrument?"

"Guitar," he said, grabbing the item off the top shelf for the lady. "And piano."

Deb laughed as the woman leered at his butt. The old lady looked back at her and said, "Very lucky girl."

"You don't have either one," Deb observed.

"I do at my parent's house. I figured they just take up room," he smiled. "Here you go, Ma'am. Good enough view, or can I get you something on the bottom shelf?" He winked, and the old woman giggled like a schoolgirl.

"You realize had you utilized these skills, it wouldn't have taken 6 months?"

"What wouldn't have taken 6 months?" asked the woman, her eyes wide.

"YOU know," Deb teased.

"I wouldn't make him wait six minutes," the woman said behind her hand.

Gavin laughed.

Marcus walked around the endcap of the aisle.

"Hello, Gavin," he said, looking at the lights overhead.

"Hey, Marcus! Have you met Deb and Jason?"

"No. Hello, Deb and Jason." He rocked back and forth between his feet. 'What's her name?" He motioned to the lady.

"Um, I don't know. We just met," Gavin replied.

"Violet Ash," she answered good-naturedly.

"Her name is Violet Ash," Gavin repeated.

"Hello, Violet Ash," Marcus said. Then he continued, "I'm happy you are here. Mr. Smythe, my boss, says I can't work here anymore. I like working here. I don't understand what he's telling me. Can you help me? My cousin Dan says I can ask you for help when he's not here. And you said you are my friend."

"I am your friend, and I'm happy to help. Violet, lovely meeting you. Get my number from Deb. I am with the FPD. You need anything…you call me. Jason, wanna come with Marcus and me?"

  "Can I get a toy?"

  "Sure can."

  "Then, yas."

  Gavin scooped up the child. "Lead the way, Marcus."

  "You made him wait six months?"

  Deb burst out laughing. "I had to make the first move. He's completely clueless to his sex appeal."

  "Not completely," Violet said, watching him leave.

  "Yeah. Sometimes, he knows very well," Deb agreed, also watching him leave and thinking of nothing but the sound of his voice and the sway of his hips. Lucky girl indeed, she thought.

CHAPTER 47

"His caretaker was withholding his meds," Gavin explained. "That situation has been resolved. He's in a new private group home and has a guardian who is actually looking out for his best interests. He likes his job."

"I don't care what the problem was. It's not MY problem," Mr. Smythe said, dismissing Gavin.

"Fine. I'll just call his lawyer. You can explain to him the grounds for dismissal," Gavin threatened.

"Go ahead," said Mr. Smythe, not backing down. He was fairly certain the cop was bluffing. He was surprised when he pulled out his phone and actually made a call.

"Hey, Sam. Doing well. — Actually, I'm calling on Marcus's behalf. Walmart has terminated him because of the issues with his medication and arrest. — Yep. — Sid Smythe. — He's right here."

Gavin held out his phone to Mr. Smythe. "He wants to talk to you."

Mr. Smythe took the phone. "Hello? — That's not my problem. — I don't care who you are or who you represent. Until my manager tells me otherwise, my decision stands. — Francine Gimmel. — The regional VP — Brian March. — Yeah, you do that." He disconnected and handed Gavin back his phone. "Wow, that was…underwhelming."

Gavin smiled. "Come on, Marcus. Let's go get this boy a toy and go out to lunch. You'll have your job back by tomorrow."

The phone on Smythe's desk rang.

Gavin laughed and walked out the door.

"Hello," Smythe said into the receiver. "Um, yes, Mr. March. — Of course. — Tomorrow. Yes, sir." He hung up. Where had Marcus found that barracuda? He walked to the door and leaned out. "You're on the schedule for the 8 am shift tomorrow, Marcus!" he called to their departing figures.

"He'll be here," Gavin called over his shoulder with a wave.

"Can we go to McDonald's?" Marcus asked.

"Sure. Anything you want."

"There are a few songs called that. One is very naughty," Marcus said with a laugh.

"I bet," replied Gavin.

"I heard you singing."

"Yeah. What did you think?"

"I think girls like you," Marcus said.

Gavin laughed and patted his shoulder. "Well, that would be the reason I bothered learning."

"Do you know 'Dos Oruguitas'?" Marcus asked.

"I have two nieces under 12…So, yes."

"Do you speak Spanish?" Marcus asked as they entered the toy department. Gavin sat Jason down.

"Dude, look at me," Gavin laughed.

"Your name is Irish."

"You're right. My name is Irish. Sorry. Yes. I speak Spanish. My mother is Mexican American. Her name was Gabriella Fuentes before she married my father."

Jason returned with a Hot Wheels track and a hopeful look on his face.

"Oh, cool! You need some cars to go with it!" Gavin said.

"It has one," Jason said, pointing.

"I can't race against you if you only have one," Gavin replied.

The child's face lit up. He ran back over to the cars and started picking out several.

"Get that wheel-shaped case for the cars too, Jason!" Gavin said, pointing.

"Are these for him or you?" came Deb's voice from behind him.

CHAPTER 48

Deb stared at the design she'd drawn back when she was still LARPING. She'd lost interest after Mark had died. It was a part of her life that belonged to him. It felt wrong to do it without him. And it honestly wasn't fun anymore. The drawing for the gown had fallen out of the sewing machine box when she pulled it out of the storage closet. Fiona had brought some things up to hem for Christian that had belonged to Jeff after she'd told her she could do it.

"That's pretty," Fiona had said, glancing at it. "That would make a gorgeous wedding gown."

And ever since, it had been just about the only thing on her mind. The Empire waist and long, full skirt would disguise her expanding belly. She'd have to make some adjustments…the wings were not necessary, the crown…a bit much. She grabbed her sketch pad and reworked the design, using angel sleeves instead of wings, changing the neckline to show off her bigger bustline, a princess veil instead of that garish gown, and a sash to match the princess veil. She smiled at the results and jumped up, grabbing her purse.

She went to the antique store first. Gabriella had found that lace christening gown there and swore there was a ton of lace to be found. And she was right. She found two gorgeous lace tablecloths that she could transform. She bought them and headed to the fabric store.

She found a champaign blush silk and a tulle fabric that would work for the gown and a light pink silk to use for embellishments, along with all the beading and threads she'd need.

At her minivan, she loaded all the fabric into the back and shut the back gate. Shannon Magill stood there next to her van. Shannon was stunning, no doubt. She had long, curly black hair, green eyes, that flawless porcelain complexion.

"Ug. What do you want?" Deb huffed.

"Whatcha makin?" Shannon asked with a sugary, sweet voice.

"My wedding dress," Deb replied with an equally sickly sweet smile. She held up her hand, revealing the diamond ring. She was rewarded with Shannon's horrified gasp. "And he proposed after less than a year. Wait. That has to be fake. He can't afford that on a cop's salary."

Shannon was visibly gutted, but she quickly recovered and screwed back on the fake smile. "Can't afford to buy a dress?"

"I can afford anything I want. I want to make it." She sighed, tiring of the game Shannon was playing. "What do you want, Shannon?"

"I just wanted to say hi. I got a job. Department of Child Services. I'll be working closely with the police department."

"Head Detectives deal a lot with social workers, do they? I'm the one with the ring. And I'm the one he comes home to. Congratulations on your new job." She turned and opened her driver's side door. She climbed in, closed the door, smiled, and waved goodbye.

Across the parking lot, Mason Miller laughed from the cab of his pickup. Point pretty blonde. Goose egg, pretty brunette.

CHAPTER 49

Deb worked daily on her gown in secret. She packed it up every afternoon before Gavin got home.

Their plans all came together. Uncle Frank and Aunt Millie couldn't make it out for the Thanksgiving thing. They were already committed to hosting Aunt Millie's family in California. Her grandmother was looking forward to watching virtually but could not travel as she was recovering from Covid. Uncle Tom had recently retired, and he and Ava Bradley were in Greece. Uncle Bob was happy to be invited. His sons all had invited him, of course, but he would go where Mrs. Ulrich went, and she wanted to be with her daughter, so he'd be in attendance. Katelynn, of course, was coming. Gavin had been right; his mother would have felt left out if they hadn't planned on her being present for dinner when they got back from the quick trip to Vegas. His parents, sister, brother-in-law, nieces, and nephew all booked rooms at a nearby hotel and a flight out to Dulles on Tuesday. Dan and Miranda would be there on Wednesday morning and take them to Vegas that afternoon. The rest of their friends and family would be there virtually but had their own Thanksgiving plans. They'd get married Wednesday night and be back Thursday morning in time to watch the Thanksgiving Day parade.

It took her two full weeks to finish the gown. She tried it on for Fiona, with Miranda and Camille Camacho via Zoom. She'd converted the lace into a long veil. The gown was stunning.

"Wow!" said Miranda. "If I knew you could do that, Deb, I'd have had you do my gown. It's beautiful!"

"You could be a designer!" Camille agreed. Camille was about to pop. Her baby was due any day.

"Do I look…is it too noticeable?" Deb asked, smoothing down the fabric over her own baby bump.

"Well, when you do that!" Fiona laughed, smacking her hands away and fluffing out the skirt.

"Wait! When did that happen?" Camille shouted. "Nobody tells me anything!"

"You really couldn't tell?" Deb asked, biting her lip.

"No! Dang. It's a magic dress, Deb!"

The women laughed.

"Wow!" came the unexpected masculine voice from the bedroom door.

"Jesus!" Fiona jumped. "How does he do that?"

Miranda covered her mouth with her hand. "Has he been taking lessons from Bob?"

"No," Deb said, disappointed. "He figured out the trick on his own. You weren't supposed to see it."

Gavin walked over to her and took her in his arms. "Wow!" he said again. She smiled.

"Yeah?" she asked.

"Yeah," he replied, kissing her.

"Hey, that's why she needs a magic dress to begin with," Camille warned.

"You're doing it wrong, Camille," he answered.

"Well, I'm doin' somethin' right," she laughed, rubbing her own belly.

"Me too," giggled Miranda.

"Noooooo!!!" shouted Deb and Camille.

"And with that, I'm out," Gavin said as he edged toward the door.

"Hold it!" Deb said, putting up her hand, and grabbing his collar, looking him in the eyes. "Crap! You knew!"

"No, I didn't," he replied too quickly.

"Daniel Joseph Bradley!" Miranda yelled.

"He didn't tell me!" Gavin blurted out. "Your father did." Then he ran.

CHAPTER 50

"I don't know what to say, Sam. She's a bruja. She can read my mind. She actually answers questions I think, but don't say out loud all the time," Gavin said into his phone as Rudy Vance knocked at his office door. He waved the officer in. "Yeah. I'm really sorry. I couldn't let Dan take the fall." He laughed. "But I didn't tell anyone. Miranda told them."

Rudy stood there, waiting patiently.

Gavin finished his call and turned his attention to Rudy. "Yes, Officer Vance!" he said cheerfully.

"You're in a good mood, Detective."

"I'm getting married tomorrow, Rudy."

"Congratulations, Sir," Rudy replied.

Gavin handed him a stack of paperwork. "Here's the assignments while I'm gone. Keep a man on Mason Miller."

"Do you really expect anything to happen?"

"Nope," Gavin answered. "I still want to know what he's doing."

"Besides following you and your fiancé around?"

"Yeah. Besides that."

"You got it," Rudy said, leaving the room.

Gavin watched him leave and walk across the floor to his own desk. His eyes narrowed. He trusted that boy less and less, but thus far, he'd managed to keep his mistrust to himself. It killed him to give the officer the lead on this case, but he wasn't ready to confront Rudy yet. He'd be fine for two days.

Chief Lindstrom knocked. "Hello," he announced, sticking his head in the door. "I understand you're taking a few days off to get married."

"Uh. Yes, Sir," Gavin replied, motioning for his boss to enter and have a seat. The Chief entered and put a gift on the desk in front of Gavin. "Congratulations, Detective."

"Thank you. You didn't need to do that," Gavin said, indicating the gift.

"Ah. It's just a vase or something. My daughter picked it out. She moved in with me last week. Problems with her stepfather."

"Well...thank her for us," Gavin said. He sat looking at his boss. He wasn't sure he trusted him completely yet either, but he'd started to a little since the whole Marcus debacle. He'd checked Lindstrom's story, and he'd been telling the truth.

"Well. Just wanted to give you that. And let you know you can take the rest of the week...Come back on Monday."

"Thank you, Sir. Is there anything else? I need to get to Dulles to get my family..."

"Oh, no, that's all. Congratulations again." He waved and left.

Gavin smiled. He picked up the gift and headed out.

CHAPTER 51

Tuesday evening, Gavin's family arrived as planned. Katelynn arrived about an hour later. The apartment was full to bursting.

They were a boisterous group.

It was about 7:15 pm when there was a knock at the door. Julieta, Molly's oldest daughter, peeked through the peephole. "Hey, Tia Debbie," she called. "There's a weird old lady with a pumpkin pie at your door!"

Gavin stood with Jason hanging on his neck, his niece, Susanna, hanging on one leg, and his nephew, Georgie, on the other. He gently but hurriedly extricated himself from the tangle of children. The last time an old woman knocked, Jerry "Bonnie" Boniface had nearly killed his bride-to-be. He looked through, seeing Violet Ash waiting on the other side. He opened the door. "Ms. Ash!" he said with a smile. "Hello!"

"Oh, Hello, Detective. It looks like I'm interrupting a party," she said, peering at the crowd within.

"It's fine. Just family. Come in," he offered.

"I really am sorry to bother you at home, but Deb gave me your address and said I could stop by."

"Of course. Welcome."

"I actually have a small problem I was hoping you could help me with."

"I'll do what I can," he offered.

"Somebody's been looking in my windows," she said, handing him the pie.

"What? Have you called the police?" he asked.

"Oh. No. I haven't seen the person. Just where he or she has trampled my mums. I wouldn't want to get kids in trouble for being kids. But I'd like them to stop. I was hoping you could…"

Gavin nodded. "Sure, Ms. Ash. Dad, wanna come with me to check Ms. Ash's house for a peeper?"

"Sure," Dave replied, standing and walking over.

"What's your address, Ms. Ash? You can stay here and have some tacos. Dad and I will check it out for you."

"Oh, thank you, Dear. I really appreciate it," smiled the old woman, patting his cheek. "Such a lucky girl!" She looked over his shoulder at Deb who smiled and waved to her.

Dave chuckled. Gavin got the address and headed over to Ms. Ash's home.

It was just a few blocks away. Ms. Ash's house was a red brick ranch, probably built in the late 50s or early 60s. She had mums in planters around her front door and under every window. Several had indeed been crushed by someone standing in the planter, peering in over her windowsills. Dave looked in the closest.

"That's no kid. Size 12 at least," he told his son.

"Yeah, that's what I was worried about," Gavin sighed.

"What haven't you told me, Son?" Dave asked.

"Mason Miller."

"What about him?"

"You recall my asking about Maurice?" Gavin asked.

"Yes. I also recall you told me not to worry about it."

"Yeah, well, maybe worry some. He's here. And I think he's my serial killer," Gavin explained.

Dave's face lost all color. "Gavin! He's always had it in for you! Even before Ellen. Do you remember the goose?"

"The goose? No. I don't think so," Gavin replied.

"You were like three, so I'm not surprised. There was a family of geese that swam in the spring that bubbled up in the field across the street. Your Nan and Da were visiting from Dublin. Da told you that geese mate for life, like people. You were very protective of those geese. You checked on them every day. Then, one day, the female goose was nowhere to be found. Your Da took your wee hand and went with you into the field, and the two of you searched for her. Ya found her, sure enough. Her head had been rung clean off and tossed to the side. You cried for a week. And Mason Miller taunted ya over it. Him a big boy of 14 and you, just a tike. He was relentless. He'd honk at ya and laugh."

"What happened to the goslings?" Gavin gasped.

"Eventually, the father goose pair bonded with another male goose with goslings and no mate. They raised their goslings together. And the next year, they came back together, and every year after…until they didn't," he chuckled. "But my point is, boy-oh, Mason Miller only picked on you. From the day ya found the gander until ya left home, you were his target."

"Yeah. I still am, Dad," Gavin admitted.

"And this little lady?" Dave asked, pointing at the house.

"He watched me talking to her in Walmart. She was nice. A little naughty. She reminds me of Mrs. Ramirez and her BUNKO ladies. I was in a good mood. The damage was done by the time I noticed him." He sighed deeply. "I told Deb to give her my contact info."

"What are ya goin' do?"

Gavin sighed again. "Get some uniforms to do drive-by checks. He won't make a move until after Christmas. See if she has someone who can stay with her in the meantime." He shrugged. "Dad?"

"Yeah?"

"He killed the gander, didn't he?"

"Aye."

"Dad?"

"Yeah?"

"Why is it the younger I am in your stories, the more Irish you sound?"

Dave laughed. "I dunno, but it's surely true."

CHAPTER 52

Dan and Miranda arrived at around 9:30 on Wednesday morning. Dan arranged for a limo to take him and Miranda to pick up Gavin and Deb.

Gavin asked them to make a stop at FPD headquarters. He wanted to make sure that checking on Violet Ash was a priority while he was gone.

He hopped out of the limo, declaring he'd be right back. He ran inside.

Andrea Grimes greeted him as he entered. "Detective! What on earth are you doing here today?"

He smiled, "I'm not staying. I just needed to check on something."

He made his way to Chief Lindstrom's office and knocked on the door.

Damnit, he thought as the door swung open. There was Shannon Magill, tears streaming down her face.

Chief Lindstrom looked positively befuddled.

"Gavin, what are you doing here? I just told Ms. Magill here you were off to get married today." His eyes pleaded with Gavin for help.

"I'm on my way out. I just wanted to make sure you got my message about Ms. Ash."

"Yeah. I took care of it." The Chief looked at Shannon.

"Ms. Magill here, had a bit of bad news this morning. She was looking for you, she says, because you're the only person she knows in town." Subtext: get this crazy broad out of my office.

"What is it, Shannon?" Gavin asked, knowing it was a trap but not knowing how to escape it.

"Barry filed for divorce!" she wailed.

"Okay?" he replied coldly.

"How can you be that way?" she sobbed. "I know I'm not your favorite person, but we did care for each other once! He wants to take my child from me!"

"We both know he can't because she's not his..." he started.

She stood up and moved toward him. He backed up. She backed him right into the wall.

"Please, Gavin, just show me a little compassion!"

He was cornered.

She pounced and kissed him on the mouth, wrapping her arms around his neck.

"Agggggggggggghhhhhhhhh!" Deb screamed from outside the Chief's door.

"Oh, Dear," said the Chief.

Shannon's tears stopped and were replaced by an evil smirk.

Deb ran out of the building. Gavin chased after her. She got into the front seat of the limo. "Take me home," she said.

"What happened?" asked Miranda.

Gavin pounded on the window. "Deb! Please!"

She rolled down the window just a little. "Get in the damn back, and don't say a word to me," she said through gritted teeth. He stood there, dejected. Then he got in the back, tears in his eyes.

"What happened?" Miranda asked again.

"Shannon Magill."

"Your ex-girlfriend?" Dan asked.

"Yeah. She backed me into a wall and kissed me," he said, wiping away a tear and looking out the window.

"She kissed you!" Miranda exclaimed.

"Wait. What happened? Step by step," Dan asked calmly.

"I went in to make sure that Chief Lindstrom had gotten a message I left about our friend Ms. Ash. She's an elderly lady. I'm concerned Mason Miller has been…I can't even describe it… following her around, looking in her windows. I went back to his office, and Shannon was there crying. She told him she had bad news and that I was the only person she knows in town. She said that Barry had filed for divorce and wanted full custody of "their" kid. She just kind of backed me into a wall and… kissed me."

"Did you kiss her back?" Miranda asked. Dan glared at her. "What? It's a valid question?"

"No. I didn't kiss her back. Deb screamed and I threw her off me and ran after Deb." He was silent for a minute. "Ever heard that song 'Anti-hero' by Taylor Swift? That's Shannon."

CHAPTER 53

Deb bolted from the limo. Gavin ran after her. Dan and Miranda followed them into the apartment. Deb went straight into the bedroom and slammed the door. Gavin leaned his forehead against the door and closed his eyes.

"Deb! Please! Talk to me. I'm so sorry. I swear. I didn't know she'd be there. She kissed me."

"What happened?" asked Gabriella, who was prepping for Thanksgiving tomorrow.

Dan shook his head. "It's nothing. She just needs a minute. I hope."

"Deb!" Gavin smacked the door with his open hand. "I love you! Shannon can't change that." He turned and slid down the door to the floor, where he sat, leaning against the door.

"Ug! What did that bitch do now?" Molly asked.

"She kissed him," Miranda whispered.

Gabriella slammed a pan down on the counter.

The bedroom door opened. Gavin looked up at Deb standing over him. She reached her hand down to him. He took hold of it and stood. She led him into the bedroom and closed the door behind them.

He opened his mouth to speak. She shushed him. He wrapped his arms around her waist and hugged her to him. She quietly slipped her arms around his neck. "I'm terrified," she whispered.

"Of Shannon?" he asked.

"Of me."

"I don't understand."

"I…I threw away my marriage. I hurt my husband," she said, pulling away and walking to the bed. She sat on the edge, staring at the floor. She caressed the baby bump.

"Deb, we've talked about this before. I trust you."

"Ha!" she laughed. "I don't."

He sat beside her and took her hand. "Talk to me."

"I don't think I would ever have cheated if it hadn't been for…"

"For?" he asked.

She cradled her stomach. "After Dan left, I was diagnosed with postpartum depression. I started the treatment…the infusion. By the time I started to feel like myself again and realized I may have been acting a little erratically, I was divorced and in a relationship with a man just as erratic as I had been acting."

"Baby, I'm so sorry you went through that. But that won't happen again."

"How do you know?"

"Because we know what to look for," he assured her. He looked down at his shoes.

"I know she kissed you. I wasn't mad at you. I looked at her, and I saw me. I saw me doing what I did to Dan to you. And I freaked out."

He held her. "So, Mark?"

"I loved him. But I loved him when I wasn't really me."

"And me?"

"I am myself. And I love you with my whole being."

"Then marry me, DeBella," he whispered, nuzzling her ear, and making her giggle.

"Okay," she replied, kissing him.

"You should tell him," Gavin suggested.

"It won't change anything," Deb said, shaking her head.

"He deserves the truth, Deb. And you need the closure."

They sat there for a moment, holding onto each other.

"Okay," she said at last. "I didn't reveal anything you didn't already know, did I?"

"No."

"How?" she asked.

"I investigated Mark's murder, remember. He made appointments for you with Dr. Naam. She specializes in PPD."

"How many?"

"At least 4. He kept rescheduling each month until…"

"Why didn't you tell me?"

"You loved him," he said quietly.

He rose and went to the door. He opened it. "Dan," he said, "Can you come in here for a minute?"

Dan looked confused but entered the bedroom. Deb moved to the seating area and motioned for him to sit opposite her. Gavin smiled, exited, and closed the door behind him.

"It's okay. They have some unfinished business to discuss before we leave," he said to Miranda. "It's way overdue." Gavin walked over to her. She looked a little scared. He rubbed her back and kissed her on the side of the head. "It's all good, Red."

She cracked a smile.

Half an hour later, Dan and Deb emerged. It was clear they had been crying, but they were all smiles now. "Vegas?" Dan said, rubbing his hands together.

"Vegas!" replied Gavin, jumping up.

CHAPTER 54

"Are you going to tell me what you two talked about?" Miranda asked, as she freshened her makeup in their hotel suite's bathroom mirror.

Dan blushed. "We talked about how I'm a dumbass," he answered.

"Danny, I know, Deb. She wouldn't call you a dumbass. She adores you," Miranda said, applying her lipstick.

"She didn't. But I am."

"What makes you think so?" she asked with a sweet smile.

"Just tell me what you're feeling, my Love. I don't want to be blind to your feelings." He wrapped his arms around her waist and kissed her shoulder from behind her. "I told you before. I had a hand in the demise of my marriage."

"I know that, Honey. Marriages don't just fail because of one person or one thing."

"Deb had postpartum depression. I never even noticed," he sighed sadly.

"Diagnosed?"

"Dr. Naam treated her with an infusion that took 60 hours. Mark took her."

"When?"

"January, 2023."

"Right after you left?"

"Yes."

"Weeks after Mike died?"

"Yes."

"Right after she had an affair?"

"Yes."

"Huh," she said with a huff.

"What?"

"I hate to speak ill of the dead, but Mark Redmond was a dick," she declared.

"Oh, I don't know. He was there for her when I wasn't," Dan said.

"Was he? Or did he take advantage of the situation and not tell you, his good friend, that your wife was having problems that you missed because you were also going through a rough time? Did he sleep with her when she was at her lowest point and then sit at your table on Christmas morning in your robe after having slept in your bed?" She was cute when she was angry. Her auburn hair bounced with each nod of her head, knocking that one piece loose that tended to fall in her eyes. She blew at it as it bounced off her nose and covered her right eye. "I don't believe Deb blames you."

"Of course not. As she always has, she blames herself."

"So, she got herself all worked up that she would make the same mistakes all over again and freaked out?"

"Pretty much."

"Deb doesn't give herself enough credit."

"She never has," he smiled. "A quality I don't need to worry about with you."

"Watch it, Deputy," she laughed. "She forgot one very important thing: she actually loves Gavin Mahoney, and he actually loves her. Further, had it been him instead of Mark, back then, he'd have talked to YOU, even if he did love her."

"Huh. You're right about that." He looked at her reflection in the mirror. "How would you react if my ex kissed me?"

"Honey, I just left you in a bedroom with her alone for half an hour without batting an eye. I'm not worried about either one of you. You love me. She loves Gavin."

"You're not surprised that she was diagnosed with PPD, are you?" he observed.

"Not really. Cheating is out of character for her. She was obviously going through something pretty intense." She smiled and winked. "This may come as a surprise, but I like Deb. I like her a lot." Then she blotted her lips on a tissue.

CHAPTER 55

The Wedding Chapel was just a wedding chapel, like the dozens of others in the city. It was decorated in white satin and silk flowers with cherub sconces on the walls and stained-glass windows depicting swans swimming under stone bridges. There was an organ and 4 small wooden pews. It wasn't meant for a large wedding party, just the officiant, the bride and groom, and their witnesses, if they brought them (or they could be provided for a fee). The officiant stood in front of the room, under the largest of the stained-glass windows. Gavin and Dan stood on his left side, Miranda on his right.

The organist played the opening bars to the wedding march. Deb appeared from a small alcove at the back of the chapel. She wore her wedding dress that she'd made herself. The champaign colored silk cascaded down from the empire waist just below the sweetheart neckline down to the floor, where it pooled at her feet. The back was waistless and flowed behind her in a short train. The sleeves were angel sleeves, made from an antique lace table cloth, tea-dyed to compliment the champaign silk of the gown. The princess veil was crafted from a wreath of the same silk with a gold ribbon strung around it. The other tea-dyed lace tablecloth was attached diagonally and hung down the back. She carried a simple bouquet of a dozen red roses bundled with the same gold ribbon. She wore her long honey-blonde hair down. For jewelry, she wore Gabriella's pearl necklace and earrings and her engagement ring. She was undeniably beautiful.

A fact confirmed by the three men at the front of the room who collectively whispered, "Wow!" as she started down the aisle. Miranda giggled and gave her a quick thumbs up.

She smiled and handed the bouquet to her bride's maid and took her groom by the hands. He beamed at her.

He was classically handsome, it was true, but she had never seen him in a suit. He hadn't put nearly as much effort or thought into his wedding attire. He had opted for a suit over a more formal tuxedo. Simple lines. Black pinstripe. She'd chosen a champagne silk tie to match her gown for him to wear. She looked twice at his tie clip. It was his first communion tie clip. She choked back her laughter. His cufflinks, at least, were his police-issue dress cufflinks, she thought. His hair was always cut short, but he'd been working so much he hadn't gotten it cut in over a month, and the top had grown out in curly, near-black ringlets. It didn't matter that he hadn't picked out a special outfit. He was effortlessly equal measures of sexy and dignified.

They exchanged their vows and placed their rings on each other's hands. Then they kissed. That was it. They were married. It had taken only minutes. But Deb felt like time had slowed down. She experienced it all in slow motion.

"Congratulations!" announced the officiant. They posed for a few pictures and toasted the marriage with the officiant and organist, the bride and bride's maid drinking sparkling white grape juice, while the others had champagne.

CHAPTER 56

The wedding party boarded the elevator in the hotel. A trio of grandmotherly women boarded with them.

"Oh, Congratulations!" the lady nearest the buttons exclaimed.

"Such a handsome couple!" said the second.

"Gavin Mahoney! Is that you?" asked the third, straining to get a closer look at his face.

Gavin blushed. "Yes, Mrs. Ramirez. How are you? What brings you to Las Vegas?"

"Wayne Newton, of course," she giggled. "Flora, this is Lucia Fuentes' grandson, Gavin. His parents live just two houses down from me."

"Oh yes. I remember him. He used to ride his bike around the neighborhood. I saw him standing on his handlebars once, going down 16th Avenue. Where have you been, Gavin?"

"Um. I grew up and moved away, Mrs. West."

"Oh, that happens, I suppose," Mrs. West chuckled.

"I've seen Molly Mahoney around. But not Gavin. Not for a while," said the third woman.

"That's Gavin there, Joan," Mrs. Ramirez shouted.

"It is? Well, what's he doing here?" Joan asked.

"He's gotten married!" Mrs. West shouted.

"Oh? Has he? About time! What's he 37, 38 years old now?" Joan announced.

Dan sputtered and turned to face the wall.

"Think it's funny? They have memories like steel traps," Gavin whispered.

Dan burst out laughing.

"You asked for it," Gavin scoffed. "You remember my friend, Danny Bradley?"

Dan stopped laughing and turned to look at Gavin with his mouth open.

"Oh, Dear! Poor boy! You have grown! And such a sweet little boy. So handsome." Mrs. West proclaimed.

"Yes, he was," Mrs. Ramirez agreed.

"He's not so bad now, if you ask me," Joan cackled.

"How's your father?" Flora West asked.

"He died, Flora," Joan reminded her.

"I thought his mother died," Flora said.

"She did. But now his father has died, too."

"Nasty business," Mrs. Ramirez sighed, "Such a terrible day."

"What, Juanita? When his father died?" Flora asked.

"No. Well, I'm sure it was, but she meant the day his mother died," Joan clarified.

"Oh, yes. And that horrid boy Mason, hitting little Gavin Mahoney like he did. You were so brave, dear, standing up to that brute."

"Wait! What?" Gavin asked.

"He punched you, Dear. Knocked you out," Mrs. Ramirez said.

"When? I don't remember that."

"I shouldn't wonder," she snorted. "Gavin was trying to get Danny into the car. Keith yelled for Gavin to go home. Gavin ran back across my yard. Keith got back in the car and drove away. Anyway, Gavin had only gone as far as my porch when Mason came out and punched him right in the face," she said to Deb, who nodded.

"You saw all this?" Dan asked. "I don't remember ever getting out from under the blanket in the back seat." He stepped forward, mesmerized.

"Oh yes. I saw it from my kitchen window," she smiled. "Oh, this is our floor!"

And the old woman stepped off the elevator.

"Memories like a steel trap?" Dan asked.

"Yep," Gavin replied, watching them walk down the hall to their room.

"You don't remember any of that?"

"Nope."

"Me, neither." Dan paused as the elevator doors closed. "But it happened, didn't it?"

"Yep."

Deb and Miranda looked at each other. "That was weird, right?" Deb asked.

"Yes," Miranda replied. "It reminds me of something."

"MacBeth. Double, double, toil and trouble," Deb suggested.

"That's it!" Miranda exclaimed.

CHAPTER 57

Gavin unlocked the door to their suite and shoved it open. He turned to Deb and smiled.

"No!" she said, backing away. "I'm too heavy."

He laughed and swooped her up into his arms. "Ugggg," he groaned.

"Shut up," she laughed.

He kissed her and carried her across the threshold.

"Ah, nothing quite like your wife questioning your ability to carry her over the threshold and three old ladies pointing out your age to make you feel old!" he teased, letting her feet drop to the floor.

"What was that?" she asked.

"Nothing we need to worry about tonight," he said, lifting her chin with his hand and kissing her. She pulled back and grinned mischievously. She ran her hand down his arm and turned, walking over to the sofa and sitting in the center. She bit her lip. "Sing for me," she demanded, the window overlooking Vegas displaying the city behind her.

Gavin shook his head. "I don't think so," he laughed.

"Oh, come on! We're in Vegas, Baby! Sing Elvis…but do that Spanish thing."

"Spanish thing?"

"Yeah."

"You mean sing it in Spanish?"

"After the English, yeah," she replied, raising her eyebrows.

He walked over and sat beside her. She turned to look at him. "Come on, Deb. That's embarrassing," he complained, blushing.

"Would it help to picture your audience naked?" she winked.

He threw his head back and laughed. "You, nymphomaniac!"

"Well, would it?" she asked, standing.

"You first," he nodded.

"Can you unhook me?" she asked, taking off her veil and turning her back to him, lifting her hair.

He stood, unbuttoned the dress, and then unzipped the hidden zipper. She let the gown fall to the floor. She stepped out of the dress and removed her shoes. He sat back down with his mouth open. "You didn't wear anything under it," he said, stating the obvious.

"Nope."

He took her hand and pulled her down beside him. He leaned in and kissed her neck and sang softly against her skin.

"'Love Me Tender.' Oh, I love that one," she said breathlessly, closing her eyes.

CHAPTER 58

Gavin walked down the hallway of the Bradley home. He shouldn't be there. He wanted to run the other way, but he forced himself to take each step forward. He was looking for Mrs. Bradley. She needed help. Nobody was home at his house. Why? Shouldn't he be in school? He scratched his arm and noticed the bumps all over his skin. Chickenpox. That's right. Molly had them last week. He had them this week. He had felt better, so he'd gone outside to ride his bike. He'd seen the old man and the guy with the hammer and the crazy, nervous man that had come, yelling at them. He had snuck into the house after the old man and the man who held the hammer had left. He had to make sure Mrs. Bradley and the baby were okay. But Mrs. Bradley wasn't okay. He opened the bathroom door. Carrie was not moving or crying, but she was wet. Mrs. Bradley was holding her in her arms. Carrie had on a little pair of blue jeans. She was covered in blood and hung limply in her mother's arms. Mrs. Bradley looked up at him. She had on a short Lurex dress. Her legs were bare. They seemed so long… and bloody. She said something. But he couldn't understand her. There was blood everywhere. So much blood. Danny. She was saying, "Danny." Gavin turned to run. Danny emerged from a bedroom. He was crying for his mommy. He had chickenpox, too. Gavin grabbed Danny's hand and ran.

He ran out the back door. Someone else was in the house. They could hear him screaming. Worse, they could hear Mrs. Bradley screaming.

Then, before they could run to Gavin's house, the wild-eyed man was back outside. Feet from them. But it couldn't be the wild-eyed man they'd heard in the house because they could still hear him in the house, and Mrs. Bradley was still screaming. Gavin put his hand over Danny's mouth and said, "Shhhhh." Then the screaming just stopped.

The crazy, wild-eyed man was still in the driveway. He'd found Mrs. Bradley at some point, too. He must have. He was covered in blood. But his car was gone. How was he still there? Who was in the house? Gavin was afraid to move from behind the corner of the house. But he needed to get Danny away. If they ran, the wild-eyed man would see them.

Then Mr. Bradley drove into the drive. Mr. Bradley got out. Gavin picked up Danny and ran. He crouched behind Mr. Bradley's car. He slowly opened the backseat door. Gavin moved very slowly. Mr. Bradley saw him. He kept the wild-eyed man talking, looking at him, Gavin pushed Danny into the car. He whispered, "Get in the car. Get under the blanket. Don't come out, no matter what." Danny was crying, but he did what Gavin said.

The wild-eyed man saw him now. He started yelling at Gavin. But he hadn't seen Danny. Danny stayed under the blanket. Gavin slammed the door. Mr. Bradley yelled at Gavin to go home. Gavin ran. The Bradleys' car sped off past him.

Mason Miller appeared out of nowhere. He had a rope over his shoulder. Money. Lots of it fell out of his pocket. He bent over to pick it up. He saw Gavin. He grinned that evil grin he always gave Gavin. Mason's fist flew toward Gavin's face! The last thing Gavin saw was that awful snake-eating snake tattoo.

Gavin sat up. The phone was ringing. He picked up the

receiver. It was their wake-up call. He replaced the receiver in the cradle and gently shook Deb awake. "Time to go home, Honey," he announced as she roused.

He rose and went into the bathroom. He steadied himself against the sink and looked in the mirror, half expecting his 10-year-old, almost 11, chicken-pocked face to look back. It was Thanksgiving. He'd just turned 37 in October. Twenty-six years had passed when the phone rang. He remembered them. His wife was beside him. She was expecting their child. They had gotten married a few hours ago. But reality felt more like the dream than the dream had.

He splashed some cold water on his face and looked at his reflection again. "He was going to kill me. Why didn't he?" Vaguely, he could see a man coming out of the Bradley house and running the opposite way. It wasn't Mason. Mason hadn't killed them. He'd been picking up the money Joe Conti had thrown or dropped. But Gavin knew without a doubt Mason would have killed him right then. Except Mrs. Ramirez came running out of her house.

Deb wrapped her arms around his waist from behind him and hugged him. "You okay, Babe?" she asked.

"Yeah. I'm okay," he claimed. "Just a bad dream."

She didn't believe him, but she didn't argue. He'd tell her when he was ready. He always did.

CHAPTER 59

They arrived back at the apartment before 10 am. They were running on just a few hours of sleep. Still, Gavin was quieter than normal, even for him. When anybody broached the subject, he simply dismissed them, saying he was tired, was all. His father saw right through that ploy. As the kids sat and watched the parade on the television and Gabriella commandeered the women to help cook, he grabbed Gavin by the arm and pulled him out onto the balcony.

Dan watched his friend and his friend's father through the glass door. Gavin took a seat in a chair at the bistro table Deb had set out there while she was decorating the small balcony with flowers. Dave blocked his egress back into the apartment, ensuring he'd get his son to talk to him. At first, Gavin stared straight ahead. Dan noticed, though, that Gavin's hand shook as he waved off his father's concerns. Then the conversation turned. Gavin was crying. Dan was sure of it. Then Dave stepped towards his son, who threw his arms around his father and cried. Dave just held on and let him.

After a minute or so, Gavin let go of his father and wiped his face with the back of his hand. Dave turned and looked at Dan. He waved to Dan to join them.

Dan made his way onto the balcony. Dave told him to take

a seat.

"I'm okay, Dave," Dan replied, smiling.

"Take a seat, Son," Dave commanded, his brogue sounding extra strong.

Dan did as he was told.

"Now, I understand ya met de BUNKO ladies yesterday, and dey told ye things dat neither of ye could remember."

"Um, yeah. I mean yessir," Dan replied, feeling like a child being lectured.

"I was not at home when dese events occurred. Gavin was home sick alone. We thought that was okay as he was nearly 11. When we got home dat evening, he had a bruise on his jaw and a goose-egg bump on da back of his head. He said he thought he got it falling off his bike. He was taken to the ER, where they told him he had a lovely concussion and a hairline skull fracture. I had avoided the topic of your mother and sister. I was on the police force, but I didn't want to scare my son since he'd been home alone. But being in the ER, he heard things. He told me about what he'd seen, and we left the ER and went to the police department, where he relayed his story to ma boss... who promptly dismissed it, listening to his own son, Mason, who claimed Gavin was lyin'," Dave explained.

"Now, we've known Juanita Ramirez for 40 years if a day. She's a gossip, but she doesn't exaggerate about what she sees wit her own eyes. So I believe her when she says she saw Gavin over there later and that Mason gave Gavin that bruise and bump. The crack in his skull surely explains why he doesn't, or didn't, remember it, but I trust my son more than her, and he tells it differently today," he continued.

"You remember it now, Gav?" Dan asked.

"Tell him, Son," Dave urged.

"Yeah. I went back after Salvatore and Geno left. I thought Joe was gone, too. His car was gone. I was worried about your mom. I snuck in the back door."

"You went in the house?" Dan asked, surprised.

Gavin closed his eyes and nodded.

"Oh, Gavin. I can't imagine how traumatizing that must have been for a kid. I mean, I saw the crime scene photos last year. It was gruesome," Dan offered. No wonder his friend had been so quiet. He was reliving something horrific.

Nothing could have prepared him for the words that came out of Gavin's mouth next. Nothing.

"She wasn't dead, Dan," Gavin announced.

Dan's heart felt like it stopped and restarted. "What?"

"Your mother was alive. Carrie was gone. But Ellen was just badly beaten…like Deb."

"So, Joe did kill her?" Dan choked out, his voice cracking, his heart breaking.

"No. I don't think so. I don't even think he killed himself," Gavin replied, his voice barely above a whisper.

Dan felt hot tears run down his face. "What then? There's more. I can see it on your face!"

"You were in the house, Dan. You weren't at school. You had chickenpox."

"No. I was in the car. I heard my father telling me to get under the blanket!" Dan protested. Gavin didn't say anything. "No. Not my father's voice. Who told me to get under the blanket? He pulled me out of the house. He hid me. He got me to the car." Still, Gavin said nothing. "You. You told me to get under the blanket. You told me not to come out, no matter what. You saved me." Dan sat back, stunned, tears streaking his cheeks.

"I think Mason Miller wanted to kill me. I think he did kill Joe. When he hit me, he had a length of rope…and a pocket full of cash, Joe's cash."

"So, who killed my mother?" Dan asked.

"Yeah. Walter Bowen was there. I saw him run away from

the house before I lost consciousness after Mason hit me." Walter had turned out to be Dan's mother's biological brother. He was the CEO of Bowen Tobacco. In the spring, Dan and Gavin had uncovered that Bowen Tobacco had, in fact, contracted Geneli to get rid of Ellen Bradley.

"Recovered memories are lousy evidence," Dan said, sighing.

"I know," Gavin nodded.

Dave turned and walked back inside, leaving the two men sitting in silence.

CHAPTER 60

Thanksgiving was November 28. Jason's 4th birthday would be on Sunday, December 1. The first anniversary of Mark's death was on Saturday, November 30th. The plan was for a family party on Sunday morning before they all left to go home. And Deb had every confidence she could muscle through Saturday with very little grief and guilt. She was wrong.

She hadn't had her nightmares ending in gunfire in months. Friday night into Saturday morning was a rough night. She would fall asleep only to wake an hour later, screaming all night. Gavin would hold her, ask her about the dreams, suggest she address the real problem, and acknowledge the anniversary. Somewhere around 4 am, she finally acquiesced if he also opened up about what had been bothering him for two days.

He flipped on the bedside lamp and sat up, facing her. He sighed. "It's nothing really. The BUNKO ladies just triggered some repressed memories with their talk."

"For Dan, too? Because he's acting just like you."

"Well, sort of. I told him what I remembered, and it triggered his memory," he said sadly.

She shook her head and held her hands out questioningly, saying, "And?"

"He wasn't in the car like he thought."

"Then where was he?" she pushed.

"In the house," he replied, looking at the covers.

"Dan was in the house. When his mother was killed."

"Well, no. When Carrie was killed. His mother was still alive when I found him hiding in his bedroom. I grabbed him and ran out the back when we heard someone come in. We heard her screaming as we hid behind a bush. We saw Joe in the driveway. It wasn't him in the house. We heard her stop screaming. Then, Keith got home. I got Dan into the car while Keith distracted Joe. Then I ran. I ran right into Mason Miller's fist. I don't know where he came from."

"Dan said he remembered his father telling him to get under the blanket in the back."

"Yeah. No. That was me."

"You were just a kid. Maybe 11?"

"Not quite 11. Yeah," he agreed.

"When exactly did you develop this deep-seated need to rescue everybody? Why would you go into that house after you saw what you saw earlier?" she exclaimed.

"In answer to your first question, I'm guessing at birth. I believe the first question actually answers the second."

"Gavin, I'm serious."

"So am I, Deb. I am who I am. You know that. Because you're the one who pushed me to take the Head Detective position after I tried to walk away from law enforcement. And you were right, by the way," he insisted.

She sighed. "Well, I certainly understand how you guys are feeling. It's devastating when you remember something like that. Remembering my father's murder hurt. But it also was freeing. Remembering let me deal with it. I actually stopped having that dream once I faced what it was about," she said sympathetically.

"Speaking of which?" he prompted, taking her hand.

"It's nothing so profound. I'm just doing normal, happy

things. And then there's gunfire and Mark dying.

"Normal, happy things? Like getting married, having a baby, birthdays?

She started to cry. "How do I have the right to be happy? When he's…"

"Dead? Because you're not."

"Well, that's callous," she huffed through her tears.

He nodded. "Yeah. Maybe. But it's also true. It's okay to be happy, Mi Vida. It's okay to feel loss and grief. Here's the real kicker: it's okay to be happy and feel loss and grief at the same time. We're complex beings," he said, hugging her to him and kissing the top of her head.

"How can you stand to watch me cry over him?" she cry-laughed.

"Because I love you."

"Doesn't it hurt you?"

He didn't answer right away. His silence told her it did hurt him. Finally, he replied, "I wish I had followed you out of that Halloween party instead of letting you walk away. Let's put it that way. But I didn't. And if I had, there'd probably be no Jason… so things happen for a reason. Just like Shannon."

"Ha! It's not the same."

"Not exactly, no. We're different people. We come to this relationship with different emotional baggage. For example, I am apparently motivated by the need to be seen as a hero, who feels embarrassed to appear as less than that," he blushed.

"Yeah. That's for certain," she laughed, for real this time. "I am a hot mess, Gavin." She laid her head on his chest.

"Yeah. But you're my hot mess now, Baby."

CHAPTER 61

Deb's frame of mind didn't improve as the day progressed. And that put Gavin in a mood as well. He did his best to let her feel what she needed to feel, but the feeling that he was competing with a ghost still nagged at him all day. It didn't really seem fair. He couldn't really fight a ghost. He couldn't even criticize Mark and not appear petty.

And, oh, how he longed to criticize Mark. He'd been the officer who investigated Mark's death. He didn't like the man he uncovered. Maybe he would have felt differently had he not felt so strongly attracted to the woman Mark left behind. He was willing to admit that. But added to his initial impressions, Deb's battle with postpartum depression and Mark's involvement before and after treatment left him with a really bad taste in his mouth, as regarded Mark Redmond.

Deb saw him as fun-loving, impetuous but harmless, kind of goofy. This was not his impression of the man. Through his postmortem investigative lens, he saw a highly ambitious and manipulative officer. He was charismatic, no doubt. He was charming. He had boyish good looks. He used those qualities to manipulate people, mostly women. He was indeed in an exclusive relationship with Deb at the time of his murder. Gavin found no evidence of any infidelity after he had started 'dating' Deb. But until just before that Christmas Eve, when she had succumbed to his charms, he had clearly been a bit of a man-whore. Gavin tended to share Miranda's view that Mark took advantage of Deb's state of mind to get what he wanted.

Of course, he was conflicted that someone, looking from the outside in, might conclude that he, too, had positioned himself so that the grieving woman would turn to him. Mainly because he thought that may have been exactly what he had done. It hadn't been a conscious decision. He had just longed to be near her, and she seemed to enjoy his company. But in retrospect, he had just been waiting for her to indicate even a little interest.

Deb enjoyed sex. She was truly uninhibited. Inevitably, the first glimmer of interest from her had resulted in a sexual encounter that, despite his surprise at its timing and suddenness, had been life-altering.

His fair-minded nature wanted to allow Mark the same possibility. She admitted she was the one who pursued him. But Mark's history with women belied that courtesy. Deb wasn't the first married woman he'd slept with. Not by a long shot. More like the fourth. That wasn't counting the numerous unmarried women, several of whom, though not technically married, were in committed relationships. It didn't seem to matter to Mark whether a woman had a significant other. And that was where he couldn't reconcile Mark's situation to his.

As the day wore on, his patience grew shorter and shorter. By noon, he found he needed a little distance from his brooding bride. So, as he often did when he felt stressed, he went for a run. His feet pounding on the ground in a steady rhythm that matched his heart and his breathing, the sweat dripping from his skin, his muscles straining, performing almost mechanically all worked with the chemical reactions in his brain to dull the stress. The runner's high was real, and it was all that was holding him together today. He ran further and longer than normal.

Deb was not a runner. When Gavin left for a run and didn't come back after his normal running time, she huffed and asked Molly to watch Jason, stating she wanted to go get things for his birthday celebration the next day. What she really wanted was a reprieve from the grief and conflict. She decided a little retail therapy was in order.

She found herself in Target. She hated to start getting Maternity clothes already, but she couldn't deny the need. She'd been wearing skirts for a month now because she couldn't comfortably close her pants. So, after she got birthday party supplies, she looked in the maternity clothes and picked out several outfits. She realized she also needed a coat, so she headed over to the coats. She found a cute bomber jacket and held it up to herself.

"Oh, Sweetie, no. That'll never fit you. With that gut, you'll want a parka," said the voice of her nemesis.

"I don't have a 'gut,'" Deb moaned.

"I hate to tell you, but that's a gut," Shannon smirked.

"That's a baby," Deb retorted, giving her tummy a loving caress.

Shannon's face froze. "Oh," she said, sounding a little defeated.

"Don't you have one of your own somewhere?" Deb asked, relishing her small triumph.

"Well, congratulations, I guess. Whatever it takes to get a man." It was the knockout blow. They both knew it. Shannon grinned and walked away.

Deb hung the coat back on the rack and checked out.

CHAPTER 62

Deb returned home in a worse mood than when she left. Gavin greeted her cheerfully, obviously fresh from the shower. His hair was still wet, and the apartment smelled of Irish Spring. She glared at him and took her purchases to the bedroom, slamming the door.

"What did I do?" he asked his brother-in-law.

"No idea," George replied.

"Dad?" Gavin asked.

His father shrugged.

His sister walked over and smacked him across the back of his head. "What difference does it make? She's pregnant. She's your wife. You apologize."

He rubbed the back of his head. "Ow, geez, Moll. Okay. I'll go." He stood and followed Deb into the bedroom.

She was sitting on the settee, pulling the new clothes out of the bags and folding them to put away. "Shannon Magill called me fat, and when I said I was pregnant, she insinuated I used that to trap you," she announced before he even said a word.

"So? You're not fat, and you didn't trap me. Who cares what Shannon says?" he asked, perplexed.

He immediately realized this was the wrong response. Her eyes flashed. Her jaw clenched.

"Oh. No. I'm sorry!" he backtracked. "I didn't mean to sound dismissive. I just mean…well, she doesn't really matter."

"I'm not having the best day, Gavin. I don't need her bullshit. And I'd really like for you to just give me some space right now," she said through gritted teeth.

"Okay," he said, backing out the door. He grimaced to his father and brother-in-law as he sat back down.

"What did you do?" Molly demanded.

"Ohhhhh. I messed that up royally," he replied.

He tried again at dinner. They had ordered Chinese delivery.

As she leaned forward, he noticed a silver strand of hair among the honey gold. He had several himself. He smiled and laughed. "Look, married two days, and you already have a gray hair," he teased. His sister shot him an evil eye. His brother-in-law shook his head. His father buried his face in his hand.

"Great!" Deb huffed. "I'm a fat slut with gray hair."

"Um. I…Uh…Wow. I'm a moron," he surrendered.

CHAPTER 63

Jason woke up screaming. Deb rushed to him.

"There's a monsta at the door, Mommy! Don't let it hur you!"

She took him into her arms and wiped his tears. "The monster is gone, Sweet Pea. Look. I'm okay. See?" She lay in his bed beside him, soothing his fears until he fell back to sleep.

She quietly rose from his bed, tiptoed out, and pulled his door closed once he'd drifted back off to sleep. Instead of going back to bed herself, she went into the bathroom.

Deb stared at her face in the bathroom mirror. The swelling was gone. She had a touch of yellow under her eyes still and a small bruise on her jaw. Still, all she saw were the bruises. Her roots were showing, too. Not that anyone but she could tell. Her natural shade was just a shade darker than the color she used, but being pregnant, there was little she could do about that. And there was that silver strand, standing out like a beacon. She saw every flaw.

Shannon Magill was a psycho bitch, but she was a flawless psycho bitch…a flawless psycho bitch with designs on Gavin, she might add.

She stood back and smoothed down her pajama top. The baby bump was impossible to hide now. How dare that bitch imply Deb was fat? She caressed her tummy lovingly.

She sighed heavily and opened the door, shutting off the light and walking into the bedroom. Gavin was sitting in the bed, watching the evening news.

"Jason went back to sleep," she said, climbing into bed beside him.

"Good news," he said quietly. He sat there in silence for a few minutes. "You shouldn't worry about her, Deb. I really couldn't care less about her."

"Uh-huh," she said, fluffing her pillow and turning away. "Your mom will be here early to help me get the party set up. Can you turn off the TV, please?"

He sighed and clicked off the television.

CHAPTER 64

Katelynn Kaminski had spent her Thanksgiving break quietly in the background. She was a shy, introverted girl. She adored her older sister. She liked Gavin, certainly more than she had Mark or Dan. What she saw from the corners of their relationship was his total devotion, a trait neither of the other two had shown to Deb. Dan loved somebody else. Mark loved himself. Gavin, however, looked at Deb like she was the center of the universe. Her fear was Deb was screwing this up.

While her sister was being a cold fish for some unknown reason, Katelynn said nothing. But she listened. Over Thanksgiving dinner, she listened to Marcus talk about how Gavin sang, and how Deb liked it. She listened to Molly tell how all the girls swooned when he played the guitar.

Gavin had obviously been in a strange mood that day, but he still had made an effort.

Deb, she concluded, was being entirely unreasonable today. She seemed to be taking out what someone else said on Gavin. She had never experienced that kind of love herself, but she didn't imagine that was a good way to keep the flames burning.

As her sister closed her bedroom door, she rose from her place on the sleeper sofa, took her guitar out of its case, and placed it on a guitar stand. Then she went back to bed.

The next morning, Gavin's family arrived, bags packed for their 6 pm flight home.

Deb rose from bed without speaking to her husband. She walked away, and his heart broke a little. He had a feeling he was losing to the ghost. Somehow, in a day's time, she had begun to doubt him. He knew her grief was the reason for her ire. He understood Shannon was an excuse, but he didn't know how to bring her out of her funk.

He followed Deb. He grabbed her hand as she reached the door. "Please. Talk to me. Please."

She felt the warmth of his touch and heard the love in his voice. "Why do you love me?"

"Because you are my life. I need you to breathe."

"Gavin, you breathed just fine before you met me," she replied.

"True, but when I saw you, you took my breath away. I'm sorry. I wish I could give you what you want, Deb. But I'll never be Mark."

She gasped and turned to him. "I don't want Mark. I wish he had lived. But I love you. I think you deserve better than me!"

"There's no one better than you," he said.

"I need to work on believing that. But you still left me alone yesterday when I was feeling sad."

"I just went for a run. I'll never leave you, Deb. I'll always come back."

"And for the record, if he was alive and I had to choose, I'd choose you."

"That's easily said, Deb."

She glared at him and pulled her hand away. "He asked me to marry him the day before he was killed. I said no." With that, she left the room.

He watched her leave, realizing the ghost had vanished.

He smiled.

CHAPTER 65

Sometime around noon, Dan, Miranda, and Marcus arrived. Fiona and her kids, Uncle Bob and Barb Ulrich, came up. Jason enjoyed his party. The kids went to his room to play with his new toys. The adults sat in the living room for some coffee.

Gabriella noticed Katelynn's guitar. "Oh! You have to play it, Mijo!" she exclaimed. Gavin blushed.

"It's not mine. Mom," he protested, frowning.

"Oh, please! 'Blue Eyes Crying in the Rain.' Please," his mother pleaded.

Dan said enthusiastically. "I didn't know you played!"

Katelynn didn't speak, but she handed him her guitar. She smiled a small, secretive smile.

He blushed deeper but took the guitar, tuned it, started, made a mistake, stopped, and started again. Then he played and sang.

Deb knew what was about to happen. He was about to turn her brain to mush, along with her legs. She bit her lip, and her breath quickened. What was she mad at him for? He had doubted her love. But hadn't she done the same to him? His head bowed slightly to watch his fingers make the changes. A single curl fell forward over his forehead. His golden-brown eyes peered through a curtain of long, dark lashes. Her heart started to race. He had explained it, hadn't he? She wasn't really mad at him. What was wrong with her? He was all she wanted. And he wanted her.

Katelynn actually looked up for a change. Miranda grabbed Dan's hand. Fiona closed her eyes and listened. His voice had a deep, even tone. He played the guitar like it was part of him. When he'd finished the song in English, he sang it again in Spanish. His mother applauded and smiled proudly.

Deb caught her breath and took the guitar from him, handing it back to Katelynn. She then sat in his lap and kissed him full on the mouth, taking him by surprise.

"Well, that was good, but that's a bit of an overreaction," Dan teased.

George shrugged in response to Dan's look. "I'm married to his sister. It doesn't affect her. But last time he sang at a family picnic, I had to dump a bucket of cold water on my sister."

"That's the single sexiest thing I've ever heard in my life," responded a mesmerized Miranda.

George nodded knowingly, raising an eyebrow.

"Uh-huh," said Fiona.

"Wo-wow," said Katelynn, clearing her throat.

"The single sexiest thing you've ever heard?" Dan repeated, giving Miranda a little push and making her laugh.

Deb pulled away and whispered, "Do it again."

He laughed. "You took the guitar, Babe. Am I forgiven?"

"Uh-huh. Am I?"

"Nothing to forgive," he replied as she kissed him again.

Katelynn smiled.

"Hey," he said as he climbed into bed that night after everyone had gone, "How about we let each other in instead of shutting each other out from now on?"

"What happened to better out than in?" she laughed.

He made a face. "Bad stuff out. Good stuff in. I think we're good stuff."

"Yeah. Me too. Sounds good."

CHAPTER 66

Monday morning, Gavin awakened to three text notifications. The first was from Pete Camacho. Camille had given birth to Michaela Ann Camacho at 2:35 am. She weighed 7 pounds 3 oz and was 18 inches. Mother and baby were doing well. The second was from Dan. Salvatore Geneli passed away in Dixon Correctional Center at 5:18 am at the age of 88. He had a heart attack. Geno and Tony, however, agreed to see Dan later in the week. The third was from Sam Davis, who gushed over the baby girl just named after his beloved son and then informed him that based on Mike's notes hidden throughout his things in the attic and Dan's memory of the day of the murders of Ellen and Carrie Bradley, Gavin had been identified as "the neighbor boy" listed in Dominica Geneli's will, and in accordance with the will, Sam would be in Fredericksburg later in the day to deliver the $7,000,000 bequeathed to Gavin.

"Holy crap!" Gavin exclaimed, sitting bolt upright.

"What? What's the matter?" Deb started awake at his voice.

"Oh, sorry, Sweetheart." He handed her his phone. She looked at it and handed it back. "Say something!" he laughed, giving her a gentle push. "What do you think?"

"I think we can afford a house,' she said, lying back down.

"We could always afford a house," he said, confused.

"A house?" he repeated fifteen minutes later as he looked at his freshly shaven face in the bathroom mirror. "That's all she had to say…a house."

At police headquarters, he added Deb as his beneficiary and to his insurance. Dan provided Jason's coverage, so there was no need to add him.

It was midmorning when Andrea Grimes called to say that he had a visitor, expecting Sam, he told her to bring him back. Andrea laughed, "He's a she, Detective."

God, not Shannon, he prayed. But Andrea continued, "It's a Mrs. Ash."

"Oh, of course. Bring HER back, Andrea."

Moments later, Mrs. Ash sat across from him.

"I just wanted to let you know I made a decision. I'm moving to North Carolina with my son. I placed my house on the market this morning. I had been thinking about it for a while. You can call off the cavalry," she laughed.

"It's not a problem. Mrs. Ash. Did you have any more problems with your peeper?"

"Oh, no. The officers seemed to have successfully scared whoever it was off."

He smiled. "Hey, how much are you asking for your house? I'm looking for a really special wedding gift."

She gave him her realtor's card and left.

His father had sent him the crime scene photos of the Bradley murders.

He carefully hung the photo showing Joe Conti's feet, one bare, the shoe and sock never found at the crime scene, something Maurice Miller never even tried to explain, next to the photo of Jeff's one bare foot. He hung the one of Mrs. Bradley in her Lurex dress next to that of Yvette's. He hung the picture of Carrie's blue jeans next to that of Christa's.

September 10, 1998
Sterling, IL

At 3:15 pm, Keith Bradley returned home from work to find Joe Conti pacing in his driveway, drenched in blood. Conti made a cryptic comment about Ellen Bradley giving the baby a bath. He demanded money. Keith, with his 5-year-old son hidden in the back of his car, drove to the fire station under the ruse of going to the bank. There, he called the police. Responding officers found Ellen Bradley clinging to Carrie, who had been drowned and then beaten with a hammer. Ellen was likewise bludgeoned to death with the same hammer. Joe Conti, her ex-husband, it was later revealed, was found hanging in the garage, where it was presumed he had committed suicide in a fit of remorse. He had scrawled a note in the blood of the victims on the garage floor.

He stood back and stared with his mouth open. "He reversed them. Why?" he asked out loud to nobody.

"Wow, what ya got here?" The Chief asked, sticking his head in the door.

"A 26-year-old crime scene in my hometown. Two houses down from Mason Miller.

Gavin pointed as he named off the victims, " Jeff, Joe, Yvette, Ellen, Christa, and Carrie."

"You familiar with the case?"

"My best friend's parents and sister," Gavin replied.

"Can you place Mason there?"

"He was there. I was there. I saw him. But I suffered a concussion and a fractured skull that day. My memory won't stand up. Dan was there. He was five. He doesn't remember much from that day. Then there's the word of an octogenarian who lived next door. Oh, and Geno Geneli, who has already been convicted of the crime, though he denies guilt."

"What was that about reverse?" the Chief asked.

"Carrie was first. Then Ellen. Then Joe."

"Like a whatchacallit…um…palindrome?"

Gavin turned and stared at the chief. "It's exactly like a palindrome!"

"What? I thought music was his thing."

"It is but there are musical palindromes: Bach's 'Crab Canon' for instance. It's music that's played the same backwards as forward. Bach isn't exactly Mason's cup of tea, of course. But the Beatles did it quite often…'As My Guitar Gently Weeps,' 'Don't Let Me Down,' 'Sgt, Pepper's Lonely Hearts Club Band,'" Gavin explained.

"So, what musical palindrome is this horror show?"

"Good question. It would have to be something…no… wait. It's a signature. He signed his work. Does that mean he killed Carrie, too…Not Geno?"

"What are you talking about?" the Chief asked.

"Yeah, what are you talking about?" Dan asked. He was standing at the door with Sam behind him. Andrea having brought them back, knowing Gavin was expecting them. She smiled and backed away, returning to her post.

"'I Palindrome I' by They Might Be Giants." He pulled up the lyrics. Dan looked over his shoulder at the computer screen. His eyes widened.

"Holy…That…that's…Geno, Tony, and Walter's motive!" he exclaimed.

And check out the chorus." He scrolled down.

"Hey, that's Maurice's…I mean Mason's…tattoo!" the Chief observed.

CHAPTER 67

Sam opened his briefcase and withdrew Dominca's will, of which he had been named executor by the court of Cook County when the executor named, Ruth Messick, was among those murdered in the Genelis' search for the heir. "Here is the provision," he said, pointing to the text he had highlighted. Dominica set the money aside in trust in 1999. She provided this photograph to indicate who 'the neighbor boy' she meant is. She claimed to have no further information as to his identity. The photo was in Mike's things. We actually came across it in May. We just didn't know what we were looking at. Is this you?"

Gavin took the picture in his hand. "Yeah. That's me. And I can prove it." He was a little surprised, to be honest. He hadn't really believed Sam's text. How would Dominica even have known to leave him anything?

"That sure would make this a lot easier," Sam laughed.

Gavin logged into the website for the local Sterling library and searched for a particular story in the local paper, "The Sterling Gazette." It had apparently been a slow news week. There it was, the exact same picture attached to the caption, "Eleven-year-old Gavin Mahoney of Sterling practices wheelies in preparation for the Fiesta parade this Saturday." He looked more closely at the caption, "photo by Harmony Rose." Dominica should have known his name then. She was paranoid, but apparently with cause, so he'd give her a pass.

"That'll work," Sam said. "Sign here." He shoved a legal form in front of Gavin. Gavin read and signed. Sam handed over a check. An actual check. Gavin stared at it. "This closes the trust. The taxes have been paid for this year, and you'll receive a k-19 form. Now it's yours to do with as you please. It was still over $5,000,000.

"Not enough if you ask me," Dan said.

"Give it to whatever charity you like, Sam. I've got to go," Gavin said, signing the back of the check. Then he looked at his watch. "Eww. Like now. I got a class at 2." He rushed out the door.

"Gavin, you should take it," Dan insisted, starting to follow.

Sam reached out his hand, stopping his son-in-law from following. "He really doesn't need it, Dan."

CHAPTER 68

Deb met Gavin and the realtor that evening at Mrs. Ash's house at 5 pm, having left Jason with Fiona. Mrs. Ash opened the door with a smile and a plate of gingerbread cookies.

"Hello! Hello!" she greeted them.

"Generally, we like to show the home when the homeowner is out, but Mrs. Ash insists she knows you two, and wanted to be here," Miss Gilbert explained.

"I do, indeed," she smiled. "These are two of my favorite people. This young man is with the Police and teaches at the University. And this lucky girl is his wife, Deb." Her voice was warm and friendly. She slipped her arm through Deb's. "Oh, look how beautiful you are! When is the baby due, Dear?"

"Late April," Deb blushed.

"Well, I imagine my décor won't be to your taste, my being 79 and your being not 79," she laughed, but it is really a great house for a growing family. It's really too much house for me anymore. It's 4 bedrooms, 5 if you count the extra one in the basement. 2 ½ baths. There's a formal living room and a less formal family room. Oh, and a big fenced back yard."

And while Deb had to agree her taste in décor did not mesh with Mrs. Ash's, she saw the house had great potential.

Once they had toured the house, she took Gavin's arm and

said excitedly, "She's right. It's a great house for a family."

Miss Gilbert smiled. "Would you like to make an offer? The asking price is $779,499."

"Sure," Gavin said looking to Deb, who nodded enthusiastically. "What do you think, Honey? Split? $400 each?"

"I'm sorry? You wish to offer over asking?"

"Yes, in cash. How fast can we close?" Deb answered.

"Um. Mrs. Ash?"

Mrs. Ash sat down wordlessly on her sofa with her mouth open! "Oh my! Did you win the lottery?" she asked after she composed herself.

Gavin looked bewildered. "No. Why would we need to win the lottery?"

"It's just...you're new to the area and not that established," Miss Gilbert said.

"You need a financial analysis?" he asked earnestly.

"It would help," Miss Gilbert replied.

He pulled out his phone and called Sam Davis. "Hey Sam, can you email those documents to..." He looked at the realtor, questioning.

"Leona Gilbert, Lgilbert76@Starrealty.com," Miss Gilbert replied.

Minutes later, her phone beeped. She opened the email. She gasped. "You're on the Board of Directors at Fuentes International!"

"My grandfather's company. It's mostly a titular position," he said.

"Titular?" Miss Gilbert asked.

"In title only," he explained.

"You don't talk like a cop," Ms. Ash laughed.

"I don't? How do cops talk?" he asked, winking.

"Well, I can be out by over the weekend," Mrs. Ash agreed.

"Wow! Okay, I'm going to be honest; this is my first sale.

Mrs. Ash and you two are my first clients. Um…Is next Monday good?"

"After 3 pm, yes," Gavin agreed.

CHAPTER 69

Gavin looked at the pictures again. Twenty-six years was too long. No way Mason had waited this long to recreate the Bradley murders. He searched for cold cases on infants in the US. The list was depressingly long. He sighed and dove in, meticulously reviewing each one that was a possible match. He narrowed the list down to 10 that were connected to multiple murders.

Rudy Vance knocked on his door.

He waved him in.

"Nothing on Marlene Travis. She hasn't returned to work, and she hasn't surfaced at her apartment," he explained.

"What about her parents?" Gavin asked.

"They live in Wilmington, Delaware. We've contacted them. Wilmington police confirm she hasn't contacted them."

"Okay, keep me in the loop," Gavin said.

An alarm went off on Rudy's watch. Gavin looked up questioningly. Rudy blushed. "Sorry, time for my medication."

"Mind if I ask?" Gavin queried.

"Oh, no. Phenobarbital. A fairly low dose. I have epilepsy. But it's fairly well controlled. I haven't had a seizure in 6 years. I'm actually weaning off the medication."

Gavin smiled. That explained the emotional reaction delay he'd noted previously. He would have sighed in relief had Rudy not been standing in front of him.

After you've taken your medication, start comparing these cold cases to our murders. See if we can narrow this list down some more. I emailed you the files," Gavin said.

"Yessir," Rudy replied.

"Rudy!" Gavin called out as Rudy was walking out the door. "Do you think you could... Could you help us move on Saturday?"

"Sure, Gavin. I'd be happy to. Why are you moving?"

"Oh, we bought a house. My sister-in-law is transferring to UMW next semester. She's taking our apartment."

Rudy blushed again, "Oh, is she? Well, that's great. I mean... I hope she likes it at Mary Washington."

Gavin smiled. "Do you have a little crush on Katelynn, Rudy?"

"No. I mean, she's cute. But no. No sir," he blushed even deeper.

"Okay. Go," Gavin said, waving him out and chuckling. Thank God. He liked Rudy. He hated suspecting him.

He packed up his things and headed to campus.

CHAPTER 70

Sam sat across the table from Miss Gilbert and her employer, Fred Jackson. Fred was skeptical about this deal. He found it hard to believe the buyers actually had the cash. When Sam Davis entered the room in his $5,000 suit, he was pleasantly surprised. Sam handed him a card. He discreetly checked the man's credentials on his laptop while they waited. Sam had chops. Top of his class at Northwestern, the youngest partner in his firm's history. Recently, he'd applied to practice in Virginia and appeared to be preparing to open an office in the area in the next couple of years. Who was this cop that he could come up with the cash and hire this lawyer? he wondered. In the end, he didn't really care. He'd congratulated Miss Gilbert on her first deal. She'd done good.

Mrs. Ash sat happily beside Miss Gilbert, her son on the other side of her. She was pleased. She'd moved out over the weekend. She couldn't wait to get to North Carolina.

They all rose as Gavin and Deb Mahoney entered the room. "Hey, Sam. Thanks for coming," Deb said, kissing the attorney's cheek. She grinned. "Congratulations, Grandad!" she teased, elbowing him in the ribs.

"Ah, thanks, Sweetheart. Miranda's doing great. Look at you! When are you due?" her lawyer replied.

Mr. Jackson nodded in satisfaction. There was obviously a

personal relationship between this attorney and the buyers. That explained how they'd been able to retain him.

"End of April," she replied, taking her seat.

They went through the closing. Money, keys, and title were exchanged. It took about an hour and a half.

"Dinner, Sam? I promise we'll go out. I won't cook," Deb teased.

"Sounds great. My flight is tomorrow morning. I'd be happy to join you for dinner. I have paperwork for you both to sign, anyway: Revised will, revised beneficiary on the trust."

Mr. Jackson beamed at Miss Gilbert. "If only they were all that easy! Congratulations!"

She blushed. "I wish I could say it was because of me. I just lucked into this one."

CHAPTER 71

Most of the furniture was staying in the apartment. Jason wanted his bedroom furniture. Deb wanted the Bureau and armchairs, and settee from the bedroom. The gun safe and gun rack were coming, and of course, their clothes were packed up. The rest could stay for Katelynn. Deb had purchased new furniture for the rest of the house, including a nursery for the baby. That was all set to be delivered on Saturday.

Saturday morning, Dan, Miranda, Pete, and Camille flew in to help with the move. Camille was to watch Jason, her twins, and baby Michaela while the others did the heavy lifting. Rudy was there bright and early, happy to be back in his mentor's good graces. Marcus showed up to help as well.

They loaded everything being moved onto the U-Haul, the men doing the heavy lifting, Deb and Miranda carrying the smaller, lighter boxes.

They drove over the few blocks to the house and went to work unloading the truck.

Dan and Rudy lifted the heavy bureau. Marcus was directing them off the truck. Rudy's hand slipped. He jumped out of the way of the heavy bureau that went crashing toward Marcus.

"Marcus!" Gavin yelled, jumping sideways and tackling

Marcus out of the way. Gavin felt his Achilles tendon snap. "Ahhhh! Damnit!" he screamed in anguish, grabbing his leg.

The bureau crashed to the ground, undamaged. "Sorry!" Rudy exclaimed, horrified.

Dan jumped off the truck. "Achille's?" he asked, standing over his friend.

"Yes!" Gavin yelled.

"Deb, you're going to have to take him to the ER. Do you trust Miranda to tell us where to put everything?"

"Of course!" Deb said, grabbing her keys.

"Marcus, help me get him up and in the van," Dan said.

Marcus stood up and grabbed Gavin by one arm. Dan grabbed the other. They pulled him up and carried him between them to the passenger seat of the minivan.

"How do I get him out?" Deb asked, concerned.

"You let the orderlies do that," Dan replied.

Deb drove to the hospital in silence. She looked terrified. Gavin looked over at her. "I'm not dying, Hon. I just tore my Achille's tendon. I'm not going to be a big help moving, but I'll be okay."

She smiled, "I know. I guess I was just having a flashback to your being shot."

"Nothing like that. Heel. Shoulder," he laughed, pointing to the different parts on his body.

"You're a laugh a minute," she joked.

"You've been through a lot this year, Deb. It's okay to feel overwhelmed. But I promise, this is nothing."

"Nothing that's probably going to require surgery and a long recovery."

"Yeah. Can you stand by me through it?"

"Try getting me to be anywhere else," she smiled.

CHAPTER 72

Gavin's MRI revealed a complete tear of the Achilles tendon. He was scheduled for surgery on Tuesday morning. In the meantime, they cast his leg, and he was given crutches with instructions to stay off his leg as much as possible. They were able to rejoin their friends within a couple of hours.

The family room furniture had been delivered, and Miranda had arranged it so that the sectional sofa faced the fireplace. Dan was installing the television over the mantel. Gavin made his way to the corner of the sofa on his crutches and sat. Pete moved the oversized ottoman over so Gavin could put his leg up on it. "You know, you could have just said you didn't want to do any of the heavy lifting," he teased.

Gavin smiled. "Yeah, a year of recovery and no running sounded like a better plan."

Pete patted him on his shoulder and went back to work.

Deb sat down next to Gavin, placing her hand on his thigh. "You need anything, Honey?"

"Nah, I'm good, Babe," he replied, looking at her. She leaned in and kissed him before she stood back up and went to work herself.

Gavin tried to be involved, but eventually, he fell asleep.

He was roused by Deb's hand on his shoulder.

"Hey, it's dark out," he murmured, opening his eyes.

Deb ran her hand down his arm and sat in his lap, taking his hand in hers. "Yeah, you got bored and dozed off about 2 hours ago."

"Where is everybody?" he asked, kissing the inside of her wrist.

"Rudy and Marcus went home. Everybody else went to the beach house," she replied.

"Jason?"

"Went with them."

"So, we're alone?"

"Uh-huh," she said, kissing him on the lips gently.

"I'm so sorry, Babe. I wanted to carry you over the threshold," he said.

"Yeah, well, that's not going to happen," she laughed. "But I can think of a few things we can do that doesn't require you to stand."

He grinned mischievously. "Do tell."

CHAPTER 73

Gavin reached out for Deb, to find her side of the bed empty. He opened his eyes and called out, "DeBella? Where are you?"

There was no answer. He reached for his crutches and pulled himself out of bed.

He found the note in the kitchen on the fridge door, "Gone to pick up breakfast for everybody. Be back soon. Love you."

He started a pot of coffee and sat down at the island, waiting for it to brew. He picked up his phone and saw a text from Rudy. "Marlene Travis showed up at her boyfriend's house in Boston."

"Initiate process to get her extradited back here," he responded.

He poured himself a cup of coffee and stirred in the cream and sugar. He managed to take a single sip before the doorbell rang. He had security cameras installed before they moved in, so he checked the doorbell camera. Jason stood on the porch, making faces at the doorbell. Deb had explained the camera to him. Dan and Miranda were halfway up the sidewalk, arm in arm. The Camacho twins, Annalise and Liam, were chasing each other around the front yard. Camille was getting baby Michaela out of the Escalade. Pete was trying to wrangle the twins. Gavin laughed. Deb drove into the drive and called out for help with bringing in breakfast. Dan broke away from Miranda and ran over to Deb, taking the bags. Gavin made his way to the door and swung it open.

Deb kissed him as she entered. "Finally awake, Sleeping Beauty?" she teased.

"Yeah, well, I slept a lot yesterday, and my damned foot ached all night, so I didn't fall asleep until almost 5 am. You're lucky, I'm semi-functional."

"Well, I've been up for a while," she grimaced.

"Why? What did you do?" he asked, panic in his voice.

"I ordered a ton of Christmas decorations for the house on Instacart," she said, rolling her head toward Dan. "Since we have friends here today who can help set them up." She raised her voice playfully.

Dan threw a handful of napkins at her and smiled.

"Great, I don't even get to decorate my own house on our first Christmas in it," Gavin sighed, moving back to the island barstool and taking a second sip of his coffee.

"It's okay, Man. You can sit in a chair and point," Dan said, pushing Gavin's shoulder playfully.

Deb started setting out the breakfast she'd picked up at a local diner.

"Can you grab this coffee for me and bring it to the family room, Dan?" Gavin asked. Getting his crutches and standing again.

"Sure," Dan said. "Who made this pot, you or Deb?"

"Me. It's safe for human consumption," he replied.

"Ha!" said Deb, handing Dan a mug. He poured himself a cup and carried both his and Gavin's to the family room, where Gavin was maneuvering himself into an armchair. Dan handed him his coffee and took a seat on the sectional.

"What's on your mind?" Dan asked.

"Geno and Tony," Gavin replied.

Dan nodded. "I saw them. Tony claims he knew nothing about Marcus but asked about his well-being. I told him I'd take care of him. He actually thanked me. Geno is still Geno. Still claims he didn't kill my mother or Carrie. Said he was there. Even admitted Walter Bowen was there. He claims they were just supposed to find Ellen. But he admits he did give some big, scary, muscle-bound kid $10,000 to take care of the problem. He says he picked up the hammer and handed it to the kid."

"Did he give any description other than 'muscle-bound?'"

"Yeah. He said he had a tattoo, two snakes eating each other in a Celtic knot."

Gavin grinned. "Will he testify?"

"Like I said, Geno is still Geno. He'll do anything that benefits him," Dan replied, shrugging. "You're worried?"

"I'm a little incapacitated. I think Mason's coming after me. I don't think he can outsmart me, but I'm worried about Deb and the baby and Jason. She's as stubborn as a mule. I want to find evidence on him before December 30th."

Dan nodded. "Yeah, you'll never get her to leave your side, and I'd trust Jason with you with no legs. You and Mike are the closest I've ever had to brothers. Jameka is sweet, but it's just not like having a brother."

Gavin grasped Dan's arm. "Same, man, same."

The Christmas lights and outside decorations arrived shortly after they'd finished breakfast. Dan and Pete put them up where Deb told them to. Gavin asked Miranda to take him to his office at police headquarters.

CHAPTER 74

"Jesus, Detective Mahoney, what happened to you?" asked the desk duty officer, James Gilmore, an older officer, slightly overweight.

"I'm older than I think I am," Gavin laughed. "I think I'm twenty, then body says, nope, you're thirty-seven. I tore my Achilles tendon."

"Ha! You're still a kid!" the officer laughed.

He looked down the hall toward his office. The yellow "wet floor" placard was up. "You've got to be kidding me!" he exclaimed. "How long ago did they mop?"

James looked back. "'Bout 15 minutes ago. Sorry, Detective."

Gavin groaned and sat down in the chair outside the desk.

He sat there for fifteen minutes when the Chief came in. Chief Lindstrom did a double take. "Hello, Detective. I'm hiding from my daughter. What are you doing here, and why are you sitting out here?"

"I'm hiding from Christmas decorating, and I'm out here because the floor's wet, and I can't get to my office on my crutches."

"Crutches? Well, what you'd break now?" the Chief laughed. "Come on, I'll get you back there."

Gavin grabbed his crutches and pulled himself to standing. Together, he and the Chief made their way slowly to his office. Once inside, he sat unceremoniously in his chair and leaned his crutches against his desk. He opened his computer. He saw that Rudy had narrowed the list of similar cold cases down to five. He picked up the phone and started making calls. By one pm, he had eliminated one of them. The other four…he needed to place Mason in Portland, Louisville, Raleigh, and Madison at the times of the murders.

Portland, WA
June 10-12, 2002

6/10: At 6:30 pm, 9-year-old Josiah Forman disappeared from his backyard in Rose City Park. He was found at 6:45 am when a baker on NE Sandy Blvd took the trash out to his dumpster. He had been strangled. He was found wearing one shoe. The day before he disappeared, his father, an English professor at Lewis and Clark College, received at his office in the mail sheet music for "One Shoe."

6/11: At 11:53 pm, Erin Mitchell, a freshman at Lewis and Clark College and daughter to Chemistry Professor Gary Mitchell, was found in her dorm room. She was wearing a Lurex short dress. She had been strangled. The day before, Professor Mitchell had received in the mail at his office the sheet music to "Beautiful."

6/12: At 7:00 am, 8-month-old Chelsea Morgan was reported missing from her home. Her mother was Felecia Morgan, an administrative assistant to the Registrar at Lewis and Clark College. She was found drowned, then strangled post-mortem. She was wearing blue jeans. The sheet music for "Tiny Dancer" was received in the mail the day before by her mother at her office.

Gavin was able to place Mason in Portland, Oregon, in May 2002 but was having trouble placing him there in June.

He wanted to punch something. Plus, his leg felt like it was on fire.

"You're supposed to have that leg up," his wife chided him from his office door.

"Hey, Babe. What time is it?"

"Six," she said, walking into the office. She looked at the pictures on his board. Carrie, Chelsea, Christa. Ellen. Erin. Yvette. Joe, Josiah, Jeff. She pointed to the last three. "I don't get it. Other than the shoe. I mean, those are kids. Joe was a full-grown man."

Gavin winced. "Joe wasn't his intended victim."

"Dan?"

"No. Dan was only 5."

She spun around, eyes wide. "You? Why do you think that?"

"When I was 9, Mason stole my shoe."

CHAPTER 75

"Excuse me?" Chief Lindstrom was walking past the open office door. At Gavin's quiet pronouncement, he pulled up short. "You mean you think Mason Miller meant to kill you when you were a child? Isn't that something we, the Police Department, should know?"

Gavin shrugged. "I don't see what difference it makes. He got me here by bringing me to your attention and to the Dean's attention at UMW. He'd just keep trying until he got me in this position. Better I'm sitting here than somewhere else."

"Wait. What do you mean he stole your shoe?" Deb asked, sitting on the sofa.

"Just that. I got a new pair of Nike Air Jordans when I was 9. We had this basket where we put our shoes by the door in the garage. My mom wanted our shoes off in the house. I took them off in the garage and threw them in the basket. When I went to put them on, the right one was gone. We looked everywhere and couldn't find it. I was grounded for a week for losing my shoe. Then, one day later that summer, I saw Mason getting into his car. He smiled at me weirdly because he never liked me. He held up my missing shoe as he drove by me. That's the last time I saw my shoe."

"This says, 'One Shoe,' not 'One Shoe Blues,'" The Chief

observed.

"'One Shoe Blues' wasn't released until late 2009," Gavin explained.

"So, this is clearly the work of the same guy. When and where?" Chief Lindstrom asked, indicating the pictures Gavin had just put up.

"Portland, Oregon, 2002," he replied. "And then there's these: Louisville, Kentucky, 2009. Raleigh, North Carolina, 2012, and Madison, Wisconsin, 2016. He reverses the order each time."

"The palindrome thing?" the Chief asked. "Why didn't this come up before now?"

"Because the method is different in each case. Strangled, stabbed, poisoned, buried alive, and shotgun here. In each case, though, the baby was drowned and then 'killed' postmortem in the same manner as the others," Gavin explained.

"Can we place Mason Miller in these cities at the time of the murders?"

Gavin shook his head. "Not yet. Just before or after, but so far not at the time, except for Sterling and here, of course."

CHAPTER 76

Gavin arranged for his TA to administer his final exams.

On Tuesday morning, his wife took him to Mary Washington Hospital, where his Achilles tendon was surgically repaired. His foot was put in a cast again. He would be in the cast for two weeks, when he could switch to a walking cast. Until then, he was on crutches. Unfortunately, two weeks was Christmas Eve. He couldn't get an appointment to remove the cast until the 27th.

Fortunately, that was before the new moon. Still, he wasn't cleared for duty. Rudy Vance would have to be his proxy.

On December 24, Marlene Travis, the daycare worker who had been in charge of baby Christa, was extradited back to Virginia as a person of interest in the kidnapping. Gavin convinced the Chief that listening in on the questioning from the next room was not violating his not being cleared for duty.

Marlene was a complete wreck. She had made sure all the babies were accounted for, she swore. She had handed Christa to an officer who was helping evacuate the building.

"So, a police officer took Christa?" Rudy asked.

"I don't know. I only know I handed her the baby!" Marlene insisted in tears.

Gavin's head shot up at that. Her. He broke into the

interview over the intercom, "Rudy! There was only one female officer at the scene. She had been dropping off her son. Andrea Grimes."

Andrea had been on duty when Marlene was brought in, but she had since left her post. Her car was gone. And so was she. A BOLO was issued, but she and her toddler son were missing.

Gavin sat in his office, pissed. How had he missed it? Her son's name was Davison Grimes. Dave's son. Damnit.

"Is Mason the boy's father?" he asked the Chief.

"I don't know. It's possible, I suppose. But I never noticed any kind of a relationship."

Neither had anyone else.

Before he headed home, he went to his office. Rudy had added photos from Louisville to the board,

Louisville, Kentucky
January 26, 2009

At 1:30 am on January 26, the alarm sounded at the residence of Professor and Mrs. Forrest Hemsworth. Their infant daughter, Cassandra, was taken from her crib. She was found the next morning at the Rounsavall Fountain at the Louisville Botanical Gardens. She had been drowned and then stabbed. She was found wearing a pair of jeans. Her family said they were not part of her wardrobe. Her father was an art professor at the University of Louisville. The Friday before he received a letter containing the sheet music to "Tiny Dancer."

On January 27, Ella Boyer, 24, was found stabbed to death in the dumpster behind her apartment building. She was the daughter of the Dean of Students at the University of Louisville, Jillian Boyer. Ella was an ER nurse. She was found wearing a Lurex mini-dress. Her mother received a letter at the university containing the sheet music to "Beautiful" on Monday morning.

On January 28, the body of 11-year-old Jeremy Gosling was found in the playground of his neighborhood park. He was the son of Professor Drew Gosling, who taught Elizabethan Literature at the University of Louisville. He had been stabbed to death and was found wearing only one shoe. His father had received the sheet music to "One Shoe" the day before in the mail.

CHAPTER 77

Gavin sat on the sectional in his family room. He promptly propped his leg up on a pillow on the ottoman in front of him and winced in pain.

Uncle Bob asked from the corner, "Do you need some Tylenol?"

"Hey, Uncle Bob. I didn't know you were coming. Yeah, some Tylenol would be nice, thank you."

Bob smiled. "I rather miss being able to startle you. Then again, I don't recall your ever really being startled." He rose and walked to the other room in his silent way, returning quickly with Tylenol and a glass of water. He seemed rather down.

"What's the matter, Uncle Bob? You aren't your normal morose. You're positively gloomy," Gavin asked, making conversation.

"I followed your example. Barb and I got married," Bob replied. Bob sat back down in the corner he had risen from.

"Congratulations!" Gavin offered. "Not to appear too dense, but isn't that good news?"

"Oh, yes. I am quite happy about it. My sons, however, are not so celebratory as you and I."

"Ah. Gotcha. Well, you know, it's your life," Gavin said, sympathetically.

"Yes, it is! They have made their positions quite clear, though. So, I made some changes. I signed over the Santa Fe store to Eric and the Seattle store to Seth. They can flourish or fail on their own. Demitri asked for his student loans to be paid. So, I did. The rest...I sold, except for the furniture manufacturing division. I have listed you as my executor, Gavin. I trust you to take care of my wishes."

"Oh sure, Uncle Bob. I'm honored. But that's a long way off."

"Not so very," Bob announced.

"Oh? I'm so sorry! What's wrong?"

"Leukemia, for many years now. I'm running out of fight."

"Damn Bob, I don't know what to say," Gavin said, taking the Tylenol and swallowing with a sip of water.

"There is nothing to say. I have chosen to live my last days happily. I chose to surround myself with those who will share in my happiness. That's you and Deb. Deb said that Barb and I can stay here. I hope you don't object."

"Of course not. As long as you like."

"Thank you. You have shown me more affection than my own flesh and blood. I won't forget it."

"Where is Barb?" Gavin asked.

"Mass. With Deb and Fiona and the children."

"I thought it was quiet," Gavin said sadly. He hadn't expected Bob to be here or to come bearing such grave news. He liked Bob.

They sat quietly for the next half an hour when Deb and Barb returned with Jason. They watched Elf. They ate takeout for dinner. Deb gave Jason his bath. Gavin read him three Christmas books from the sectional. Uncle Bob took him by the hand and put him to bed.

Barb followed with a sad smile. "I'll go with them. I think Bob has had enough for today. Goodnight. Merry Christmas!"

Then Gavin and Deb were alone. Wordlessly, she got the Christmas gifts from their hiding place. She brought out the wrapping paper, scissors, and tape. Again, wordlessly, they wrapped the gifts together. And then, she placed them under the tree in the family room.

She wept softly, looking at the tree.

"DeBella?" Gavin said finally.

"Yes," she answered.

"I'm so sorry, Mi Vida."

She turned and looked at him, "Me, too. He's as close to a father as I've had since my dad…"

Gavin patted the sectional beside him. She walked over and sat beside him. He wrapped his arms around her and pulled her close. "I know. You don't have to cry alone, Sweetheart. I can't fix this, but I can help you bear it." He kissed her forehead.

"Mmmmm," she murmured, snuggling into his embrace. "You have from the moment I met you." Once again, as he had done when she cried over Mark, her mother, her father, he held her while she cried, letting her vent her grief in the safety of his arms. He was her refuge. She honestly didn't know how she had survived 31 years without this man in her life.

CHAPTER 78

Christmas morning came, as it does in every home with a small boy of 4 years, early. The sun was barely up when Jason bounded excitedly into the family room. His squeals of joy roused, if somewhat reluctantly, the rest of the household.

After Jason opened all his gifts from Santa, while Barb fixed breakfast and Uncle Bob played with Jason, Deb sat beside Gavin with his foot propped up. He pulled a small box from his robe pocket. "Merry Christmas!" he whispered.

She smiled and opened the box. It was a simple floating diamond solitaire on a gold chain. "It's…it's…beautiful," she stammered. He took it from the box and fastened it around her neck. The diamond nestled in the divot at the base of her neck. He kissed her neck gently as he let go of the chain. She smiled and leaned into the kiss. "I love you, Gavin."

"I love you, too," he laughed.

She rose and left the room, returning a moment later with his gift, a Fender acoustic guitar and case. She grinned as she handed it to him. "There's room for a guitar in a house," she said.

"Oh," he marveled as he lovingly took it from its case. He adjusted his position in his seat and tuned it.

Katelynn, who had moved into their old apartment, arrived at that moment with her own guitar in tow. She blushed.

"Oh, you gave it to him? I hope I picked the right one. She asked me to help," she said, looking at the ground.

"It's perfect, Katelynn," he replied. He nodded to her case. "Play with me."

"Okay, but don't make me sing," she pleaded.

"You don't have to sing if you don't want."

She blushed but took a seat on the ottoman, facing him, and took out her guitar. "Ave Maria?" she asked.

"Sure," he answered. They played together through the song once. Then started again. Gavin sang and played. Katelynn just played. Though about halfway through, her voice joined in on harmony, her being compelled by the music.

There was silence as they finished. "Wow," came Dan's voice from the door. "You two should go on tour!"

"Daddy!" Jason yelled, running to his father.

If it were at all possible, Bob seemed paler than he even had before. He took the reprieve from Jason's attention as a chance to sit quietly in the armchair. Barb rushed to his side. He smiled. "I'm okay, my dear. No need to hover. I wish to enjoy this day."

Dan's brows knit the way they do when he was concerned. He looked at Gavin, questioning. Gavin nodded. Dan's expression fell. But Jason was demanding his attention. Miranda followed him in. Deb took her by the arm and led her to the baby's room under the guise of wanting her advice. Once they were alone, Deb hugged Miranda. "I'm glad you're here," she confided. "I thought you were spending Christmas with your parents."

Miranda smiled. "We are, but Dan was missing Jason, so we decided to all come to Virginia."

"Oh. Where are they? I hope they know they're welcome here!" Deb replied.

"Of course. They're on their way from the beach house. Mom was cooking something. Dan didn't want to wait. So, we drove separately. What's wrong, Deb?"

Deb sighed. "Uncle Bob is dying. My cousins are all being dicks about his getting married. They should be happy he's found someone who makes him happy. Instead, they're big crybabies. Gavin is working on a case in which a serial killer has an unhealthy fixation on him. He's hobbling around on one leg. Despite not being cleared for duty, he keeps going to his office. I have a houseful of people. Fiona and her new boyfriend Ted and her kids are coming, too. And Gavin invited Rudy Vance." She sat in the rocking chair and pouted. "And I can't cook."

Miranda laughed. Deb looked at her in exasperation. "Oh, I'm sorry, Deb. It's just the cooking thing seems a little...petty."

Deb shrugged. And then, after a moment of Miranda's bemused stare, she, too, laughed. "Okay. Maybe. Just a little. But I want Uncle Bob to enjoy this day. I have a nightmare that I serve a turkey burnt on the outside and frozen inside. Somehow, I doubt that will be that enjoyable."

"Oh, dear Lord! Is the turkey still frozen?" Miranda gasped.

"Shouldn't it be?"

"No!"

"What do I do?" Deb asked, panicking,

Miranda bit her thumbnail. "I don't know. I'll call Mom."

Connie Davis had spent the last 32 years as a wife and mother, but before that, she had been an interior designer. She had been good at her job. She was still talented in that area. But she had found her passion in the kitchen. She rarely hired caterers, except for Miranda's wedding, and only at her daughter's insistence. No one left the Davis house hungry, ever. At her daughter and Deb's frantic call, she calmly determined what stores were open and went into rescue mode. She detoured her husband's driving route, going first to the Food Lion in Colonial Beach. The fresh turkeys were sold out, but they still had several standing rib roasts. She threw ingredients to make mashed potatoes, gravy, fresh rolls, and a Buche de Noel. She also grabbed some butternut squash, onions, and cabbage. Realizing Deb was a novice, she bought whatever cookware they'd need. She called the girls back and advised them she had what they needed and was on her way.

Crisis averted, Deb and Miranda went out to the family room. Fiona, Ted, Mavis, and Christian had arrived and were about to start opening gifts from Granny Barb and Bob. Deb looked at the empty spot on the sectional. She gasped and pointed, showing Miranda. Miranda looked around and noticed her husband had also disappeared. "Ug, men!" she commiserated.

CHAPTER 79

"You're not cleared for duty, Detective," chided Officer James Gilmore.

"I'm just checking my email," Gavin lied.

"I'm old, but even I know you can do that from home," the older man said, shaking his head.

"Fine. But I'm not on duty. I'm just looking at the evidence. I just need to think. I can think without injuring myself further."

"You can think at home, too," laughed the officer.

"I have a house full of relatives, a pregnant wife, a four-year-old stepson, and two of his friends at home. The Thinker couldn't think there."

"You have a small point. And your friend?"

"He drove," Gavin replied. Dan saluted.

"Fine, but if your wife calls lookin' for ya, I'm not lyin' for ya," the officer said.

"Fair enough," Gavin agreed.

Gavin moved quickly for a man on crutches. James Gilmore chuckled, thinking he was racing his wife, figuring out he'd snuck out to work on Christmas. He'd seen the detective's friend with him before. Office gossip said he was a deputy in Illinois but filthy rich. All he knew was the detective seemed to trust his friend more than he trusted anyone on the FPD. Given

Andrea Grimes's disappearance and apparent involvement in the kidnapping of the murdered baby, he couldn't say he blamed him. Gavin disappeared into his office. The rich Yankee deputy followed him. Gilmore returned his focus to his work.

Gavin switched on his office lights. Rudy had gone through one more city's cold case on their killer. He sat in his chair, flipped over his empty trash can, and propped his leg up on it. "Let's see what we've got," he said, focusing on the board.

Dan sat on the sofa and stared at it, too. He saw what Deb was worried about immediately. Joe had been a substitute. Gavin was clearly who Mason had wanted to kill that day. This was all a build-up to completing that goal. And here was Gavin, on crutches nearing the expected date of the Songster's next attack. "Yeah, I'm sticking around until after the new year," Dan announced.

Gavin opened his mouth to protest, but Dan shot him a side eye and pointed to the board. "I'm staying. If this were me, you'd stay."

Gavin nodded. "Okay. Thanks." Then he picked up the summary report Rudy had prepared on Raleigh's cold case.

October 15-17, 2012

Raleigh, North Carolina

At 6 am, Professor Haywood Fillmore, Head of the Engineering Department at North Carolina State University, arrived at the home of his ex-wife Meg to pick up his 11-year-old son Jarod to take him to school. Jarod was not in his bed. After a cursory search of the house and calling neighbors and friends, he was reported missing at 7:15 am. At 12:30 pm, his body was found in a dumpster on campus. He was wearing only one shoe. His jaw was broken, as were several teeth. The coroner concluded a glass bottle containing sweet tea and cyanide had been forced into his mouth. His father had received a letter containing the sheet music to "One Shoe Blues" on Friday afternoon. He died of cyanide poisoning.

On October 16, at 9 pm, Edith Hundley, the 19-year-old runner for the NC State Wolfpack Women's track team, was found in her car in an on campus parking lot. Her workout clothes, which she had left home wearing, were missing. Instead, she was wearing a short black Lurex dress. She had drank from her water bottle. It was determined to contain water and cyanide. Her mother was a librarian at the University and received a letter containing sheet music to "Beautiful," in the mail at the library the day before.

On October 17, at 2 pm, Colleen Jessup, 10 months, daughter to Math Professor Diane Harding and her husband, Doctor Neil Harding, an ER doctor at Duke Raleigh Hospital, who was home alone with their daughter after a 29-hour shift, was reported missing. He had fallen asleep and awoke after several hours when the baby hadn't made any noise. The back door had been broken into. The baby was found at 4 pm at Lassiter Mill. She had been drowned. Cyanide was forced down her throat postmortem. She was wearing jeans her family claimed were not hers. Professor Harding received the sheet music to "Tiny Dancer" in the mail at the university that morning.

Gavin handed the summary over to Dan. He'd placed his cell on silent, but the office phone rang. He winced.

"Busted," Dan laughed. Then his own cell rang. "Ewww. We gotta go!"

CHAPTER 80

Deb glared at Gavin as he came through the door. "I'm sorry. I know. I know," he said.

"Do you?" she sneered.

He looked down at the floor. "Yes, I do. I didn't plan to be gone for long. But I really do have to concentrate on the serial killer who hates me."

"And the family who loves you?" She retorted. She had noticed he'd started carrying his service weapon all the time over the last few days. She knew he was anxious, not just for his own safety but for hers and Jason's, but he needed to recover from his surgery. He needed to let others worry a little. He thought she was mad that he'd left her alone on Christmas, and she was, but that wasn't really what bothered her about his frequent escapes to his office. She was worried he wasn't letting anybody help him because he sure wasn't letting her.

He shrugged.

"Remember when you took me to the gun range after... Mark?" she asked.

"Of course," he replied.

"I'm not helpless, Gavin. And I carry. Stop worrying so much," she said.

Bob appeared behind Dan, placing his hand on Dan's

shoulder. "Ahhhh! Jesus… Bob!" Dan jumped.

Bob smiled and said, "I have missed that. This one says hello before I get up on him. But I wanted to say Deb's a great shot. She's better than any of my boys."

"It makes sense. Your mom was a marksman. I imagine she taught you," Dan said.

"What's your point, Deb?" Gavin asked.

"That you aren't alone. That I'm not helpless. That you aren't solely responsible for my safety. Yes, bad things happen. I got beaten up pretty darned badly because I wasn't paying attention. I am now. Please stop worrying so much. Take care of yourself. Let your leg heal. I have every confidence you'll catch Mason before he hurts any of us. And if he somehow slips past you, I'll kill him myself. Trust me, I'd have rather had a gun than a frying pan when I took out Theo."

Gavin sighed. "I can't promise I won't still obsess about this, but I promise, I won't for today…well, the rest of today."

"I'll take it," she said, kissing him.

CHAPTER 81

Connie set the grocery bag on the counter. Sam dropped the five other bags on the floor.

"Okay, Girls, unload the groceries, and let's get started," she said with authority.

"You aren't going to cook, Mom?" asked Miranda hopefully.

"Nope," she replied. Deb felt panic rising. Connie grabbed her hand. "Don't worry. I'll tell you what to do. You can do this." She winked. "And Miranda will help."

"Oh, sure. I can help," Miranda offered.

Within minutes Connie had the two of them preparing a meal.

Gavin was true to his word. He sat with his leg up until they were called to dinner. He stood and started to make his way to the dining room. Christian and Jason suddenly ran past him. Jason tripped on one of his crutches. The child fell in front of him. He twisted to keep from tripping over his stepson and started to step backwards. He put his weight on his leg and, as he twisted, felt the telltale pop in his knee. "Son of a…" he muttered, hobbling back to the chair and dropping back into it, grabbing his knee.

"I's sorry!" Jason yelled, running to him, starting to cry.

"Oh, it's okay, Honey. It was an accident. Don't cry," Gavin said, picking him up and hugging him. "Are you okay?"

Jason nodded and hugged his neck. Gavin kissed his head.

Deb came running in from the kitchen. "What happened?" she asked frantically.

"I twipped Gabin," Jason cried.

"He tripped on my crutch and fell. I managed to not fall on him. We're fine."

"No, Mommy. Gabin's not fine. I huwt his leg," Jason said.

Deb turned back to Gavin. "My knee, not my foot. I twisted it…" he said. She continued to stare at him. "I felt something pop," he admitted. "Let's just eat, okay. I'll ice it. If it still hurts after we eat, I'll go to the ER. Okay?"

Dan came in behind Gavin's chair and handed him an icepack over his shoulder. "Come on, Jay, Let's go eat," he said, taking his son in his arms and heading back out of the room.

"Fine, but you're staying in here," Deb replied.

"I don't want to eat alone!"

"You won't eat alone, "she smiled. She tousled his hair and kissed him.

She walked out and returned with two full plates. "Here goes nuthin' My first big dinner." She handed him a plate, a fork, and a knife.

He sat the plate down and adjusted the ice pack on his knee. He picked up the fork and knife, and cut into his slice of rib roast, which he found cut incredibly easily, much to his surprise. He took a bite. It was delicious. "You made this?" he asked.

"Yes!" she said indignantly. Then she took a bite. Her expression was also one of surprise. "Oh, my God! I did it!" she squealed, pleased with the outcome.

Gavin laughed and leaned forward, kissing her. "You sure did! It's delicious, Querida."

Bob quietly carried his plate into the family room and sat

in the corner.

"Come sit with us, Uncle Bob," Gavin invited.

Bob smiled and joined them on the sectional.

After dinner, they all congregated in the family room. Deb brought in the Buche de Noel on a wooden cutting board. She was so proud of herself. They cut it and served it. She picked up the cutting board to take it back to the kitchen.

"This is wonderful, Deb," Fiona exclaimed.

Deb swung around to thank her, smacking Gavin in the face with the heavy cutting board as she turned.

"Oh my God! I'm so sorry." She dropped the cutting board and grabbed for the icepack on his knee to put it on his eye. It landed on his good foot.

"Jesus, Deb, stop trying to help me!" he yelled. She jumped back and covered her mouth with both hands. She looked like she was about to start to cry. He started laughing. "I was safer at work." Dan stood and walked over to check his knee.

"Yeah, that's not right. Come on. I'll take you to the ER before something else happens to you," he laughed.

CHAPTER 82

Miranda went back to the beach house with her parents. Bob and Barb retired to the guest room. Fiona, Ted, and the kids left. Rudy Vance stopped by, but Gavin wasn't there, so he stayed for about 20 minutes, leaving at the same time Katelynn went back to her apartment. Deb cleaned up. She found Jason asleep under the Christmas tree when she was done. She picked him up and carried him to bed before going to bed herself.

At 2 am, Dan dropped Gavin off before driving back to Colonial Beach.

Gavin climbed into bed beside Deb and snuggled in against her back. Laying his arm over her.

"Are you okay?" she asked sleepily.

"Yeah. I dislocated my knee. Two more weeks on crutches," he replied.

"I'm so sorry," she repeated.

"It's okay, Honey. Just a series of unfortunate events," he laughed.

They drifted off to sleep, but rest was not in the cards. At about 3:30 am, Barb screamed, "Gavin! Deb! Come quick!"

Deb jumped out of bed. Gavin grabbed his crutches and followed. They went to the guest room, where Barb was lying in bed beside Bob, her arms wrapped around him tight.

She was crying. He appeared to be sleeping. But he was cold. Boban Zamphir had passed away in his sleep sometime around midnight.

Deb made the calls to her sister, her cousins, her Uncle Frank, her Uncle Tom, and her grandmother. Uncle Frank volunteered to call the rest of the family. Gavin took care of calling the coroner. Barb sat quietly, looking at the Christmas tree. She cried herself to sleep in the chair. Deb covered her with a blanket.

When Katelynn returned after her sister's call, she was accompanied by Rudy Vance. Gavin raised an eyebrow to that situation. Rudy went and sat quietly in the corner Bob had seemed so fond of all day. Katelynn blushed.

"What? What are you embarrassed about?" Deb asked her sister. "You're an adult. He's cute. People have sex, Katie. It's no big deal."

"Does anything embarrass you, Debbie?" Katelynn asked.

"Not sex," Gavin confirmed. He sat in his spot on the sectional and closed his eyes.

"Not much, really," Deb answered. "That's not to say there aren't things I've done that I'm ashamed of. Ashamed is different from embarrassed. But smacking Gavin with that cutting board and then dropping it on his foot was fairly embarrassing."

"But sex isn't?" Katelynn asked.

"Are you kidding? Look at him!"

"Yeah. I see your point," Katelynn replied, apparently losing all her shyness, looking him up and down.

"Sitting right here. Hearing every word," Gavin said.

The Davises and the Bradleys arrived. Dan kissed Deb's cheek, "I'm sorry, Honey. I know he was like a father to you." He sat beside Gavin. "What's going on, Man?"

"You don't want to know," Gavin replied, nodding toward Rudy Vance, who half smiled and waved.

"Oh, crap," Dan said.

"Oh, crap, what?" asked Sam, entering the room.

"When we called Katelynn, she wasn't alone," answered Gavin.

Sam turned and looked at his daughter and wife as they sat next to Deb and Katelynn. "Oh crap," he said.

"What are we talking about?" Miranda asked.

"Katelynn had sex," Deb answered.

"Oh my God, Deb!" Katelynn exclaimed, wanting to disappear.

"Really? With whom" Connie asked.

"Rudy, there," Deb answered, motioning to the young man in the corner.

"Oh, he's cute," Connie said, squirming into her seat.

"Acck," squeaked Rudy.

"Sorry, son. It's going to get worse before it gets better," Sam said, shaking his head and taking a seat.

"Katelynn's a little embarrassed," Deb offered.

"It's just private, Deb!" Katelynn protested.

"It was private. Then he came here with you. Now it's not."

Miranda snickered. "Came…"

Dan winced and buried his head in his hands.

"I'm sorry. Are you Beavis or Butthead?" Katelynn asked.

"I must be Beavis because you appear to be Butthead," Miranda retorted, sticking her tongue out and laughing.

"Honestly, Katelynn, you have nothing to be embarrassed over," Connie said, putting her hand on the young woman's knees.

"That's what I said," Deb reiterated. "I mean, it's not like Jason walked in on you during the actual act and then asked if you were going to marry Rudy."

"Jason walked in during?" Katelynn asked, wide-eyed.

Gavin shook his head.

"The first time?" Miranda asked, smiling.

"Well… third or fourth. It was a good night."

"Oh, Jeez," Gavin moaned.

"Third or fourth?" Dan asked incredulously. Gavin shrugged.

"My dad interrupted us. That's always fun," Miranda giggled.

"Yes, let's relive that pinnacle moment," Dan sighed sarcastically.

"Not at the top of my list of things I want to remember, either," Sam said.

"My parents and their friends caught Sam and me in the pool," Connie added.

"Nor is that!" Sam bellowed. Connie waved him off.

"Jason's caught us a few times, too. He's a quiet little bugger," Miranda mused.

"Wait, why would Jason catch you?" Rudy asked Dan.

"He's my son," Dan replied. "Deb's my ex-wife."

"More of that thread you didn't want to unravel, Professor?" Rudy asked Gavin.

"Yeah. My wife's ex-husband is my best friend."

"Ah, thanks, Man. You're my best friend, too."

"And none of you are embarrassed by any of this?" Katelynn asked.

"Totally embarrassed," Sam replied.

"Mortified," Dan agreed.

"Wish the floor would open up and swallow me," Gavin nodded.

"Of course not!" exclaimed Connie.

"Why should I be?" declared Miranda.

"Never," replied Deb.

"Then, can I ask a question?" Katelynn said, leaning in.

"Oh God!" Rudy yelped.

"Told you it would get worse," Sam snickered.

"Shoot," "Of course," and, "Ask away," came the chorus of answers from the women.

A collective groan sounded from the men.

"What gets…your motor running? I mean, it was so silly. I was just normal, shy me. Then he…said my name against my neck, and I was like a different person. My full name. Kata Linda. Not my everyday name."

"Yeah, that usually works," Gavin gave a thumbs up. Dan and Sam nodded in agreement.

"The Spanish thing is pretty darned good, too," Deb said wistfully.

"The Spanish thing?" Sam asked.

Gavin gave a slight sly grin and raised his eyebrows.

Dan smacked him on the back of the head.

"Keep that one to yourself from now on. Sexiest thing she'd ever heard," Dan grumbled.

"I was singing for my mother," Gavin laughed.

"I call bullshit," Dan said. "You were seducing your wife. And every other woman not related by blood to you got caught in the crosshairs."

"Hey! You got the benefits of it!" Miranda protested.

"There you go. You're welcome," Gavin quipped.

Dan shrugged. "The benefits were actually pretty good."

"You people are really weird," Rudy announced.

Deb moved over and sat next to Gavin, dropping her hand on his knee. "Did you really sing 'Blue Eyes Crying in the Rain' to seduce me?"

Gavin burst out laughing. "Yes."

"Right in front of your mother! Gavin!" she giggled. "You were confident that would work?"

"Pretty confident. It's worked for 27 years," he laughed heartily. Dan, likewise, cracked up.

"Oh, my God. You, Casanova, you. So, you've been playing guitar and singing your way into the good graces of women since you were 10?" Deb said, feigning shock.

"Yeah." He stopped laughing. He looked at Dan and then quickly away.

"It's okay. I don't remember much about her. But I remember her. I remember her smile and her laugh, and I remember her playing the guitar."

Gavin blinked back tears. "Ah, Man, your mom was somethin' else."

"Ahhh, Honey, did you have a little crush on Danny's mom?" Deb asked. Miranda scooted forward in her seat.

"I don't know, not like that. I was a kid. She was an adult. But Mrs. Bradley was honestly the nicest person I'd ever met. Plus, she was beautiful. Curly, long brown hair. Green eyes like Dan. Great smile. And yes, she played guitar," Gavin agreed.

"So, you learned to play to impress Dan's mom?" Connie asked.

"Oh, God, no. I had a crush on Ashley Kohler, and she wouldn't give me the time of day. The Bradleys had just moved in. So, I was like 9. Molly was over there playing with Dan. Your mom was still pregnant with Carrie. It was summer. Anyway, I went over to bring Molly home or something. And Mrs. Bradley had a guitar out on her front porch swing while she watched the kids play. Ashley happened to be walking by when I picked up the guitar to look at it. I may have exaggerated my prowess. Mrs. Bradley said she'd teach me. She even had her first guitar I could have to learn on. I started going over every day to get lessons. By Christmas and the time Carrie was born, I was pretty good. I am saving the guitar for Jason."

"And did you get Ashley to notice you?" Deb asked.

"As I said, it's worked for 27 years."

Thankfully, the coroner arrived, and the conversation was

dropped. Deb shook Barb awake. She had Bob's medical records. The coroner examined them and Bob and concurred the cause of death was late-term leukemia.

CHAPTER 83

In accordance with Bob's wishes, he was cremated, and his ashes were intermingled with those of his first wife, Mary Beth. He asked their ashes to be entrusted to Gavin Mahoney, his niece's husband, until such time as he could scatter them in Big Bear, where they had honeymooned. He wanted only a small memorial service.

Gavin had his appointment with his surgeon in the morning on the 27th. His cast was removed, but due to the injury to his knee, he was advised to walk on it as little as possible, and he was still not cleared for duty. He found, however, that with the knee brace and one crutch, he could manage quite well on the walking cast.

By 1 pm, Uncle Tom arrived. He brought Ava Bradley, Dan's stepmother, with whom he had entered a relationship recently. Uncle Frank and his wife, Mildred, arrived shortly after. His hair had grown out. He had been shaving his head for years, it turns out in honor of his brother, who ironically never lost his hair. Cousin Paulie, with his wife, Sophie, flew in from Chicago, bringing his Aunt Sara, Bob's mother. Her twin, Sharon, was not feeling well and stayed in Chicago. Deb's cousins, Eric, his wife Brianna, Seth, his wife Diana, Demitri, and his wife Cleo also came, though they expected nothing, considering their recent argument with their father. With all the cousins' children, plus Jason, Mavis, and Christian, the house was a bit chaotic.

Bob was a generous and loving man. He didn't hold grudges. And he had been quite wealthy. He had just liquidated his business holdings and left behind over $60,000,000. He left his house in Big Bear to his new wife, Barbara Zamphir, along with $2,000.000. He left the hearse to Fiona, which made her laugh, as well as $100,000. To Dan, he left his pocket watch. To his brothers, Frank and Tom, he left his home in Modesto. He left $2,000,000 to be held for the care of his mother. To Paulie, he left $250,000. Then he left Kata Linda Kaminski $400,000. To Deb, he left $400,000 as well. The rest was split equally between his sons, much to their surprise and shame. His other personal belongings were left to Gavin to keep or to distribute to his family and friends as he saw fit.

"Holy…" he whispered, looking at the inventory Sam handed him. "I didn't know what he was asking when he asked me."

Miranda took the pocket watch left to Dan into her hands, "Imperial Russian Army Officer's watch, 14K, circa 1910, French design, 30-40 rubies in the works. A similar one recently sold for $26.000."

"It's a lovely watch. It will go into my safe deposit box to be held for Jason," Dan said, taking it back.

"I never would have guessed he had this much money," Gavin said. "He was such a quirky little man."

"And no one who knows you would know you have money," Dan teased.

CHAPTER 84

Gavin soon had had enough of special requests. He advised everybody to write down what they wanted, and he'd figure out a fair way to decide who got what. Then he grabbed Dan and made his escape.

As they walked into the FPD headquarters, Chief Lindstrom saw them and slowed to match their stride.

"Whatcha doin' here, Detective?" he laughed. "You're still not cleared for duty."

"I'm literally hiding from my wife's relatives," Gavin answered. "Her uncle died. I'm the executor of his will. And he was loaded."

Dan chuckled. "I was there. It was pretty brutal."

"Well, hide as long as you can, but keep off that leg," said the Chief, holding the door open for Gavin.

Gavin and Dan made their way into Gavin's office. Gavin went to the sofa. He put both feet up on it and laid his head back on the arm. His jaw was tight, and his brow furrowed.

"Does it hurt, Gav?" Dan asked, sitting behind his friend's desk.

"Like a son of a bitch," Gavin replied, his eyes closed. He rubbed his forehead. "Plus, I have a splitting headache."

Dan opened the top drawer of the desk. As expected, it

was completely organized. "You'd give Connie a run for her money on organization," he said, finding the Tylenol. He tossed the bottle to Gavin. "Water?"

"Mini fridge behind you," Gavin replied.

Dan took a bottle out for Dan and one for himself. He tossed Gavin his bottle and opened the one in his hand, taking a drink. Gavin, likewise, leaned up on his elbow, took two Tylenol, opened his water, and took a swig. He then tossed the Tylenol bottle back to Dan. "Put that back where you got it, will you?"

"Sure thing,"

There was a knock at the door. "Who is it?" Gavin called.

"Rudy Vance, Sir," came the response.

"Come in, Rudy," he said, still holding his head.

"Hey Rudy," Dan said, swiveling in the chair.

"Hello, Mr. Bradley. Um, Gavin, Sir. I have the summary ready for Madison."

"Can you give me the highlights without my having to read anything?"

"Um. Yessir, if you like."

Dan smiled, "Gavin has a headache from first world problems. He has to distribute wealth among a bunch of greedy bloodsuckers. To think I called Bob a vampire," Dan chuckled.

"That's the truth," Gavin replied.

Rudy read the report.

"July 4-6, 2016

"Madison, Wisconsin

"On July 4, 2016, at 5 am, Computer Science TA, Georgia North went for a run, leaving her 7-month-old daughter Charlene North, and her long-time boyfriend, John Brown, sleeping in her apartment. When she returned, Charlene was gone. Charlene was found in Lake Mendota. She had been drowned and then shot with a hunting arrow. She was wearing jeans her mother did not recognize. On Friday afternoon, Georgia had received sheet music for "Tiny Dancer " in the mail at her office.

"On July 5, at 8 am the body of 34-year-old Emma Reyes, daughter of Psychology Professor Javier Reyes, was found at Cherokee Marsh Conservation Park. Emma was 5'11" tall and was found wearing a short black Lurex dress, instead of the hiking clothes she'd left her home wearing the evening before. She had been shot with a bow and arrow. Her father received sheet music for "Beautiful" in the mail at the University on Friday afternoon.

"On July 6, at 7pm, 10-year-old Jacob Hampton was reported missing after he failed to return home after riding his bike to a neighborhood park. He was found an hour later in a wooded area on the outskirts of the neighborhood, wearing one shoe. He had been shot with a bow and arrow. His mother, Marion Walsh, a secretary to the dean of students at the University of Wisconsin, had received sheet music for "One Shoe Blues" in the mail at her office that morning."

Gavin sat up, feeling better. "'Down by the River,'" he mused. "Portland has the Willamette and Columbia. The Ohio in Louisville. The Neuse in Raleigh. The Yahara in Madison. The Rappahannock here."

"The Rock in Sterling," Dan added.

"Yeah, but here, the river is integral to the rite. It's a deviation from the original murder, like the boys instead of a man, the connection to academia, the new moon on Monday thing. Like the change from 'One Shoe' to 'One Shoe Blues.' He is willing to deviate."

"What does that mean?" asked Rudy.

"That the rites he follows mean absolutely nothing to him," Gavin replied.

He looked at the younger officer. Rudy was probably 25. He was of average height. His hair was somewhere between blond and brown, closer to brown. He wore it short and neat. He was fit. And he was intelligent. Gavin could see where he would be appealing to women, to Katelynn. He wasn't going to presume to tell Katelynn who to see socially…or not to see, as the case may be. He thought Rudy was all right. He'd checked out his medical files and confirmed he had a history of epilepsy, mostly febrile, and none since joining the police force, which had been 4 years ago. He was a good officer with a good record. But Katelynn had a history, too. And hers was such that she was vulnerable.

"Rudy, about Katelynn," Gavin said after a moment of scrutiny. "She's 20. She can make her own decisions. Just tread lightly. She's shy for a reason."

Rudy hadn't been avoiding the topic, but he wasn't going to be the one to bring it up. "Yessir, I understand that. We've been talking since she was here at Thanksgiving. She told me about the rape. I wouldn't do anything to intentionally hurt her."

"Good enough," Gavin said with a smile. "Hurt her, and they'll never find you."

CHAPTER 85

Gavin was relieved to find no one at his house. He sat in his spot on the sectional and propped up his leg. His headache was better, but his leg was throbbing. He closed his eyes and sat in the silence.

After half an hour of quiet, he became aware of a presence behind him. He didn't even bother to open his eyes. "Hello, Frank," he said.

"Hello, Gavin. Sorry to intrude," Frank replied, stepping into the room.

"You're always welcome here, Frank," Gavin said.

"Bob has been singing your praises for months, you know. He was very fond of you." Frank's voice was tinged with sadness.

"The feeling was mutual."

"I know that everyone has been asking you for everything today. Rest easy that I don't want anything."

"Are you sure? He was your brother, Frank. I would understand if you wanted something of his. I surely don't want his things. I never did," Gavin sighed.

"Oh, I know that. He chose you because you didn't want anything. But, I am sure. I want nothing. My brother is in my heart. His things are just things. I wished to speak to you because I wanted to give you something."

"Again, Frank, I don't want…"

"Please, take it for the baby," he handed Gavin a small porcelain doll, about 16 inches, dressed in a beautifully embroidered outfit. "Our grandmother's. She brought it with her as a child from Romania. Our mother and she did not get along. She had given this to Kata when she was very little. After our father died, and Baba scared Kata so badly, my mother wanted to throw it out. But Bob said he would like to keep it, and our mother let him, on the condition she never lay eyes on it. He gave it to me several years ago. He said I had forgotten who I was. I wasn't surprised when he took back the name Zamphir."

"It's lovely," Gavin said, taking it. "It is a girl, Frank. We found out last week."

Frank smiled as if he already knew.

CHAPTER 86

The doorbell rang. Gavin looked around at the otherwise empty house. "Frank, would you mind getting the door? I've spent too much time on my leg today."

"Of course," Frank answered, gliding silently out of the room, just as Bob used to do.

"Oh, hello. Sorry, I was looking for Gavin Mahoney," came Barry Magill's voice from outside his front door. Great, he thought, just what I need, some Shannon bullshit. Then he heard the desperation and fear in Barry's voice as he continued, "It's important!"

"Come on in, Barry!" Gavin called.

Frank moved aside from the front door. Barry rushed in. "Straight back past the kitchen," Frank said.

"Jesus, what bus hit you?" Barry asked, looking at the welt on Gavin's face and his leg.

"Just a series of unfortunate accidents," Gavin sighed. "What can I do for you, Barry?"

"Shannon has Olivia for the holidays," he said, as if this explained everything.

"Okay?" Gavin asked with a shrug.

"I got these in the mail this morning!" he said, tossing down two letters. Gavin reached over and pulled sheet music out of the envelopes, one containing "Beautiful," the other "One Shoe Blues."

"Oh, dear Lord!" said Gavin. "Get Shannon and Olivia out of town, Barry."

"That's just it. She won't give me Olivia, and she won't come with me! You know, as well as I do, Olivia isn't my daughter. I don't have a leg to stand on. I don't know what to do!"

Gavin struggled to get up. "Where is Deb?" he asked Frank.

Frank pulled him up. "She's okay. She went to get dinner. She'll be home any second."

As if his word had some magical power, Deb walked through the door. Gavin, moving as fast as he could, made his way to her in the kitchen, where she was unloading the grocery bags. He grabbed her and kissed her, hugging her tight, "Oh, thank God!"

"Gavin! Jeez. What's got into you?" she laughed. Then she noticed the fear in his eyes.

"You don't understand! Shannon and the baby are in danger!" Barry exclaimed.

Gavin caught his breath. "I do understand, Barry," he said, "I'm sorry. I didn't mean to dismiss you. He wants to hurt me. And hurting Deb is the easiest way to do that." He turned back to his wife. "Are you carrying?"

She nodded.

"Let me see," he insisted.

She opened her purse and pulled out a small gun. She sat the Ruger LCP Max on the counter.

"You keep it on you! You understand?" he demanded.

"Yes. Okay." She picked it up and put it back in her purse. "What about Shannon and the baby?"

CHAPTER 87

Deb banged heavily on the apartment door. "Shannon! Come to the damn door!" she bellowed. A neighbor opened her door and glared at Deb. "Yeah, I don't care. She's going to come to the door!" she yelled.

Shannon opened the door. "What?" she said snidely.

Your husband is at my house, losing his mind," Deb answered.

"Right! I'm in some kind of danger, but they let you come here alone to get me?"

"No," she said, pointing to Gavin standing on his crutch at the end of the hall.

Shannon huffed. "Are you really concerned?"

"We're here, aren't we? Barry is so upset he came to us. At least come talk to your husband, Shannon. Don't you owe him that?" Deb asked.

Shannon looked at her feet. "I don't see why he would care. I haven't exactly been the best wife."

"Please. Come talk to him."

She sighed. "OK. Let me get Olivia." She closed her door.

Deb looked at Gavin. He gave her a smile.

Shannon followed them back to their house.

"How did you afford this?" Shannon snorted.

Gavin ignored her. Deb rolled her eyes and answered, "We have money."

Inside, Gavin headed right back to his spot on the sectional, his headache had returned thanks to the fear and irritation Barry and Shannon brought with them.

"Tylenol, Honey?" Deb asked from the kitchen.

"Yes, please," he answered as he sat and propped up his leg.

"Would you like me to watch the baby while you two talk?" she asked Shannon.

It was Barry, who answered, 'Yes, please." He took the child from her mother and handed her over to Deb.

"You guys can talk in the living room," she said, nodding in that direction. "Miss Olivia and I will go watch Baby Einstein with Gavin, yes we will," she said to Olivia who was a pretty toddler, just over a year old. She grabbed the bottle of Tylenol from the cabinet and a bottle of water from the fridge and headed into the family room. She handed Gavin the Tylenol and water, and the baby. She picked up a blanket and spread it out on the floor. Then she turned on the TV and found the show to stream. Then she took Olivia back and set her on the blanket. Gavin handed her back the Tylenol, having taken two. She carried them back to the kitchen and put them back in the cabinet. Shannon watched her as she ran back to Gavin's side and gave him a quick kiss before sitting on the floor with Olivia. Shannon frowned and followed her dejected husband into the living room. Gavin's laughter filled the house. Deb laughed, too. Shannon stared at the ground.

"Do you still love him?" Barry asked suddenly.

She looked up, startled at his abruptness. "No. I just hate that he's happier than I am."

"Well, that's really petty, Shannon. Are you willing to throw away our marriage because you don't want him to be happy?"

"I don't want to. I can't really explain it. He left me. I was supposed to be the one who had the grand life. Not the husband who works all the time and ignores me."

"What isn't grand? I give you everything you want. If you aren't happy…"

"That's part of the problem! I used to have a job and friends and a life outside!"

He stared at her. "Well, how was I supposed to know that? You never said. If you want a job, get a job!" he said, raising his voice.

"You could ask! You never asked!" she yelled back.

"The second you heard Gavin's voice, you changed toward me!"

"That's untrue! I told you that I didn't give a damn about him, and I didn't, but you kept telling me how he was happier without ME!" she retorted.

"So, this is my fault?"

"Of course not! It's our fault!" she cried. Tears rolled down her cheeks.

He stared at her for several minutes. "Are we beyond repair?"

"I don't know. I hope not." She burst out laughing. "That poor man. I've been trying to get your attention by throwing myself at him. But all he thinks about is her."

"You have my attention, Sweetheart. When I got that sheet music…"

"It doesn't make any sense. He doesn't care about me," she said dismissively.

"This guy just wants to hurt Gavin. And he does care about you. He went and got you."

They ultimately worked it out. They headed back to Green Bay together.

"I give them 6 months," Deb said, watching them drive away to go pack up Shannon's things.

"If that," Gavin agreed.

CHAPTER 88

Gavin walked through the Bradley House again, his heart racing. He had to find Deb. He could feel that she was there. He went to the bathroom door, where he had found Mrs. Bradley all those years ago, and reached out for the doorknob. He called out to her and turned the knob. He pulled the door open.

He sat upright. The bedroom was dark, but he could make out Deb's sleeping form next to him. He took a deep breath and placed his hand on her arm, just to confirm she was real. She stirred but did not wake. "I love you, DeBella," he whispered as he lay back down.

He stared at the ceiling, unable to fall back to sleep. After lying there for half an hour or more, he gave up. He reached over, grabbed his crutch, and rose. He limped his way to the family room, picked up the remote, and turned on the TV.

He stood staring at the sectional for a minute and frowned. He needed to go for a run. He needed to get away from that damned couch. Unable to meet that desire, he selected a music channel and ignored the sectional. He lowered himself to the floor and started doing push-ups.

"If you screw up your leg more, I'll kick your ass," Deb said from the kitchen entrance to the family room.

"If I sit on that sofa anymore, I'll grow roots," he replied. "I have too much nervous energy. The doctor said I could exercise as long as I stay off the leg. I am off the leg."

"Couldn't you sleep?"

"No," he replied simply.

She walked in and took his seat on the sectional.

"You've been having nightmares," she said. "You don't have to look for me. I'm right here. I'm wherever you are."

He stopped mid-push-up. "Reading my thoughts again?"

She smiled cryptically. "I know she isn't a threat. I'm not going anywhere if that worries you."

"A little, maybe. It's been a sore point for us," he said, moving to a seated position.

She blushed. "I know I come off as confident and... carefree. I'm not really. I've suffered with a bit of an inferiority complex my entire life. I force myself to be confident. The truth is, my feelings are easily hurt, and I wonder what I have to offer in a relationship. I constantly second-guess myself, but I don't know. Lately, I really do feel comfortable."

"You should. You're my world. I knew from that very first kiss."

"Come back to bed, my Love." She stood and reached out her hand to pull him up. He took it and pulled himself to standing. He pulled her close and placed his hand on her belly and his forehead against hers. Deb's belly thumped back.

"Ohhhhhh!" they exclaimed in unison.

"That was a big one!" he laughed.

"Rockette," she agreed.

He felt ice water pump through his heart as "Tiny Dancer" played in his brain.

CHAPTER 89

Miranda reached down to pick up the single Air Jordan sitting on the doorstep.

"Don't touch it!" her husband yelled, stopping her just in time.

He rang the bell. Gavin answered the door with a smile. Dan held up his hand and pointed at the shoe. Gavin's face went ashen. But then he smiled. It might be enough to get him that warrant. He headed inside, Dan and Miranda following.

He called out to Deb, "Honey, get me my bag from the closet, please!"

She emerged from the bedroom moments later with his bag. He put on some latex gloves and picked up the shoe.

"What on Earth is that?" his wife asked.

"My shoe," he answered.

"Gavin, that thing is half the size of your foot," Miranda laughed.

"Well, I last wore it when I was 9, so I'm not surprised," he replied. He reached inside and pulled out a crumpled piece of sheet music for "One Shoe Blues."

He then sat at the kitchen island and checked the video doorbell footage from overnight. At 3:45 am, Mason Miller clearly left the shoe. The man was brazen. He looked directly at the camera and gave it the finger. He sighed heavily and shook his head.

"What? Doesn't that prove that Mason Miller is the killer?" Miranda asked.

"No, Honey. It proves he put a shoe on the front porch. It'll probably get Gavin the search warrant to search Mason's house, but Mason knows that. They won't find anything," Dan said sadly.

Jason came running out of his room. "Daddy!" he called, running and jumping into his father's open arms. "Hey, kiddo!" Dan said, kissing the child's head.

Gavin looked hard at the shoe. "No. He left the evidence. We'll find it here." On the bottom of the shoe in Sharpie was an address. "He's reached the end of his game."

Gavin reached into the shoe again. This time, he pulled out a crumpled piece of sheet music for "Do It Again," by the Kinks. He smoothed it out. "I have to go home," he said.

"You are home," his wife said.

He looked hard at Dan. "You don't have to come."

Dan sighed. "Yes, I do. I should have a long time ago."

"I'm coming with you!" Deb exclaimed, terrified Gavin planned to leave her behind, which, in a manner of speaking, he did.

"No. You need to go to California with Frank!" he said adamantly. "Deb, your name is literally translated to 'Beautiful.' I don't want you anywhere near Mason Miller."

"It's not up to you. Where you go, I go. It was right there in our vows," she insisted.

"Same," asserted Miranda, taking Dan's arm.

"We're not winning this argument," Dan conceded.

Gavin was right about the search warrant panning out. The address on the shoe was for a storage unit. Inside were Mason's trophies from each and every murder. Mason himself was gone, just like Andrea Grimes.

CHAPTER 90

Dan stood quietly, looking down at his mother's grave marker, his son in his arms, his wife on his right, his best friend on his left, and his ex-wife beside her new husband, the man to his left. The last year had been leading him back here, the place he'd avoided his entire life. Ellen's grave was at the top of a small knoll directly overlooking the dirt drive that wound in a circle around this half of the cemetery, directly across from the pond and angel in the children's garden next to Carrie's grave.

"I'm not particularly religious," he said at last, "but I believe in God. I feel like I should pray or something. I just don't know the words."

Miranda took his hand. "You don't need words. You can just pray with your heart."

"Still…Gavin, do you know any hymns? You have the best voice," Dan suggested.

Gavin nodded reverently. He closed his eyes and started to sing, "Amazing Grace, how sweet the sound that saved a wretch like me…" His voice was soft and sweet, but as he sang, he began to project it. The mellifluous notes filled the air. It felt like the whole world stopped to listen. In reality, it was just the three of them and Jason, two widows at two different graves in the middle section of the circle, and a squirrel by the pond in the children's garden.

There was one other observer as well, and as Gavin finished and opened his eyes, he saw him across the cemetery, back by the fence line separating the cemetery from the cow pasture behind it. Gavin said nothing. He just put his hand on his wife's back and maneuvered her to the limo they'd taken from the small airport outside Rock Falls. He limped beside her, leaning on the crutch.

Dan saw him as well. He followed suit and kept quiet.

They made their way back to Sterling, turned left at Lynn Blvd, and then left on 16th Ave. The Mahoney's house was a two-story colonial with an attached garage. A large Magnolia graced the front yard. The limo pulling into the drive stirred curiosity in the neighborhood. Late December in northwestern Illinois was not the time of year for spending time on your front porch. And yet nearly every house's door opened and at least one occupant came out onto the porch of each home. They were more than a little disappointed to just see the Mahoneys' son exit, even if he emerged wearing a walking cast and leaning on a crutch, but rewarded when his wife of just a month stepped out, obviously way more than one month into a pregnancy. And who was that with them? The man stood and looked at the house three doors down nervously. Wasn't Gavin friends with the Bradley boy? That boy was at the center of the most sensational thing to happen in the community in the last third of a century. Poor boy. The redhead with him was stunning. And the child clinched it. He was the spitting image of little Danny Bradley, whose mother and sister had been brutally murdered in that infamous house three doors down from the Mahoneys. Then the Mahoneys' door swung open, and squeals of delight greeted the visitors, who promptly disappeared from scrutiny into the warm house. The driver returned to his post in the car to wait for them to come back out.

CHAPTER 91

At 4:27 pm, an hour after Gavin walked into his parent's house, the fire started in the house three doors down. The smoke billowed out the windows, and flames licked at the interior.

The house was currently empty, having been placed on the market again by the last owner just a few weeks ago. It had gone through at least 10 owners in the last 26 years. The kids in town talked about it being haunted. The murders committed there were the stuff of legends. Tales of an infant's cries coming from inside when it sat empty, the ghostly noose that kept appearing hanging in the rafters of the garage, or of the lady in black who walked around inside were never confirmed by any of the owners when it was occupied, but every child in either Sterling or Rock Falls needed no such confirmation. Plus, none of the owners stayed very long.

It was a small saltbox-style house with yellow siding and green shutters. It was a pleasant-looking home, kept in good repair, with a nice yard and a large, detached garage. Downstairs were the kitchen, dining, and living rooms. Upstairs were three bedrooms and one bathroom, the stairs running up the side of the large living room that ran the entire length of the front of the house. The top of the stairs emptied into a hallway that ran left off the stairwell across the center of the house, the saltbox ceiling sloping down to the right where the smaller two bedrooms were. The hall ended in a window that overlooked the drive and detached garage. The bathroom was at the end of the hallway. The largest bedroom was on the left of the hall, immediately at the start of the hallway.

As the neighbors frantically called 911, Gavin and Dan rushed outside. Gavin, still relying on one crutch, turned suddenly, yelling for his wife, who had followed him, to stay in the house. It was a direction she didn't like or intend to follow. She trailed along behind him in direct opposition to his instructions.

Gavin yelled, "Deb, I'm begging you, please go back in the house!"

"I told you I'm not leaving your side!" she yelled back.

As he turned to force her back inside, the man rose from the shadows behind the cover of evergreen bushes around the porch where she stood. Before anyone could reach her, the hulking dark figure grabbed her from behind, a large knife held against her throat. Dave Mahoney, who had come out of his garage, drew his weapon. Gavin and Dan did the same. The dark figure eased his way into the porch light, revealing his features. He was instantly recognized as Mason Miller.

A woman suddenly emerged screaming in terror and agony, fully engulfed in flames from the supposed empty house, bursting through the front door into the cold pre-dusk air and falling to the ground.

The commotion was enough of a distraction for Mason to race off, dragging the terrified pregnant woman with him. He made it to the burning structure before the fire trucks came rushing in and pulled her with him into the blazing inferno.

Gavin threw aside his crutch and ran frantically in behind them, hobbling on the walking cast, while the ranking firefighter cursed and successfully prevented Dan and Dave from rushing in as well.

The woman was extinguished, but it was too late. Andrea Grimes had cornered herself inside as she spread the accelerant, and her clothing had caught fire when she tried to get through the flames to escape. There was crying, but it came from the garage, not the house. A fireman found Andrea's vehicle inside with her two-year-old son, Davison, still in the car seat in the back.

Gavin knew the house like the back of his hand, and unless he was mistaken, Mason would take Deb upstairs to the bathroom where Ellen and Carrie Bradley had been found.

Carrie was drowned in the tub after her mother was severely beaten. Then, the killer had brutally beaten the dead infant. Gavin had come looking for them as Ellen regained consciousness and picked up her murdered child. When Gavin had opened the door instead of her attacker, she had sent him looking for her other child. The boy was so brave. She saw him grab hold of Danny and run with him down the stairs. She heard the back door out of the kitchen slam, and she breathed a sigh of relief. Then Walter was there. He had contacted her, telling her he was her brother, also given up for adoption by their unwed mother. She thought he would help. Too late, she realized, her husband had been right in not trusting him. As he lunged for her to choke the life out of her, she screamed until she couldn't anymore because his gloved hands were crushing her windpipe, and then she felt the life ebb out of her.

Gavin covered his mouth and nose by pulling his tee shirt collar up over the bridge of his nose. He hugged the wall and avoided the flames, making his way up to the second story quickly. His weapon drawn and held in front of him, he made his way down the hall to the closed bathroom door. He kicked it in, feeling that telltale snap as he re-tore the Achilles tendon. He yelled, "Damnit!"

Mason stood in the bathtub, the water from the shower running over them, holding Deb, in much the same way he had on the porch, from behind, the knife at her throat. He laughed as Gavin entered. Gavin knew he didn't have a clean shot. He needed to get Deb away from him. He needed to get Mason to lower the knife.

"Why Mason? What did I do to you?"

"You left her to die!"

"I was 10 years old! I got Dan out. I'd have called somebody to help, but I never made it past Mrs. Ramirez's porch."

"She trusted you!"

"I was a child!"

"She loved you!" Mason cried.

"Now that's just bat shit crazy!" Gavin exclaimed.

Mason lowered the knife and shoved Deb aside. Gavin raised his weapon higher. He took the shot, his weapon discharging and the bullet hitting Mason right between the eyes. But simultaneously, as Mason had lurched forward and Gavin pulled his trigger, a second gunshot rang out. Deb had pulled her pocket pistol out of her coat pocket. She shot him right through the ear.

Gavin grabbed her and pulled her out of the tub, leaning on her to get down the hall and to the stairs and out the front, meeting firefighters coming in to rescue them.

Once outside, he pulled her to him and kissed her. When she finally pulled away, he laughed, "Hope you have your FOID and conceal carry permit still."

"Of course I do," she replied, collapsing against him.

CHAPTER 92

Gavin sat holding his daughter, staring in wonder at the absolute perfection in his arms. His leg was unencumbered, though he was still undergoing physical therapy after the second repair on his Achilles tendon in January. It was late April now. The dogwoods were everywhere and in full bloom. He had to admit it was pretty in Virginia in the spring. "Hello, Estrella Moira Mahoney," he cooed. "My little angel."

"She looks like you. All that dark hair," Deb said, reaching over as her daughter grabbed hold of her outstretched finger.

"No. She's too pretty to look like me!" he laughed, leaning in and kissing his wife.

Deb's sister and her boyfriend, Officer Rudy Vance, knocked at the door to the hospital room.

"Congratulations, Detective! Everybody at the FPD sends their love. Chief wants to know when you'll be back already. Says the department runs smoother with you there. Sure, the University agrees," Rudy said, looking at Estrella over her father's shoulder. "Wow. You're right. She's too pretty to look like you."

Katelynn, whose shyness had decreased by leaps and bounds since moving to Fredericksburg, burst out laughing. She jumped to hug and kiss her much taller boyfriend's cheek.

"Not until I've used every second of leave," Gavin replied.

He leaned back in the rocker and started to sing "Too Ra Loo Ra Loo Ral" softly.

Lacynda Mathes is a graduate of Radford University in Radford, VA. She holds a B.A. in English.

She is originally from Oak Grove, VA, in Westmoreland County near Colonial Beach. She graduated from Washington and Lee High School, Montross, VA, in 1986. She attended Randolph-Macon College, studied abroad at Wroxton College in Oxfordshire, England, and ultimately transferred to Radford University, where she completed her degree.

She currently resides in Sterling, IL, with her husband. She is the mother to their teenage sons, the eldest with special needs, who has been diagnosed with Lennox Gestaut Syndrome, a catastrophic childhood epilepsy, and severe autism.

www.ingramcontent.com/pod-product-compliance
Lightning Source LLC
Chambersburg PA
CBHW050714180626
46814CB00002B/433